Grace to FORGIVE

SEQUEL TO
Grace for Tomorrow

Eva Schmidt

◆ FriesenPress

Suite 300 - 990 Fort St
Victoria, BC, V8V 3K2
Canada

www.friesenpress.com

Copyright © 2018 by Eva Schmidt
First Edition — 2018

All rights reserved.

No part of this publication may be reproduced in any form, or by any means, electronic or mechanical, including photocopying, recording, or any information browsing, storage, or retrieval system, without permission in writing from FriesenPress.

All bible verses quoted are from the King James version of the Bible.

ISBN
978-1-5255-3056-2 (Hardcover)
978-1-5255-3057-9 (Paperback)
978-1-5255-3058-6 (eBook)

1. *Fiction, Christian, Romance*

Distributed to the trade by The Ingram Book Company

And be ye kind one to another,
tenderhearted, forgiving one another,
even as God for Christ's sake hath forgiven you.

—Ephesians 4:32

DEDICATION

I dedicate this book to my readers
who encouraged me to write this sequel.
You are a blessing to me.

PROLOGUE

"B...b...b...ab..." Jacob struggled to get the word out, his face contorting with the effort.

"Take your time," his wife, Anna, encouraged. She stroked his hand as she wracked her brain. *What starts with bab? He's tried to say the same word for a few days now.*

The stroke Jacob suffered eight months ago had left him unable to walk, or speak intelligibly. Their small, isolated hometown didn't have a physical therapist or a speech therapist, so a large portion of the rehabilitation program fell on Anna's shoulders. Every day she helped Jacob through his daily speech therapy and muscle strengthening exercises. It was paying off too; he had already learned to walk again—with some help. *If only he could learn to speak,* Anna thought. He was able to say her name and their children's names and had added a few more words to his vocabulary. Anna was optimistic that it was just a matter of time. She watched Jacob take a deep breath and release it with a sigh of frustration. Anna's heart went out to him. *He tries so hard.*

"B...b...bab..." his gaze pierced Anna's eyes, willing her to understand what he was trying to say.

"It's alright, Jacob. Maybe tomorrow you'll be able to say it."

Jacob shook his head, took a breath, and concentrated hard on getting his mouth to form the word correctly. Anna saw determination in his dark brown eyes.

"B...b...ab...y," Jacob said, his eyes glowing with accomplishment. She could see he was proud of himself.

"Baby?" Anna questioned, not sure that was the word he meant to say. Sometimes the words came out wrong, and they weren't what he wanted to say at all. *Why is it important for him to say 'baby'?*

Jacob nodded emphatically. Anna laughed and gave him a hug. "That's a new word, even though I'm not sure it's the word you meant to say. Good for you, Jacob!" She was excited for each new word he added to his vocabulary. It was one word closer to being able to talk.

"M...ar...y."

"You want Mary?" Anna asked. "Mary's doing the chores. Do you want me to call her?"

Jacob shook his head. "B...b...ab...y."

"I'm sorry, Jacob, I don't understand," Anna said with a sigh. She patted Jacob's hand where it lay in his lap. "We'll stop the therapy for now. Mary and Benny will be finished doing chores soon, and I should make supper. You did very well. You'll be talking again soon." She smiled at him as she stood up from her chair.

"*Jo*," Jacob said, nodding as he smiled up at his wife, willing to let it go for now.

Lord, I know Jacob is trying to tell me something. He's been working on that word for so long, but I still don't know what he means. Why is it important for him to say 'baby'? I wish you would just heal him already. Anna caught herself. *Lord, help me be patient. I am thankful that you spared Jacob's life and that he is improving, but it's so slow.* Anna conversed with the

Lord as she cut up vegetables and added them to the stew meat already boiling on the back of the wood cook stove. She took four plates from the cupboard and set them on the table. *Lord, I am thankful I still have Jacob, Mary, and Benny. I don't want to seem ungrateful. It's just that I miss the way Jacob and I used to be. The talks we had…*

The door opened and seventeen-year-old Mary entered, carrying two galvanized pails filled to the brim with frothy, white milk.

"It sure is a nice day," she told Mama as she poured the milk through the strainer on top of the cream separator.

"I saw that our garden is coming up nicely," Anna told her daughter, who was turning the handle on the cream separator. The machine hummed noisily as the milk and cream poured into separate containers through two spouts. Anna raised her voice above the hum of the machine. "Is Benny almost done with his chores as well?"

Mary didn't need to answer as nine-year-old Benny burst into the house, slamming the door behind him. Laughing, he turned to look out the window beside the door.

"*Oba* Benny, don't slam the door!" Anna turned to scold her rambunctious son.

"Skipper and I were racing." Benny laughed at the dog through the window.

"That is no reason to slam the door," Mama said. She stirred the stew again and pulled it off to the side of the wood cook stove. "Now wash up; supper is ready."

Benny laughed again as he knocked on the window at Skipper—who was happily wagging his tail—then turned to do Mama's bidding.

Benny brings liveliness to this family. Lively—like their family used to be—before David was suddenly taken from them in a vehicle accident three years ago, and Mary ran away from home a year and a half later. She'd been away ten long months before they found her.

Actually, she found us, Anna corrected her thoughts. *It was after Jacob had a stroke and ended up in the hospital in Edmonton when John found Mary and brought her to us.* Anna reminisced to herself as she put the finishing touches to the meal. John had been David's best friend and was a dear friend of the family. *He was very selfless in helping us while Jacob was in the hospital. He insisted on taking his turn sitting with Jacob so Mary and I could rest.*

"Mama," Mary's voice broke through Anna's reverie, "should I help Papa to the table?"

Anna looked up to see Mary had finished separating the milk and had already put it in the pantry to cool.

"Yes, please. We're ready to eat."

Mary smiled at her papa as she entered the living room. "Supper time," she said, holding her hand out to him. Jacob smiled at his daughter and leaned forward. Mary tucked her arm under her papa's arm, helping him as he pulled himself up out of the chair. She kept her arm securely in place, allowing him to lean on her as he shuffled to the kitchen table.

"Mama, can I go to Billy's house after supper?" Benny asked as he dished a generous portion of stew onto his plate. "We want to hunt squirrels." Benny had loved to hunt squirrels ever since David helped him make his first slingshot years ago.

"As long as you're home by nine o'clock," Anna said. She kept a close eye on Jacob as his shaky hands made it difficult to keep food on his fork. "School tomorrow."

"Yes, I know," Benny said, buttering a freshly baked bun.

"Mama, this stew is delicious," Mary said, casting an appreciative look at her mama.

"*Jo*," Jacob agreed, smiling his appreciation at his wife.

"Thank you," Anna said, smiling at her little family. She loved mealtime when they were all together. It was a time of connecting as a family.

After supper, Anna led Jacob back to his chair in the living room, while Benny grabbed his slingshot and ran out the door.

That boy has so much energy; he'll probably run the half-mile to Billy's house, Mary thought as she watched her brother through the window. Anna came back into the kitchen, and Mary turned from the window to help clean up from supper.

"Papa said a new word," Anna told her daughter as she scraped the leftover stew into a smaller dish. "It has me confused."

"What was it?" Mary asked, sinking a stack of plates into the sudsy dishwater.

"Baby." Anna placed more dirty dishes on the counter beside Mary. "I'm not sure that's what he meant to say, but he was sure proud of himself."

Mary's heart stopped—then pounded erratically in her chest.

"He's been trying to say the same word for days now," Anna continued as she disappeared into the pantry. Coming back into the kitchen, she dipped a dishcloth into the dishwater, and then wrung it out before wiping down the table. "Then he said your name. I asked if he wanted me to call you, but he shook his head and said 'baby' again. I don't understand." Anna threw the dishcloth onto the cupboard, took the tea towel off the rack, and started drying dishes.

Mary's knees were weak as she leaned forward—supporting her elbows on the cupboard. She sank her hands into the warm, sudsy water. *Did Papa hear me?* When her papa came out of his coma after the stroke, she had wondered if he had heard her heart cry out to the Lord. She had sat with him that night and had fallen asleep with her head on his bed. She'd had the nightmare again and woken up crying. It was then that she finally cried out to God, confessing her sins and asking His forgiveness. Later that same night, her papa had come out of his coma.

"Mary."

Mary jumped as her mama touched her arm. The eyes she turned on her mama were filled with such raw pain that Anna gasped. "Mary, what is it? Are you sick?" That awful day Jacob had a stroke passed before Anna's eyes. "Here, sit down." Alarmed, she put her arm around her daughter, helping her to a chair.

"No, Mama. I'm alright." Mary shook off her mama's arm. Taking a deep breath to steady her racing heart, she picked up a dish and started washing it, her mind working furiously. *Obviously, Papa knows. It's not fair to keep it from Mama. I have to tell her. Oh, Lord, help me.* Ever since she returned home months ago, she had struggled with how to tell her parents the real reason she ran away.

Mary finished washing the dishes in silence, her brain scrambling. She wiped her hands on a towel and turned to her mama, who was putting the last of the dishes into the cupboard.

"I need to talk to you and Papa."

What is going on? What does Mary want to talk about? What does Jacob know that I don't? Anna's heart was heavy with trepidation as she followed her daughter into the living room and sat down in her rocking chair, close to her husband.

Jacob looked up from the book lying in his lap.

Mary sat down on the couch on the other side of her papa's recliner. Her heart thumped wildly in her chest—worse than when she was a little girl and feared her papa's discipline. *Lord, give me words. I'm about to break their hearts,* she prayed silently. She didn't take her papa's hand as she usually did when she talked to him.

"Papa," her voice sounded hoarse to her ears, "do you remember that I was with you when you came out of your coma?"

"Jo," Papa affirmed, nodding his head.

"Did you hear me pray?" The nurse had told them that it was likely that people in a coma could still hear. That's why her mama and John had read the Bible and prayed out loud to her papa. Mary knew she should have prayed silently, but at the time, she had been so convicted that she had cried out to God, forgetting the nurse's warning.

Jacob nodded again, his eyes misty. Mary dropped her head into her hands for a moment. When she lifted her face, her eyes were a sea of unspeakable pain and sorrow.

Anna looked from her husband to her daughter and back to her husband. *What are they talking about?* Her heart thumped ominously in her chest. She knew instinctively that she didn't want to hear whatever Jacob and Mary were talking about. She wanted to bolt from the room and hide. *Please Lord, we've been through enough!* Her mother-heart nearly failed her. Ever since Mary had run away, Anna had been afraid for this moment. Afraid there was a deeper—more painful—reason she had left.

"I wanted to tell you but I didn't know how." Mary's voice was so soft that Anna strained to hear her. Mary swallowed past the tightness in her chest. "I left because I was pregnant." Tears spilled over and ran down her cheeks. "I had a baby. A baby girl." Her voice shook as she looked from her papa to her mama, her eyes pleading for forgiveness. "I gave her up for adoption."

Anna fought desperately to control the multitude of emotions that battled for control within her. Disbelief…anger…love…sorrow. Yet her heart had known all along.

CHAPTER 1

Seven years later

"Mary, do you know where the bouquets are?"

"Sarah has them." Mary smiled as she fixed the veil onto Lena's luscious auburn curls. "Relax, Lena, everything is right on schedule."

Lena's blue eyes sparkled as they met Mary's soft brown ones in the mirror. "I guess I'm feeling a bit nervous," she admitted with a giggle. "Oh, Mary, I still find it so hard to believe that I'm really getting married!"

"Well, believe it." Mary wrapped her arms around her friend and brought her face alongside Lena's, smiling at her in the mirror. Her own normally straight, light brown hair hung in soft curls down the back of her burgundy, floor-length, empire-waist dress. "I am so happy for you."

There was a soft knock, and Sarah pushed the door open, her arms laden with red and white rose bouquets.

"Wow! You're gorgeous!" Sarah exclaimed at the sight of Lena. "Henry is one lucky fellow."

"Is he here yet?" Lena asked, slipping her feet into her delicate white sandals.

"Yes, he is. The guys are all downstairs. His mom is helping them with the boutonnieres."

Lena's long, slender fingers fluttered to her chest. "Oh, I'm so nervous." She giggled. "I hope I won't trip over my dress when I walk down the aisle."

They all laughed and assured Lena that wouldn't happen. The door opened and Mrs. Penner, the pastor's wife, entered. She was a friendly, middle-aged lady, with a mass of red curls that she struggled to contain in a bun at the nape of her neck.

"I just checked on the men—looks like everyone is ready to get this wedding started! Let's join hands and pray." She reached her hands out to the ladies. They came together in a circle, interlocking their hands in prayer.

"Lord, thank you for this special day that you have given Lena and Henry. A day of dreams fulfilled and commitments made. Bless them as they enter into marriage. May they always stay true to you and to each other. In Jesus' name we pray. Amen."

"Amen," the ladies murmured in unison.

Mary, Lena, and Sarah picked up their bouquets and followed Mrs. Penner into the church foyer to await their individual turn to walk down the aisle. Mary tried to calm the butterflies in her stomach as she watched Sarah slowly make her way down the aisle. When Sarah took her place at the front of the church, Mary stepped into the sanctuary with a smile on her face. She stopped just short of the front pews and watched John come toward her. Her heart fluttered at the lopsided grin he gave her as she looped her hand through the crook of his arm.

"You look ravishing," he murmured softly so that only she could hear. Mary felt herself blush as he led her onto the stage. John noticed, and his grin grew wider.

Pastor Penner asked the congregation to rise as Lena and her papa stepped into the sanctuary. Lena looked radiant in her flowing white gown and veil, holding a bouquet of red and white roses in front of her. She kept her sparkling blue eyes focused on Henry all the way down the aisle.

"Who gives this woman to be married to this man?" Pastor Penner asked.

"Her mother and I do," answered Lena's papa. He gave Lena a hug. Henry brushed the back of his hand over his eyes before walking forward to receive his bride. Lena's papa hugged Henry and then took a step back as Henry took his place beside Lena. Together they came forward to stand in front of Pastor Penner.

Mary's heart was overwhelmed with joy for the couple. *They'll be happy together,* she thought as they exchanged vows. She looked up and found John's deep brown eyes resting on her. She quickly averted her gaze as the familiar pain stabbed her chest. *He's so handsome, dressed up in that black tuxedo.* Giving herself a mental shake, she willed her mind to concentrate on the ceremony.

Mary had loved John since she was a young girl. She'd dreamt of marrying him some day, but her rebellion and bad choices during her teenage years made marrying him impossible. She knew John didn't understand. No one understood. None of her friends knew about the broken heart she lived with. It was only by God's grace that she was able to face each new day. She dabbed at the errant tear at the corner of her eye, glad that people would think it was a tear of happiness for Lena. She put a smile on her face. *Today is Lena's day, and I will think happy thoughts.*

They look absolutely radiant, Mary thought when the Pastor introduced the newlyweds, and they walked out of the sanctuary amid the congregation's applause. Mary fell into step beside John as they followed close behind.

Much later that evening, Mary hugged Lena goodbye and waved to her and Henry as they set off for their honeymoon. She turned around to find John standing behind her, his tuxedo casually slung over his right shoulder.

"May I give you a ride home?" he asked, as his lips turned up in that lopsided grin she loved.

"It would beat walking home in these heels," she answered flippantly, with a twinkle in her eye.

He chuckled as he caught her elbow and guided her to his car. He opened the passenger door for her before walking around the car. Opening the door, he threw his tux on the backseat before sliding in behind the wheel. Mary caught the faint smell of John's aftershave. She took a deep breath as a longing rose in her chest.

"Do you mind if we go to the river first to watch the sunset?" John asked as he turned the ignition and the motor purred to life. He noticed her body stiffen and added, "We haven't talked in a long time. I'd like to know how you and your family are making out."

She felt herself relax. "Yes, let's do that. You can tell me what's happening in your life." It had been a long time since they'd had the opportunity to talk. *I'll savour the moment.*

John smiled as he shifted into gear. They talked about the wedding as they drove to the beach on the river, where in the past they had gotten together with their friends to play beach volleyball or have a wiener roast. Those evenings had usually ended with campfire singing. That was a lifetime ago. Parking at the edge of the sandy beach, John turned the ignition off and gazed across the deep blue water. The river looked serene on the surface, but he knew that underneath were strong undercurrents that could drag you along if you weren't careful—similar to his feelings for Mary.

"We had so many fun times here," he reminisced, running his hand through his black curls. "Fishing, volleyball, wiener roasts, and campfire singing. It wasn't the same after David passed on." Mary heard the catch in his voice.

"That changed everything."

"It did." John rolled down the windows to catch the gentle evening breeze. "So how are you doing, Mary? I'm impressed with how your family has pulled together and kept the farm going after your papa's stroke."

"Mama is a strong woman!" Mary chuckled. "She rented out the farmland and put us all to work—from feeding chickens to slopping barns—we did it all." She turned serious. "I'm thankful we managed to keep the farm. Mama and Papa worked so hard to build their life there; it would have been sad to give it up. The whole community was very supportive and helped us out a lot."

"How's your papa doing?"

She turned to face him, resting her back against the passenger door. "He's about the same. His speech is difficult to understand. He still needs help walking, and he gets frustrated sometimes, but usually he's an easy patient. He's become quite emotional since his stroke. Very appreciative and loving."

"I should stop in and see him," John turned to watch the sun sinking in the west. Mary took the opportunity to study his profile. She loved the way his black hair curled around his ears. *He's wearing his hair longer than he used to.* She refrained from reaching up and smoothing those errant curls back from his forehead.

"He would love that. Mama would love to see you, too."

"How's Benny? He must be what—sixteen already?"

"Yes, he's sixteen. Two more years till he graduates. He loves the farm. Benny is so full of pranks; he reminds me a lot of David when we were growing up."

"I still miss David like crazy."

"Yeah, me too."

They fell silent watching the sun sink behind the horizon, each left to their thoughts. So much had happened since Mary's brother—and John's best friend—was killed in a car accident. Was it really ten years ago? *Sometimes it feels like forever, and sometimes it feels like it was yesterday.* Mary sighed.

"Wow, look at that." John's voice filled with awe, watching the pink, orange, and purple hues stretch across the western sky. "God's masterpiece. Have you ever seen a painting more beautiful than that?"

"I'm always amazed how beautiful God's creation is." Mary's voice was soft. "Sunsets, stars in the night sky, hoar frost on the trees in winter." They watched the sky's vibrant colours fade to pastel hues. "What are your plans now—are you going back to the city?"

John turned his attention to Mary. "The mission board is arranging for me to work at a teenage shelter for street kids in Mexico. They are in desperate need of trained counsellors."

"Mexico." Mary let the word roll off her tongue. *Leaving again.* She was glad that dusk was setting in, making it more difficult for John to read the emotions on her face. "When are you leaving?"

"It might be a few months or early next year," John said, reaching for her hand, his eyes studying her face. "Years ago, when I first told you that I was going to Bible school—you were so young—I didn't think it was fair to ask you to wait for me…"

"Please don't," Mary interrupted, trying to pull her hand away. "That was a long time ago."

"Let me speak, Mary." Even in the gathering dusk she could see a passion in his eyes. "Just before you left Edmonton—when your papa had a stroke—I wanted to tell you, but you wouldn't let me say what was on my mind. I let it go because I knew you had a lot on your plate. During the following years I could see how hard you had to work to keep the farm going and help take care of your papa—but now Benny is at an age where I can see him taking over the farm. I can't let it go anymore, Mary. We are both adults, and I need to tell you that I love you. I loved you then, and I love you now."

She knew the love she saw in his eyes would haunt her dreams. She turned to watch the colours slowly fade from the sky, just like they were fading from her heart. *If only things were different,* she thought, *but he wouldn't love me if he knew.*

With a heavy heart, she turned back to him. "You can't love me, John." She worked hard to keep her emotions out of her voice. "You don't really know me."

"What do you mean, I don't know you? I've known you since childhood! I know I love you." He tightened his grip on her hand. "Don't you have any feelings for me?"

"Oh, John." Mary felt torn between telling him she loved him and knowing she could never do that. *How can I let him go again? Dear God, this is too much. Please help me to know what to say. I don't want to hurt him, but he can't know that I love him. It wouldn't be fair to him.*

She sighed deeply and forced the words past her lips that she knew would break his heart. "John, I love you dearly—as a friend."

Mary's heart wept at the crushed look in his eyes. It was all she could do not to put her arms around him and tell him the truth. But if she told the complete truth he wouldn't want her anyways. *No, it's best this way.*

John turned his gaze back to the fading light in the western sky. He had loved Mary since grade school. Back then he was sure she cared for him as well. Then David was killed in that awful car crash. Mary had been consumed with grief and had withdrawn from her friends, while John had focused on completing his high school courses early. Within the year following the accident, he had left for Bible school. During his second year of college, Mary had run away from home and months later, John had stumbled upon her right on his college campus. Her papa had been in a hospital in Edmonton at the time, fighting for his life. John had taken Mary to the hospital, reuniting her with her parents. When her papa was finally released from the hospital, Mary went back home with them.

John shifted in his seat, started the car, and put it in gear. They didn't talk much during the short drive to Mary's house. When they pulled into her yard, John cleared his throat and covered her hand with his own. "Friends?"

Mary smiled up at him. "Friends." She squeezed his hand before letting herself out of the car. She turned to wave to him before opening the door and stepping across the threshold.

Mary was glad Mama and Papa were already in bed. It was difficult enough to shed her clothes and get into her pajamas before she allowed herself to fall into bed. She wrapped her arms around her pillow as she buried her face in it—only then did she release her pent-up tears.

"*Be not deceived; God is not mocked: for whatsoever a man soweth, that shall he also reap.*" The verse ran through her mind, like it had thousands of times in the last eight years.

I know, Lord, she cried silently, sobbing into her pillow. *What I would give if I could change the past, but I can't. I am doomed to spend my life paying for the consequences of my rebellion—without my little girl—and without the only man I have ever loved. Dear Jesus, help me bear this burden.*

"They that sow in tears shall reap in joy." Like a gentle whisper, the verse flitted through her head.

Oh, Lord, how can that be? How can I ever reap in joy? You know my heart breaks every day. If it wasn't for your love, I couldn't go on.

"Weeping may endure for a night, but joy cometh in the morning." The verses kept coming, one after another.

I have wept for eight years, Lord, when will my morning of joy come?

"For as the heavens are higher than the earth, so are my ways higher than your ways, and my thoughts than your thoughts."

I know, Lord, you alone can see the big picture. You are in control. You can take care of my daughter. You know where she is. Dear Jesus, please protect her and help her to have a good life. Please draw her to yourself so she will learn to love you and live for you. If I never see her again here on earth then we will meet in heaven. Tell her how much I love her.

"Be careful [anxious] for nothing; but in everything by prayer and supplication with thanksgiving let your requests be made known unto God. And the peace of God, which passeth all understanding, shall keep your hearts and minds through Christ Jesus."

Mary fought hard to grab onto the peace she knew was there for the taking. She emptied her heart and lay her burdens down—only then did the familiar peace steal over her, and she knew the Lord had heard her. *Lord, thank you for your peace. Please remove this love that I have in my heart for John. There is no future for us.*

Mary didn't understand all of God's promises but she was once again willing to trust him with her daughter and the man she loved. Mentally and emotionally exhausted, she prayed until she fell asleep.

After dropping Mary off, John drove his car down the dirt path to the little log cabin he and David had built in their early teens. It was still his favourite place when he needed to be alone with the Lord. As he pulled up to the cabin, he noticed a couple of shingles missing and made a mental note to come back and replace them. He opened the latch, and the door creaked. *I'll have to bring some WD-40 as well.*

John stepped through the door and let his gaze slowly sweep across the cabin that was so special to him. In one corner were the homemade bunk beds that he and David had slept in whenever their parents allowed. Their sleeping bags and pillows were still in place, as were the table and chairs they had built from their dad's leftover scraps of wood. The air tight heater was there as well. They'd had so many good times in this cabin. He sat down on the bottom bunk.

"Lord," he said, lifting his eyes toward the ceiling. "I don't understand. I felt confident tonight was the night you wanted me to declare my love to Mary—yet she turned me away. Lord, if she doesn't love me, then why did she have such a tortured look in her eyes?" He dropped to his knees beside the bed and his voice took on a more urgent tone. "Lord, I sense something is not right with her, but what is it? I feel so strongly that she is the woman you have for me, yet she spurns my love. Am I wrong in this? Is she not the woman for me? Lord, what is it? If she is not the woman for me then please remove these feelings I have for her."

"Trust in the Lord with all thine heart; and lean not unto thine own understanding. In all thy ways acknowledge him, and he shall direct thy paths."

John hung his head as the tears dripped onto the floor. "I want to trust you, Lord. I do. Help me to trust you more." His shoulders shook as deep sobs wrenched from his heart. "Lord how can I go on like this? I thought you brought me home so Mary and I could explore and rekindle the feelings we have for each other—then get married by spring and go to Mexico together. How could I be so wrong?"

"*My grace is sufficient for thee.*"

"Yes, Lord, your grace is sufficient for me. I know I can trust you. You alone know the end from the beginning. You alone can see the big picture. Lord, I totally commit my life to you. I trust you to lead me and guide me in all things." John relished the peace that flowed through his broken heart as he committed himself totally to his God once again. "Jesus, take control of my life. Lead me. Guide me. Help me not to run ahead of you. Give me patience and please Lord, if Mary is not the woman for me, then remove these feelings I have for her."

His tears subsided as he conversed with his Creator, and he felt a deep calmness steal over his soul. He lifted his eyes toward heaven. "Thank you, Lord, for hearing my prayers. I know you are in control and I praise you. You are the Creator of the universe. You alone know me better than I know myself. You created me, and I trust you."

When he got up from his knees much later, he felt confident that if Mary was the woman God had for him, then God would bring them together. If that didn't happen, then Jesus would be enough. More than anything he wanted to be fully committed to the Lord.

CHAPTER 2

Francis saw the strikingly beautiful, raven-haired woman and her little girl enter the church Sunday morning. She watched as they stopped just inside the doors and looked around. The woman's long black hair, cascading down her back, and the sad chocolate-brown eyes reminded her of someone.

Where have I seen her before? Francis asked herself as she walked across the grey carpet to greet them.

"Good morning." Francis shook hands with the woman and the little girl. "Welcome to our church. I'm Francis Webber."

"Good morning." The woman smiled a bit nervously. "I'm Gloria Simpson. This is my daughter, Emily. We just moved here from Red Deer. This is our first time here. Emily wants to go to Sunday school—can you point us in the right direction, please?"

"Let me show you," Francis offered, smiling at the little girl. "What grade are you in, Emily?"

"I'm in grade three," Emily said, looking up at Francis with big hazel eyes. "I was in grade two, but when school starts again, I'll be in grade three."

"Good for you!" Francis chuckled, flicking her shoulder-length brunette hair back with a small toss of her head. The excited little girl had an infectious smile and the cutest dimple she'd ever seen. Obviously, Emily wasn't shy. "Come this way, then." Francis led the way into the church basement.

"I went to Sunday school in Red Deer," Emily offered, her long brown hair bouncing as she walked and her beautiful hazel eyes sparkling with excitement.

"I'm glad you did." Francis smiled down at the cheerful little girl. "Then you'll fit right in."

"I didn't want to leave my friends, but Mommy says I can make lots of new friends here."

"I'm sure you will." Francis found the correct classroom and walked through the open door. Heidi, the teacher, noticed them immediately and came towards them.

"I brought you a new student," Francis told her. "This is Emily and her mother Gloria. They recently moved from Red Deer."

"I'm pleased to meet you." Heidi shook hands with Gloria before turning her attention to Emily. "I'm so happy you're going to be in my class." She took Emily's hand and together they entered the classroom.

Francis turned to go and was surprised to see Gloria's eyes glistening. "Do you want to stay here with her?" she asked. "You could—just to make sure Emily will be okay."

Gloria shook her head, blinking back her emotions. "No. Emily will be fine. I have separation issues—not Emily." She turned to leave. "I hope she won't overwhelm the teacher." Her full red lips parted in a soft chuckle as the two women retraced their steps. "My little Emily loves meeting new people. Hopefully she'll stop talking long enough so the teacher can teach the lesson!"

"Well, that will make the move a lot easier for her," Francis said, managing the flight of stairs with ease in her black dress pumps. "She seems like a very nice girl. I'm sure she'll make lots of friends." At the top of the stairs she turned her full attention to Gloria. "Do you want to join me in the adult Sunday school class?"

"I would love too," Gloria said with a smile. "Thanks for helping us out."

"Anytime," Francis said. She led Gloria into the classroom, stopping in front of an older lady with a kind face and wrinkles spreading out from the corners of her eyes.

"Dolores, this is Gloria Simpson. She recently moved from Red Deer." Francis made the introductions. "Gloria, Dolores Browning is our teacher, as well as the pastor's wife. Dolores is very knowledgeable in the Bible. You'll find that her teachings are always insightful."

"Pleased to meet you," Dolores said with a laugh, shaking Gloria's hand. "I'm happy to have you in my class, although I don't know that I can live up to Francis' introduction."

"Pleased to meet you, too," Gloria said, appreciating the warmth with which she was accepted. "Francis noticed me and my daughter come into church this morning and took us under her wing."

"Oh, you have a daughter?" Dolores asked. "How old is she?"

"Yes, Emily—she's almost eight," Gloria told her. "She was very excited to start Sunday school."

Francis introduced Gloria to the other ladies who were trickling into the classroom, before taking their seats to start the lesson. They opened their Bibles to Genesis—they were studying the story of Joseph.

After class, Francis waited in the foyer for Gloria—who had gone to fetch Emily—then they entered the sanctuary together. Francis' children, Brad and Chantel, had grown up in the church and joined them in their pew before the service began.

After church, Gloria and Emily found themselves surrounded by people welcoming them in the foyer. Francis smiled as she turned away, confident that Gloria and Emily would be made to feel welcome—the same way Francis and her children had been made welcome when they started attending years ago.

"Let's go for pizza," fourteen-year-old Brad suggested as they walked to their car.

"Yes, let's!" Chantel, his eleven-year-old sister agreed quickly.

Francis laughed. "I think that's a good idea. I don't really feel like making lunch. Let's ask Mr. and Mrs. Pitman if they want to join us."

"I'll go ask them." Brad sprinted across the paved parking lot back to the church, returning with Dale and Maggie Pitman in tow.

"We would gladly join you for lunch," the elderly lady told Francis. "But Viona and her children are visiting us. Do you mind if they come as well?" Viona was the Pitmans' married daughter, who lived out of town.

"That's even better," Francis assured her. "It'll be nice to catch up with Viona."

That evening, after her children had gone to bed, Francis fixed herself a cup of tea and curled up on the living room couch with a book; she liked to unwind before going to bed. She had just started reading when the telephone rang.

"Who would call at this time of night?" she muttered to herself. Jumping to her feet, she hurried to answer the call before the ringing woke the kids.

She snatched the receiver off the wall phone. "Hello."

"Francis? Is that you?" The voice from her past flew through the telephone line—and into her life—like a missile at warp speed. Pain slashed through Francis' chest like a sword as she groped the cupboard for support.

"Mike?" she croaked, her throat constricting. She clutched at her chest as the old wound burst wide open, exposing her bleeding heart.

"Francis, it's so good to hear your voice." She remembered the voice well. Her fingers clutched the receiver as the years fell away.

"Francis, are you there?" Mike asked, his voice soft and low. "Francis, I'm sorry."

She felt his strong arms around her—loving her. She felt his fists punching her—the pain, the blood. The room spun out of control. Her knees buckled as she crumbled to the floor. The telephone receiver, which had slipped from her fingers, dangled helplessly on its spiral cord. Her body trembled as she huddled there, clutching her knees to her chest. Memories tripped over each other as they tumbled from the recesses of her mind, where they had been locked away for years. Ten years. Her breath came in short gasps, forced past the tightness in her chest. Time slipped away as she relived her nightmare—her aching body, her swollen eyes, her blood-sticky legs—as her unborn baby paid the ultimate price of her daddy's rage.

The room had grown dark by the time Francis slowly got to her feet and placed the dangling receiver into its cradle. *I have to keep the children safe!* The thought suddenly hit her. Heart pounding, she hurried to check the deadbolt on the front door. She peeked into the children's bedrooms—both were sound asleep. Relief flooded over her. Retracing her steps, she sat down on the living room couch and picked up her Bible, clutching it to her chest. *It's been ten years! Why now?* She thought she had forgiven Mike years ago. Hadn't she prayed for him often? Why then, did her body react like it was yesterday?

"Lord, I need you," Francis pleaded quietly, rocking back and forth as she fought for control over the waves of anxiety attacking her. "Protect me and the children. Please keep us safe. I feel so weak and helpless. Lord, give me strength and wisdom."

"Be of good courage, and he shall strengthen your heart, all ye that hope in the Lord."

"Thank you, Lord." Francis felt a degree of calmness steal over her. "Jesus, I need you more than ever," she whispered as she turned to Psalm 31:24 and read the words the Lord gave her. She continued reading and praying for a good part of the night, drawing strength from the living Word.

Mary pulled on a knee-length navy skirt and a pale pink blouse the next morning. She studied her face in the mirror as she pulled her straight brown hair into a pony-tail at the nape of her neck. Her soft brown eyes were very ordinary, as was her heart-shaped face. Her small, straight nose and full lips were probably her best feature. If she had a volume of gorgeous curls like Lena, then maybe she'd take more time with her hair, but as it was, she looked quite plain. She'd accepted that she was no beauty a long time ago.

"Looks don't matter to me anyways," she muttered to herself as she laid down her brush and turned from the mirror. "It's not like I'm trying to snag a guy."

"Good morning, Mary," Anna said as her daughter entered the kitchen. She was stirring a pot of porridge on the gas stove they had installed a few years ago. It was a huge improvement from the wood cook stove they used to have—especially during the heat of summer.

"Good morning," Mary said cheerily, including her papa with her smile. He was already sitting at the head of the table, waiting for breakfast to be served. Retrieving dishes from the cupboard, she started setting the table.

Benny came through the front door with a galvanized pail of fresh milk, which he set on the counter. "Chores are all done," he announced.

"Thanks Benny," Anna said, placing a steaming pot of porridge on the table. "Wash up then—breakfast is ready."

As he passed Mary, Benny poked her in the ribs—laughing when she jumped—then made a quick retreat into the bathroom, slamming the door behind him. Mary was waiting for him when he came out and cuffed his ear.

"You watch out, boy, or I'll..."

"You'll what?" Benny laughed, dancing in front of her like a boxer in a ring, his fists making short punching jabs at her. Benny was tall for his age and towered over Mary's five feet two inches.

"*Oba*, Benny," Anna scolded her son with a chuckle in her voice. "Now sit down and let's eat."

They were still laughing as they sat down at the table. They bowed their heads and, as was the Mennonite custom, silently thanked the Lord for the food.

"How was the wedding?" Anna asked her daughter, dishing up porridge for herself and Jacob.

"It was wonderful," Mary said, buttering her toast. "Lena was radiant—they both looked fabulous." Jacob smiled, nodding his head at her from where he sat at the head of the table.

Mary reached over and patted his hand. "You want to know all about the wedding?"

Jacob nodded his head again. His speech hadn't progressed the way they would have liked but—between hand gestures, facial expressions, and a few words—the family could usually figure out what he meant. Jacob was difficult to take care of away from home so Anna had decided they wouldn't attend the wedding.

After Mary finished talking about the wedding, Jacob turned his attention to Benny.

"Cows?" he asked; it was his way of asking about the farm.

"I turned the cows out to pasture," Benny said, between bites of oatmeal and toast. "The horses need their hooves trimmed. I'll talk to Mr. Regier about that today." Jacob nodded his approval. He was proud of his son's interest in farming and happy knowing that Benny would follow in his footsteps. They still rented their land out, since Benny was still in school, but Jacob could see the day coming when Benny would take over.

After breakfast, Mary pushed her chair back from the table and carried her dirty dishes to the cupboard as Benny headed out the door. He had taken a job working for Mr. Regier, the local veterinarian, for the summer. Anna helped Jacob to his recliner in the living room, where he spent most of his time.

When Anna came back into the kitchen, she started clearing the table. "Did John bring you home last night?" she asked her daughter.

"Yes he did." Mary's tone was guarded as she strained the milk into one-gallon jars. They didn't use the cream separator in the morning.

"He doesn't have a girlfriend?"

"No, Mama."

Anna set the dirty dishes on the counter, then turned to carefully search Mary's face.

"I was hoping that you and John would start dating," she confessed. "He would be good for you, Mary."

"*Oba*, Mama!" Mary exclaimed, trying to keep her tone light.

"Seriously, Mary, I worry about you. Your friends are getting married, and you are so engrossed in your work and helping me and Papa that you never even date. I worry that we've put too much responsibility on you, and you are missing out on your own life."

"I don't want to date, Mama." Mary set the milk in the fridge. It was unusual for her mama to speak up like this. "I don't want to get married, so I see no reason to date."

"Don't you really, Mary?" her mama questioned earnestly, watching her closely.

"Really, Mama." Mary gave her mama a quick sideways hug in passing. "And for the record, you're not putting too much responsibility on me. I don't mind helping out."

"I just want you to be happy." Anna sighed as she turned the faucet on.

"Don't worry about me, Mama," Mary said, picking up her keys as she headed towards the door. "See you later."

Mary rubbed Skipper's ears as she headed to her car. The old golden retriever padded alongside her, stopping when she opened the car door. "See you later, Skipper," she said, closing the door and starting the engine.

She had taken a job at the only accounting firm in their small town after her papa had his stroke. Originally she was hired as a part-time filing clerk for the growing business—probably out of compassion for her family's plight—but her employers quickly discovered her knack for numbers and her ability to learn quickly. They had trained her and now she had an office and her own regular clients.

As she drove into town, Mary's mind drifted back to how difficult the adjustment had been on the family. Her papa had always been their tower of strength until the day he had a stroke. Their family dynamics had changed drastically overnight. Mary stayed home from school to do the chores and take a part-time job. She had finished high school by correspondence. Her mama had rented out their land and, as soon as Benny was old enough to do the chores, Mary started working full time at the accounting business. *It was hard but we squeaked by,* Mary thought as she parked her car in front of J&H Accounting. She was proud that they had pulled together as a family to keep the farm.

The community came together for us, as well, she thought to herself as she walked across the dirt parking lot to the brown brick building. Men from the community had volunteered to renovate their house, making it easier for her papa to manoeuvre around in his wheelchair. They added a bathroom and indoor plumbing—making it easier to take care of her papa. The electrical company installed power lines so they were able to get electricity, and they had installed a gas furnace.

Through it all, God has been good to us, Mary mused as she opened the door.

"Mom, do you know where my glove is?" Brad asked, entering the kitchen where Francis was busy making lunch. "I can't find my glove." Brad had a minor league baseball game that afternoon.

"Have you looked in the entrance closet?" As Francis tucked a strand of shoulder-length brunette hair behind her ear, she heard him open the closet doors and rummage around. After a fitful night filled with nightmare extensions of Mike's phone call, her heart was palpitating and her hands were shaky. This morning, her mirror had told her she looked frazzled around the edges; her blue-grey eyes had a frightened look and worry lines creased her otherwise flawless forehead. *I have to keep it together for the kids,* she told herself as she took a deep breath and willed herself to calm down.

"Found it," Brad called.

"Good, then come and eat." Francis set a pot of soup and hotdogs on the table.

"Chantel," Francis called down the hall, "lunch is ready."

"I'm coming."

When Chantel joined them at the table, Francis asked Brad to say grace.

"Lord, thank you for this food. Please bless it to our bodies, and bless Mom for all she does for us. Help us to win the baseball game today. Amen." Brad winked as Francis turned to him. "I couldn't help it, Mom. We need all the prayers we can get." Francis had taught her children not to pray for winning, but rather to pray for a good game.

"It's not about winning, Brad," Francis said, as she dished soup into her bowl. "The other team wants to win, too. It's way more important to have a good game where everyone can have fun."

"Mom, remember I'm going to spend the night at Sydney's house," Chantel said, crumbling crackers into the bowl of soup her mom set before her.

"Oh, that's right. Sydney's having an overnight birthday party," Francis said, fixing her hotdog. "Do you have your bag packed?"

"Yes, I do." Chantel's long blonde curls cascaded down either side of her face as she reached across the table for a hotdog. "We're going to have a pajama party."

"Don't stay up too late," Francis cautioned her daughter, then turned to her son. "Brad, are you mowing the Fraser's lawn after the game today?"

"Yep," Brad said around a mouthful of food. He took another huge bite from his hotdog.

"Chew your food, Brad. It's not healthy to eat so fast," Francis admonished her son. *That boy can't sit still long enough to enjoy his food.*

Brad grinned at his mom, his blue eyes twinkling. "I'd be late for my game if I slowed down."

"You have a point," Francis admitted, smiling at her son. "The amount of food you put away could feed an army!"

"He just wants to be the first one ready for dessert," Chantel said, still fixing her plate.

"You're going to have to start eating, Chantel, or you'll go to the game hungry." Francis reached over and poured Chantel a glass of water.

The two children were opposites in so many ways—Brad was tall with a husky build and lived for sports, while Chantel was petite and content to play with her dolls.

"We better get going." Francis downed the last of her coffee and went in search of her purse.

"Shotgun!" Brad called as the two children ran out of the apartment complex ahead of their mother. Francis followed them, double checking to ensure the door was locked before heading down the stairs and out to the car.

At the baseball diamond, Brad grabbed his glove and ran to join his team, leaving Francis and Chantel to find good seats in the stands. The opposing team was up to bat first, so Brad's team jogged to their positions on the field. Brad stepped onto the pitcher's mound and threw a few practice balls to the back-catcher.

When the first batter stepped up to the plate, Brad wound up and released a fastball over the edge of home plate. The batter swung and missed. The second pitch was a ball. One strike, one ball. Brad wound up again and released the ball in a straight shot across the plate. The batter knocked a low ball into left field. In one fluid motion, the left-field man picked up the ball and threw it to first base. Batter out.

Francis and Chantel cheered with the rest of their team's parents. The second batter made it to second base but the third batter struck out. The fourth batter popped a fly ball, which the short stop caught in his glove. Three down. Brad's team was up to bat.

"Hi Francis." Francis turned to see Gloria and Emily coming towards them. "May we sit with you?"

"By all means," Francis said, moving over to make room for them. "It's good to see you." *Where have I seen her before?* Francis wondered again, racking her brain. She was overcome by the feeling that she knew Gloria from somewhere. *Maybe she just looks like someone I've seen before.*

Francis shook off the feeling as they turned their attention to baseball, where the first batter from Brad's team took his stance. He popped up a fly ball, which the pitcher caught. A collective sigh emanated from the stands. One down. The second batter hit the ball into right field and made it to first base. The third batter drove the ball beyond the left fielder and made it to second base. The next batter walked. Bases loaded.

Brad stepped up to the plate, took a few practice swings, and took his stance—a semi-crouch bent slightly forward, legs spread apart, hands firmly clutching the bat.

"That's my son," Francis whispered to Gloria. She held her breath. The pitcher wound up, Brad swung, and hit a foul ball.

"Strike one!" the umpire shouted, jabbing his finger into the air above his head.

Brad took his stance again. The pitcher wound up and released the ball. Brad didn't swing.

"Ball," the umpire shouted. "One strike, one ball."

Francis felt her heart racing. "Come on, Brad, you can do it," she said more to herself than to anyone.

Brad resumed his stance. The pitcher wound up and released the ball, followed by a solid thump as wood hit leather and the ball went flying high over the pitcher's mound and far into centre field. The crowd was on their feet, cheering as the runners from all three bases sped around the diamond and touched home base. As Brad rounded third base at full speed, the crowd yelled for him to watch out—the ball was being thrown toward home! With a few yards left, Brad flung himself to the ground—stretching his arm out ahead of himself—sliding into home base a split second ahead of the back catcher.

"Safe!" the umpire yelled.

Chantel and Emily jumped up and down, cheering and clapping. Francis sank back onto the bleachers, her heart pounding.

"He's good," Gloria said, resuming her seat beside her newly found friend.

"He's going to give me a heart attack one of these days!" Francis exclaimed. "He takes so many chances."

"The only way to play the game." Gloria chuckled.

"He usually makes it, too." Francis smiled, her chest filled with pride. "I must admit, it makes the game exciting."

Brad's team stayed far enough ahead that the rest of the innings were easier on Francis. As they carried on a conversation between plays, Francis noticed dark circles under Gloria's eyes that she hadn't noticed in church the day before. *Maybe it's the difference in lighting,* she thought.

"There's a ladies' Bible study at church Wednesday evening," Francis told Gloria as they walked to their cars after the game. "You're welcome to come."

"I would love to go," Gloria assured her. "What time?"

"Seven-thirty," Francis told her, rummaging in her purse for her keys.

"I'll see you there," Gloria called over her shoulder as she continued to her car.

After dropping Chantel off at Sydney's house and Brad leaving to mow the Fraser's lawn, Francis dialled Maggie's number. If there was one person she could count on, it was Maggie.

"Hello." Maggie's cheerful voice greeted her after the second ring.

"Hi Maggie," Francis said, massaging her throat. "Could you come over for tea? I need to talk to you."

"Is something wrong?" Maggie asked, concern lacing her voice.

"Something came up yesterday that I need advice on," Francis told her. "I need to talk to you in private. The kids are both out of the house, but I need to be here when Brad comes home."

"I'll be there in a couple of minutes," Maggie told her.

"Thanks, Maggie. I appreciate it." Francis returned the receiver to its cradle. "What would I do without Maggie?" she asked herself as she put water on to boil. She grabbed a couple of mugs from the mug tree on the counter. Teacups were for leisurely, relaxed occasions. Today was serious talk time—they would need the bigger mugs.

It didn't take long before a knock at the door announced Maggie's arrival. Francis opened the door and invited her into the kitchen.

"I'm so glad you could come at such short notice." Francis pulled out a chair at the table for her friend, before pouring tea into the mugs.

"I don't leave the house enough," Maggie said, stirring a dollop of honey into her tea. She studied Francis, who joined her at the table. "What's up?"

Francis sat opposite her elderly friend, who was more a mother to her than her own mother was. She had met Maggie at the diner where she worked when she and Mike first moved to Edmonton. Maggie had been a cook and Francis a server. She had taken Francis under her wing when she found out Francis' mother had disowned her when she married Mike. Now Maggie was retired, her hair a beautiful snow-white, and she walked with a limp due to arthritis in her knees.

"Mike called," Francis blurted out, her fingers wrapped around the mug in her hands. "I don't know what to do."

Maggie's eyes grew wide, her mug freezing in midair, as she stared at her friend. "Mike?"

Francis nodded.

Maggie slowly brought the mug down and set it on the table. "When did he call?"

"Last night."

"Why? What did he want?" Maggie's mind raced in a million different directions.

"I don't know." Francis' voice trembled as she shrugged her shoulders. "I was shocked. I couldn't talk to him."

"What did you do? What did he say?"

"He said it was good to hear my voice. That he was sorry." Francis looked down at her hands—they had started shaking again. Maggie noticed and covered them with her own. "My head started swimming, and I ended up on the floor. Memories overwhelmed me, and I sat there a long time. When I got up, the house was dark. I made sure the deadbolt was locked and the children were safe." She raised pain-filled eyes to Maggie. "What will I do?"

"Does he know where you live?" Maggie asked, her own eyes filled with concern.

"I don't know," Francis answered. "Like I said, I couldn't talk. The receiver must have slipped from my hands as I crumbled to the floor. It all came back to me in a flash."

"Would you feel better if you came to stay with us for a while?" Maggie asked.

"I don't want the kids to find out," Francis said, shrugging her shoulders. "They would have a lot of questions if they were uprooted from their home."

"They don't know he called?"

"No, they were already in bed."

"I'm at a loss, Francis," Maggie admitted. In all her seventy years, she had never been so unsure of what to do. "Maybe you should call the police."

"What would I tell them? That my husband called? I don't think that's against the law."

"You could get a restraining order."

"What good would that do if he shows up? Anyways, I don't want to involve the police." Francis stood up and walked over to the window overlooking the parking lot and the playground beyond. She had moved into this apartment after Mike left, so he wouldn't be able to find her and the children. The thought that he might be looking for them hadn't crossed her mind in years.

"Why would he call after all these years?" Maggie wondered out loud, still trying to wrap her head around it. "I certainly didn't expect it anymore." She had been the one to find Francis beaten up in her apartment. After Francis called in to work sick for a couple of days, Maggie had gone over to see if there was

37

anything she could do to help. As it turned out, there was plenty. Francis had hardly been able to see out of her swollen eyes, and she had bruises over most of her body. But the most heartbreaking had been that through it all she had miscarried her third child. Maggie and Dale had taken Francis and her children to their house, took her to a doctor, and nursed her back to health. They had even found this apartment for her when she was well enough to take care of the children again.

"I think you should talk to Pastor Bob," Maggie suggested. "He has a lot of connections. Maybe he knows someone who could help you."

Francis turned away from the window. "Yes, maybe I should," she agreed with a sigh.

Maggie prayed with Francis before she left and promised to keep praying for them. Francis knew it was not an empty promise.

CHAPTER 3

Mary locked the door to J&H Accounting. The hot July sun beat down on her, and she searched the sky for any sign of clouds as she walked to her car and opened the door.

Lord, please send rain, she prayed as she slid into the driver's seat.

"Eiyeeyee!" she exclaimed as she came in contact with the hot seat. She wiggled her skirt into a better position between her thighs and the seat, then she turned down the window. Leaning across the passenger seat, she turned that window down as well. Turning the key in the ignition, she backed out of the parking stall and pulled onto Main Street.

Springwater was a small farming town—more like a village but everyone called it a town—where everybody knew everyone else. A handful of businesses were set back haphazardly on either side of Main Street, which consisted of a gravel road running the length of town and beyond into the rural area. Neatly kept yards and bungalow-style houses made up the residential area down a few gravel side streets. The largest buildings were the red-brick school and white church.

Mary turned off of Main Street and parked in front of the general store. She had promised to pick up groceries for Mama before heading home.

"Hi Mary." Her friend Martha greeted her cheerily from behind the counter. "Hot enough for you?"

"Sure is," Mary said with a smile. "I wish it would rain."

"You and everyone else," Martha said, concern creeping into her voice. "Papa says the crops are beginning to suffer."

"We've been watering our garden, but that doesn't help as much as the rain would," Mary said. She walked down the aisle to pick up a few baking supplies.

"Hi Mary."

Mary turned to the sound of a familiar voice behind her.

"Hi Annie, how are you?" she asked. "I haven't seen you in a long time."

"Yeah, I mostly stay at home." Annie looked tired. She wiped a few moist strands of red hair from her forehead. The little girl in the cart she was pushing started whining. It looked like she would be a big sister soon.

"Congratulations!" Mary said with a smile, nodding towards Annie's protruding midsection. "I didn't know you were expecting."

"Thanks." Annie smiled and her shoulders lifted a little. "It makes for a very hot and tiring summer."

"I bet," Mary said, remembering the heat she felt that July her baby was born. "Is there anything I can do to help out?"

"Oh no, we'll be fine," Annie told her. "Thanks anyways. This heat is just getting to me." The toddler whined louder, and her mother took her leave. Mary turned back to the baking supplies.

The car kicked up a plume of dust as Mary drove down the gravel road. The fifteen-minute drive to the farm gave her time to reflect on her teenage years when she had been drawn into Annie's party scene.

"I don't blame Annie," she told herself. Mary had been unable to come to terms with David's tragic death so—turning her back on God and her parents—she had started hanging out with Annie and her partying friends.

"I was worse than any of them," she muttered. Getting drunk out of her mind, she got pregnant and, at the request of the baby's father, ran away to the city to have an abortion. "But God looked out for me and brought Francis into my life."

Francis, a friendly Christian lady with two small children, had literally rescued her and convinced her to give her baby up for adoption instead of aborting it. Mary's heart carried a constant pain ever since her little girl had been taken from her arms. Only a few people in Edmonton knew about that part of her life. She had eventually told Mama and Papa about the baby but not about the depth of depression she had sunk into that summer and fall. *It's only by the grace of God that I didn't end my own life,* she thought to herself as she wiped an errant tear from her eye.

Annie had married Isaac—who still couldn't stay out of the bottle. She was already expecting her third child and, if there was any truth to what the local gossips said, it sounded like their marriage was suffering. Mary sighed as she turned into her driveway. She wished there was some way she could help Annie. She had tried talking to her about God, but Annie wanted none of it, saying that people who called themselves Christians were hypocrites.

What can I say to that? Mary thought as she picked up the bag of groceries and walked to the house. *Am I a hypocrite because I haven't told anyone about my daughter? How can I witness for the Lord when I'm not honest with my friends? Jesus has forgiven me, but I don't trust others to do the same.*

"Francis, wait up."

Francis was just leaving the church after Wednesday night Bible study. She turned and saw Gloria hurrying to catch up.

"What's up?" She asked when Gloria fell into step beside her.

"I'm so glad you invited me for Bible study." Gloria flung her black curls back with a quick twist of her head. "I really enjoyed it. I was sad to leave our church family in Red Deer, but I feel so welcome here. It's more than I could have asked for."

"That's how I felt when I first started attending here," Francis said. "They helped me out so much when I felt like I was all alone in the world."

"Yeah, that's how I feel." Francis thought she detected sadness in Gloria's voice. "I have a doctor's appointment tomorrow afternoon and need someone to keep Emily. Do you know any good sitters?" Gloria asked.

"What time?"

"Four o'clock."

"Bring her over to my house," Francis said. "I'll be home and Chantel would love playing with her. They seemed to hit it off at the baseball game."

"Oh, I don't want to impose on you!" Gloria exclaimed, but Francis saw the relief wash over her face.

"It's not a problem," Francis assured her with a smile. "We would love to have her."

"I really appreciate that. Chantel was all Emily could talk about after the game."

They had reached Francis' car by the time she had given Gloria her street address and directions.

"Thank you so much," Gloria said as she turned to go.

"I'm looking forward to it." Francis opened the car door. "See you tomorrow."

Francis turned up her car radio and sang along with the familiar Christian songs as she turned her car into the street. She felt a calmness in her heart since she had talked to Pastor Bob before Bible study. He had encouraged her and prayed with her.

"Let's stop at A&W for a burger," Brad suggested when Francis picked him and Chantel up from their friend's house.

"Yes, let's," Chantel piped up from the backseat. "I want a milkshake."

"No, we need to get home so you kids can go to bed," Francis said. If he had his way, Brad would never let her drive past an A&W without picking up something to eat.

"Please, Mom?" they pleaded in unison.

"I said no. You can eat something when we get home." She hated saying no to them, but they'd had a big supper and she knew they weren't hungry.

"Awe, Mom," Chantel pouted. "You never take us to A&W."

"That's not true; we were there just last week," her mother said. "We need to get home so you can go to bed. By the way, Mrs. Simpson is bringing Emily over tomorrow afternoon."

"Who's that?" Brad asked.

"Mrs. Simpson and her daughter Emily just moved here from Red Deer. Remember, they sat with us in church last Sunday?"

"We sat with them at your baseball game," Chantel said, cheering up. "I like Emily."

Francis turned into their parking lot and parked the car. The children scrambled out and raced towards the grey-brick apartment building, through the double glass doors, and up the single flight of stairs. Francis followed at a slower pace.

After the children were in bed, Francis made herself a cup of tea and was on her way to the living room when the phone rang.

"Hello," she said tentatively into the receiver, setting her cup on the counter.

"Francis, please don't hang up." Mike's voice came across the line.

"Why are you calling me? Why now?"

"It's a long story, but I cleaned up my life. I realize you don't want to see me or hear from me, but I need to know that you and the kids are alright. I need to ask you to forgive me."

Mike has no right to ask about the kids—or forgiveness! Francis fumed inwardly as the walls around her heart stood tall and strong. There was a hard edge to her voice when she spoke again. "After all this time, why are you suddenly interested in the kids? They don't even know you."

"Francis, I've changed. I need to talk to you. Please." He paused. When he spoke again, his voice was just above a whisper. "The baby, was it a boy or a girl?"

Francis gasped at the sharp pain that seared her chest. *He doesn't even know he killed the baby!* Pure, unadulterated rage ripped through her.

"Please don't call me anymore." Francis' voice sounded strangled as it squeaked past the tightness in her chest. "If you've really changed, you can talk to my pastor. Then I'll decide what to do." She tried desperately to control her voice as she gave him Pastor Bob's name and phone number before slamming the receiver into its cradle.

Francis picked up her cup of tea and carried it into the living room with her. *Forgive Mike? How can I forgive him?* She sank onto the couch as the memories washed over her.

"You are not going to ruin my life, sweetheart," he had snarled, pulling her up against his chest. He had smelled of alcohol and perfume. It had made her sick to her stomach. "You want another baby? You take care of it!" he had shouted in her face, grabbing her shoulders. "You're not going to trap me with your little schemes."

"Mike, stop—you're pulling my hair," she had whimpered.

The punch to the side of her head had sent her sprawling, and her head hit the rocking chair. She had screamed as he landed a kick in her right side and another in her back. He had yanked her up by her hair. Totally out of control, his eyes blazing, he had punched her over and over, releasing his pent-up fury on her. Blackness had engulfed her.

Francis had slowly made her way out of the dark fog. She had tried to open her eyes, but her eyelids felt thick and heavy. The bed felt too hard. She had rolled over to find a more comfortable position, and a sharp pain shot through her abdomen. Instinctively, she had curled her legs up to her tummy. They felt wet and sticky. Her head throbbed, and her body ached. She had forced her eyelids open and realized she was lying on the floor. *Mike.* Slowly, she had turned her head and searched the room for him as memories flooded back. He wasn't there.

Where is he? She had wondered. She pulled herself up into a sitting position but immediately doubled over and clutched her abdomen. She felt as if a vise clasped her midsection in its grip.

No! Oh God, no! Not my baby! A sob caught in her throat as she had realized what was happening. She clutched her abdomen and doubled over with another searing contraction.

No! Francis had cried silently. *Please, no!* Tears poured down her face. A sharp pain stabbed through her breaking heart. Her unborn baby had fallen victim to her daddy's rage. The tiny life had been snuffed out almost before it began.

How could Mike do this to me? To us? Sobs had wracked her body as she half sat and half lay on the floor with her head propped up on the side of the couch.

Francis wiped at the tears streaming down her cheeks. That had been the most awful night of her life. She hadn't realized until the following day that while she was lying unconscious on the floor, Mike had packed his clothes and left. She hadn't heard from him since. It had been difficult bringing up the children on her own but—with the help of friends—she had not only made it, she had also found the Lord. Why was Mike coming back into her life now?

John ran up the grey cement steps to the white church building two at a time. Pastor Penner had called him in for a meeting about his upcoming mission to Mexico. He opened one of the double glass doors and walked quickly across the grey carpeted floor to the pastor's office.

"Good afternoon, John." Pastor Penner got up from behind his wooden desk to shake John's hand. Mr. Anton Wieler, the head of the mission board, sat in a chair across from the pastor.

"Thank you for coming on such short notice. Please have a seat." The pastor motioned to an empty chair. Mr. Wieler stood up and shook John's hand.

"I'm afraid Mr. Wieler has some bad news," Pastor Penner said, sinking back into his chair. "I'll let him explain since he got the phone call."

"I received a call from the mission centre in Mexico yesterday evening," Mr. Wieler said. "A couple of counsellors at the shelter have fallen sick to malaria. Nobody knows when they'll be able to return—so they need reinforcements." Mr. Wieler studied John with kind eyes. "Since you are planning to go anyways, we thought you might be willing to go right away."

John felt as if he'd been punched in the stomach.

"Go right away? What does that mean?" he asked the two men who were watching him closely.

"As soon as you can reasonably do so," Mr. Wieler answered.

"You don't have to answer right now," Pastor Penner said. "Think about it. Pray about it. Then let us know. Just remember, they need help as we speak."

John turned his gaze to the window. *I was looking forward to spending time with Mary. Maybe if we could spend the winter seeing each other, she would realize that we are meant to be together.*

"This is a big decision," John said, running his hand through his hair. *God, do you really want me to go to Mexico now?* He swallowed hard. "I don't know what to say."

"Son, we realize this is a big decision," Mr. Wieler said, nodding his silver-covered head. "You weren't scheduled to go until spring, and we realize that you were looking forward to spending some months at home with your family. I hate to rush you, but we need to know by the end of the week."

John promised to think it over, pray about it, and let them know. He shook hands with both men and left the church, deep in thought. He stopped at the post office before heading home and almost ran into Mary as she came out of the building.

"Hi John," she greeted him, a smile lighting up her face.

"Hi Mary," he said, holding the door open for her. He walked her to her car.

"Do you mind if I come over later tonight?" he asked. "Something has come up that I would like to discuss with you."

Mary searched his serious eyes and knew she couldn't turn him down. *Why am I so weak?*

"Yes, of course," she said. "Has something happened?"

"It's about my upcoming mission trip. I'll see you later." He turned to leave.

"See you," Mary called after him as she opened her car door.

"Something is bothering him," Mary told herself as she backed out of the parking stall and turned onto Main Street. "He looked so serious. I hope it's not bad news."

Skipper wagged his tail at Mary from where he lay on the lawn as she drove up to her house. Mary parked the car and got out.

"Hi Skipper," she greeted him. "How are you?" Skipper answered her with a steady thump-thump of his tail, but he didn't bother to get up. Mary stooped down and scratched his ears. "You poor dog," she told him. "Arthritis bothering you or is it too hot for you, too?" Skipper kept thumping his tail as he looked up at her with sad eyes. Mary left the dog and ran up the steps to her house.

"Hi Mama, Papa," she called, closing the front door behind her.

"M...Mary," her papa said from his chair in the living room. Her mama was nowhere in sight. She walked into the living room and sat down beside her papa.

"How are you doing today, Papa?" she asked as she rubbed his hand. He nodded and smiled at her.

"I had a busy day," she told him. "After work, I ran into John at the post office. He wants to come over tonight." There was a definite twinkle in her papa's eyes.

"Oh Papa, not you too!" she exclaimed, rolling her eyes at him in mock exasperation. "He said it had something to do with his upcoming mission trip. Remember, I told you he's going to Mexico on missions?"

Her papa squeezed her hand and nodded.

"Where is Mama?"

Jacob pointed to the door. "Out."

"Outside? Is she in the garden?" Jacob nodded again.

"I'll go see if she wants me to start supper." She patted her papa's hand as she left in search of her mama.

She found her mama bent over in the garden, picking peas, her head invisible under her big straw hat. Mary chuckled to herself. Her mama always wore a straw hat when she worked outside in the summer.

"Do you want me to start supper or pick peas?" Mary asked as she got closer.

"I made a potato salad, and there's leftover meatloaf in the fridge." Anna straightened up. "You can help me finish picking these peas if you want. You better get out of your work clothes first, though."

"Alright, I'll be right back." Mary turned and jogged back to the house only to return in a few minutes in her work clothes.

"Sure wish it would rain," she said as she bent over the peas. "It's been awfully warm lately."

"*Ach jo*, rain would be good, both for the crops and gardens," Anna said.

"There's just no escaping the heat."

"All in God's time. We must be patient."

"I'm surprised our garden is still doing so well."

"*Jo,* the water Benny pumped onto it has helped a lot."

"Where is Benny?"

"He's helping Mr. Regier deliver calves at the Friesens'."

"Benny's helping Mr. Regier quite a bit lately."

"Mr. Regier isn't getting any younger, and Benny loves animals."

"Yes, he does," Mary said, chuckling. "Remember how he always wanted to be outside with the cows and horses when he wasn't even going to school yet?"

Anna picked the last peas from the plant and straightened up, rubbing the small of her back. She had a faraway look in her eyes.

"*Ach jo.* David always teased him about it. David didn't have the same love for animals—he wanted adventure."

"Did you know David wanted to be a missionary?"

"No, I didn't." Anna turned to face her daughter, a faraway, misty look in her eyes. "It doesn't surprise me, though. Our David had such a zeal for God!"

"Don't you wonder sometimes why God took him home when he was so on fire for the Lord?"

"*Ach* Mary, who can understand God's ways?" Anna asked wistfully. "God's ways are not our ways. We can't see what he sees, so we just have to trust him. God knows what's best for us."

"I know, life is just hard to understand," Mary said as she picked up two brimming five-gallon pails of peas. She knew Mama missed David just as much as she did.

After the supper dishes were done, Mary took her book outside and sat on the lawn swing to wait for John. It was almost nine o'clock when she heard John's car drive up. She closed her book and got to her feet, her heart beating a little faster, like it always did when she saw him.

"Hi John," she greeted him with a smile. He looked good in his blue jeans and Western style shirt. "I had almost given up on you."

"Hi Mary." A grin spread across his face as he closed the car door. Turning his back to the door, he leaned against it nonchalantly, folding his arms across his chest as he watched Mary approach. She had changed into a yellow-flowered shift dress that complimented her figure without being suggestive. "You look great," he said appreciatively.

"I was just thinking the same," she answered, laughing up at him.

"Really? Then we're agreed that you look great," he teased, his eyes glinting with laughter.

Mary cuffed his arm indignantly. "You know what I mean. You look great."

John laughed as he stepped forward. "Let's take a walk to the cabin."

"That's a great idea," Mary agreed, turning in that direction. "We might as well enjoy the long summer days while we have them. Winter will be upon us soon enough."

Mary enjoyed the light banter between them, the sun on her shoulders, the deep green of the tall poplars on one side of the dusty path, and the golden blossoms of the canola fields on the other. She could almost forget her sorrow as she looked up into John's clean-shaven face towering over her by a good ten inches. He caught her hand and for a moment they stood gazing into each other's eyes. A powerful connection sizzled between them. Mary was helplessly mesmerized as John's head bent closer to hers, his cologne filling her senses. Her hand reached up to touch his face. The memory of a soft, tiny, newborn baby flitted through her mind. She dropped her eyes and her hand.

"What's wrong, Mary?" John asked gently, rubbing his thumb across the skin of the small, soft hand still clasped in his own. *Something is holding her back. I saw the yearning in her eyes.* "What is it?"

"I'm sorry," Mary mumbled. Mortified by her lapse, she pulled her hand free and started down the path, her heart thumping in her chest.

John swept his fingers through his hair in frustration before following her. The carefree mood was broken, and they walked in silence the rest of the way.

"Have you been working on the cabin?" Mary broke the silence as John swung the cabin door open for her. "The door didn't creak."

"Yes, I fixed it up a bit." John admitted, letting his gaze sweep across the room. "I oiled the door hinges, put up some new shingles, and cleaned up in here. I can't let this place deteriorate; it's too special to me."

"Me too." Mary agreed, running her hand over the wooden table top. "It makes me feel close to David." She sat down on one of the two wooden chairs. John pulled the other chair out from the table and sat down across from her.

"You wanted to tell me about your mission trip," Mary prompted, looking towards him without meeting his eyes.

John leaned forward, his arms resting on the table. "First, I need to know what happened back there on the path." He paused, searching for the right words. "I know what I saw in your eyes," he insisted. He reached across the table and took her hands. "Please look at me." His voice was so gentle that she couldn't resist looking up and meeting his soft brown eyes. "I'm sorry if I frightened you back there. I promise I would never do anything inappropriate."

"It was nothing. A moment of weakness." Mary shrugged, dropping her eyes to her hands. She lifted her eyes to meet his momentarily. "I wasn't frightened. I know I can trust you." She owed him that much.

John sighed as he leaned back in his chair. "Okay then." Frustration was evident in his voice. He took a deep breath and changed the subject. "I had a meeting with Pastor Penner and Mr. Wieler at the church this afternoon. Apparently there has been a malaria outbreak amongst the missionaries at the boys' shelter in Mexico. They asked if I could go immediately." John kept his eyes focused on Mary's face, trying to read her thoughts.

Shock registered on Mary's face. "When are you going?" she choked out.

"I don't have anything keeping me here. I talked it over with my parents at supper tonight, which is why I was so late getting here. They agree that if there's an escalated need then I should go."

Mary looked down at her hands. A sinking feeling of loneliness in her heart. *He's leaving again. Why shouldn't he? I can't keep him here.* She would miss him terribly. She felt his hand under her chin, lifting her face to meet his eyes. She blinked back the unbidden tears.

"Mary, if you don't love me then why is my leaving so hard for you?" Her eyes were sad and misty.

Mary shook her head slightly, unable to speak to the raw emotion she heard in his voice.

"I've loved you since David and I built this cabin, and you came around to help out or just watch us," John told her. "You were so pretty, trying your best to lift those heavy logs. I was impressed by your strength, your humour, and your stubborn drive to get things done. At first David was annoyed that I fell in love with you, but later on he decided it would be cool if we were brothers."

"You told him?" Mary was astonished. *No wonder David always teased me about John!*

"We were best friends, of course I told him. My feelings have only grown deeper over the years. I have prayed that the Lord will remove these feelings I have for you—if you are not the person he has for me—but so far that hasn't happened." John wiped at a tear that escaped the corner of Mary's eye.

"I'm so sorry, John." She reached up and touched his dear face. "You mean so much to me. I don't want to hurt you. I love your friendship, but trust me, I'm not the right girl for you."

"I think you are," John said, exhaling rather forcefully. "But if friendship is the best you can offer then I'll settle for that. I don't want to lose you completely."

"You will always be very dear to me," Mary promised, willing her eyes to keep the secrets of her heart. She had to convince John that he was only a dear friend.

"May I write you when I'm in Mexico?"

"Yes, I would love that. You can tell me all about your exciting adventures." Her smile was a bit shaky, but she managed.

John stood up and pulled her out of her chair and into his arms. "I have to hold you this once before I leave."

Mary laid her head on John's chest. She could hear the regular thump-thump of his heart. His strong arms around her felt so right, even while her heart was breaking. *If only I could tell him about my baby. If only he would understand! But he would never forgive me, and I would lose him completely. This is the only way I can keep him in my life.*

Hand in hand, they walked back in the dusk, talking about his upcoming mission trip and what might be waiting for him once he got to Mexico.

CHAPTER 4

Mike held the receiver to his ear even after he heard the click on the other end. With a sigh, he hung up. He poured himself a cup of coffee, adding a little milk. Crossing the floor, he sat down at the small table in his cozy, one-bedroom apartment, overlooking a busy city street. *If only she would hear me out.* He ran his fingers through his thick blond curls as he watched the traffic below. So many people were rushing to go somewhere, to someone. He looked down at the slip of paper in his hands. Her pastor's phone number. *So she has a pastor. That must mean she goes to church. I wonder if she's become a Christian.* Thoughts tumbled over each other in his mind.

Ten years. Mike sighed deeply, feeling the familiar loneliness settle over him. It had been a long ten years. He picked up a family picture and traced Francis' face, then Brad's and Chantel's. The picture was taken when Chantel was just a few months old. *What do they look like now?* Brad and Chantel would have changed, of course—they would have grown up. What about Francis? Was she still the same beautiful lady he had married? *Why didn't she tell me if the baby was a boy or girl?* His heart ached for his family.

He felt bad for having called her on the phone—it seemed so cowardly. He should have approached her in person, looked her in the eye, manned up, and begged her forgiveness. That's what he'd meant to do. He'd gone to their old apartment, only to have a stranger answer the door. He had asked for her at the diner she used to work at, but the staff couldn't recall anyone by that name. Out of options, he had finally given in to calling their phone number. He'd almost started bawling at the sound of her voice. It was just as he remembered. His sweet, darling wife.

He couldn't fault her for hanging up on him—he had treated her despicably. Mike hung his head in his hands as memories flooded his mind. He had been so angry with himself for not being able to take care of his family adequately. Guilt had eaten away at him when Francis was forced to go back to work only a short month after Chantel was born. Unable to deal with the pressures, he had allowed his work buddies to talk him into having a drink with them after work to ease the stress. Just once, he had told himself. The fiery liquid had warmed him from the inside out and made him feel happy again. It allowed him to laugh and carry on with his buddies. It didn't take long before he was going out almost every night. He would stay out late, hoping Francis would be asleep when he got home, but she never was. Then he'd be overwhelmed with guilt, knowing that she had to get up to go to work in a couple of hours.

Cheryl's birthday party was a turning point for him. Cheryl was the opposite of Francis; she knew how to enjoy life. She was funny, flirty, and hot. A free spirit she called herself. Feeding his ego, pouring his drinks, coming onto him—she had drawn him into her evil web. He began to stay out later and later, knowing the guilt that would consume him when he got home. He'd taken his frustrations out on Francis—the one person who had always been there for him.

Jason had warned him that he was just a fling for Cheryl—that she'd drop him like a hot potato—but he shrugged it off.

The night he left replayed in Mike's mind. That night a ruggedly handsome stranger had entered the bar and ordered a drink. It didn't take Cheryl two minutes to sidle up to him, leaving Mike to watch her play the game she was so good at. Angrily, Mike had stormed out of the bar and driven home.

When he got home, Francis had told him she was pregnant. He lost it. In his drunken state, he felt backed into a corner. He hadn't been able to take care of the family he had, never mind another baby. The rage that had been building up inside of him for months had exploded, and he remembered punching Francis over and over. When he saw her lying unconscious on the floor, he got scared. He had grabbed a big garbage bag and stuffed his personal belongings into it. He had checked to make sure Francis was breathing, then high-tailed it out of there before she woke up. Knowing she would call the police and send him to jail, he ran.

Mike wiped the sweat off of his forehead. He hated what he had done. He had no excuse. He gulped down his now cold coffee and paced up and down his small apartment, but the memories would not leave him alone.

He had gotten into his car and driven for hours before stopping in a vacant parking lot to sleep. When he woke up the next morning, he found a liquor store and bought a bottle of Crown Royal. He went to a drive-through to pick up some breakfast—looking over his shoulder—sure that at any time the police would pick him up.

Days turned into weeks, weeks turned into months, and months turned into years. He lived in his car, struggling to feed himself. He'd pick up odd jobs here and there, but they usually only lasted a couple of weeks. He would go on an alcoholic binge and, when he didn't show up for work a couple of times, he'd get fired. The story repeated itself over and over—in town after town.

Then one day, Mike signed on with a road construction company as an equipment operator. Dan, the foreman, was a friendly guy, but he was very particular about being on time and doing the job right. There was no slacking off on Dan's crew. When Mike didn't show up for work one Monday morning, Dan showed up at Mike's trailer. He'd been living in a decrepit trailer in the far corner of a tired-looking trailer park. Mike was passed out on his faded couch. He woke up to a loud banging at his front door that rivalled the pounding in his head.

Dan took one look at Mike's dishevelled appearance, took Mike by the arm, and marched him into the bathroom.

"You will take a shower right now," Dan had commanded, turning on the shower. He grabbed a towel from the closet and threw it at Mike. "Then we'll talk." He turned and left the room.

Mike yelped as he stepped into the shower under a full blast of icy cold water. He scrambled back out and adjusted the water temperature. The guy hadn't touched the hot water tap at all!

Mike stopped short when he entered his kitchen. There was his boss, fixing eggs and toast while humming a song Mike had never heard before.

"Get yourself a plate for these eggs," Dan said, turning the eggs over with a flip of the wrist. "You can't go to work on an empty stomach." Mike retrieved a plate from the cupboard, and Dan dumped the eggs into it. He buttered the toast that had popped out of the toaster, placing the slices on Mike's plate.

Mike stared at his plate of food in amazement, not sure what to make of his new boss.

"When you finish eating I'm taking you to the job site," Dan told him in a tone that left no room for argument. "After work, you and I will have a talk."

Mike had worked hard that day. He had made sure he kept up with the rest of the crew, all the time wondering about Dan's actions. Any other boss would have fired him on the spot—he knew that from experience.

After work, Dan picked up Chinese food on his way to Mike's trailer.

"I am an alcoholic," Dan told him after he had prayed a blessing on the food, and they had dished up their plates. Mike's fork froze halfway to his mouth.

"No you're not." How could Dan be an alcoholic? Hadn't he just said grace? Wasn't he the supervisor of a construction crew?

"Yes, I am." Dan's eyes looked sad. "I had a beautiful wife and a month-old baby girl." Dan's fork rested on his plate and his eyes took on a faraway look. "I loved them more than anything else in the world. Jolene had long black hair that curled down over her shoulders to her waist. When she smiled, her eyes squinted as if they were laughing. She was a great mother to our little Shauna—such a sweet baby—her whole face scrunched up when she howled." Dan grinned as he looked at Mike. "Little Shauna didn't cry—she howled."

"What happened?" Mike asked, supper forgotten. He had his own memories of a beautiful woman and two small children.

"I loved them, but I loved the bottle more. One snowy December night, we came home from a Christmas party at a friend's house. I had been drinking, so Jolene offered to drive, but I insisted I wasn't drunk. I took the corner too fast. The road was icy, and I lost control of my car. We rolled over into the ditch. When the car came to a standstill, I could tell Jolene was in a bad way. I tried to free her from the wreck, but both my legs were broken. I will never forget how Jolene looked up at me and said 'I love you'. Then she stopped breathing. The baby was killed instantly."

Silence stretched between them as Mike struggled to come to grips with Dan's story. He pushed his plate back. He wasn't hungry anymore.

"I'm sorry, man." He didn't know what to say. "What did you do?"

"I got arrested for drunk driving causing death and got thrown in jail. I was ordered to join Alcoholics Anonymous. I sank into a deep depression, but I always went to the AA meetings. When I got out of jail, I met James. James told me about Jesus and took me to church. Man, I'm telling you, I didn't become a Christian overnight, but I was attracted to the gospel. It was like something, or someone, was pulling me in that direction. I couldn't forgive myself, and some days I still can't, but I know that Jesus has forgiven me and that's why I can go on. I still go to AA meetings, but now I go to tell my story so those people will know there's a better way."

Mike had agreed to attend AA meetings with Dan, and slowly he was able to break his own addiction.

Mike ran his fingers through his hair. Sometimes it seemed like that had all happened long ago, and then other times, it seemed like it was just yesterday. Dan had been by his side every step of the way. Mike picked up the phone to call Dan. He could use some encouragement.

Francis could see Gloria had been crying when she came to pick up Emily. Chantel and Emily were busy playing dolls in Chantel's bedroom, and Brad was outside shooting hoops with his friends, so Francis invited Gloria to stay for a cup of tea.

"Do you want to talk about it?" Francis asked when they were seated at the kitchen table.

"I had a series of tests done, and I got the results today." Gloria's eyes grew moist and she took a minute before she continued. "I have cancer."

"Oh no!" Francis' heart dropped to the floor. How could this be? Is that why Gloria had those dark circles under her eyes? "What kind?"

"Breast cancer," Gloria said, stirring honey into her tea. "I already knew I had cancer. That's the main reason Emily and I moved to Edmonton, so we would be close to my parents, and I could get the medical attention I need."

"Does Emily know?" Francis asked, her mind grappling with what Gloria was telling her.

"No," Gloria said. "The poor girl has been through so much already, I didn't want to tell her unless it was absolutely necessary. The doctor told me I need radiation to reduce the size of the tumor. After that, I'll need surgery."

"I'm so sorry, Gloria." Francis felt terrible for her new friend. "If I can be of any help, please tell me. Emily can stay here whenever she wants to or whenever you need someone to take care of her."

"I appreciate that. My parents are very supportive and will gladly take care of her, but being an only child, she enjoys playing with other little girls."

"I know they're having lots of fun," Francis said, smiling. "I've hardly seen those girls since you dropped Emily off. You can leave her here anytime. Even when you go for surgery."

"I appreciate the offer more than you know." Gloria looked down at her hands clasped on the table in front of her. "If only Richard was still here." Her voice was wistful.

"Richard?"

"My husband. He passed away from a heart attack two years ago."

61

"That's awful! No wonder you said Emily has been through a lot. So have you."

"It was totally unexpected. Richard was a paramedic. He was in good shape—worked out regularly and everything. Then one day he was gone." Gloria's voice held a volume of sorrow. "Emily was devastated." Her voice caught in her throat.

"I'm so sorry." Francis stood up and wrapped her arms around Gloria. "How awful for both of you!"

Gloria returned the hug, then wiped the back of her hand across her eyes. "I'm hoping I can beat this cancer without having to tell her. She's just started enjoying life again." She drank the last of her tea and composed her face. "I should get Emily. Mom invited us for supper."

Francis went to get the girls, who were busy playing Barbie dolls, while Gloria went to the bathroom to repair her face. She stood at the door, watching them play. They had the pool set up in front of the Barbie doll house and were so engrossed in playing they didn't even notice her.

"Emily, your mommy is here. She's ready to go home now."

Startled, the girls looked up.

"Mommy's here already?" Emily asked.

Francis chuckled. "She's been here for a while. We already had a cup of tea."

Francis left the girls to clean up and went back to the kitchen. "Emily was surprised you were back already," she told Gloria.

"Sounds like she had a good time." Gloria smiled. "I knew she would. She's been talking about Chantel nonstop since we sat with you at the baseball game. She really likes Chantel."

Francis started making supper after Gloria and Emily left. Her heart felt sad, and she wondered how she could help them. *I obviously can't do anything substantial except to love them and be there for them.* "Lord, be with Gloria and Emily," she prayed as she worked in her kitchen. "They have a lot on their plate. Wrap your arms around them and comfort them. Touch Gloria with your healing hand."

Her mind went back to her own broken marriage. A flood of resentment and bitterness welled up in her chest. How often in the last ten years had she wished Mike would call and say he was sorry, that he had changed, and they would start a new life? She had imagined it all—that they would get back together. They would love each other like they had when they first got married. Brad and Chantel would have their daddy back, and they would be a happy family.

Then he called. Memories washed over her like it happened yesterday. The rejection. The pain. The baby. Anger built up in her chest. *How could he? How dare he? The kids don't even know him. We've made a good life for ourselves. Why now?*

"Forgive us our debts, as we forgive our debtors." Part of the Lord's Prayer popped into her mind.

I can't! Her mind screamed back. *Lord, you can't possibly ask that of me. Not after what he did. He doesn't deserve it.*

"This is my commandment, that ye love one another, as I have loved you," the still, small voice echoed in her head.

CHAPTER 5

John stepped off the Greyhound bus in Edmonton. Grabbing his luggage after the driver pulled it out of the storage compartment, he headed through the glass doors into the terminal. He set the luggage down and quickly scanned the large room for his friend Patrick. He spotted him coming in his direction with two disposable cups in hand.

"Hi John, sure is good to see you!" Patrick greeted his friend, handing one of the drinks to John before shaking his hand.

"Sure good to see you too," John said, pumping his friend's hand. "Thanks for the coffee." He lifted the disposable cup up in a gesture of gratitude. "That is one long ride."

Patrick laughed. "Tell me about it. I used to take the Greyhound all the time when I worked in the oilfields up north. Not a pleasant experience."

"I was almost sorry I'd left my car back home," John admitted as he bent over to pick up his luggage. He looked up to find Patrick staring at a couple of guys in the far corner who were talking with a heavily made-up young girl. One of the guys kept looking over his shoulder nervously.

"What's up?" John questioned, confused at the angry look that had come across Patrick's face.

"My guess is they're trying to pick up that girl. I'm going to find out."

John watched as Patrick strode over to the small group, throwing the disposable cup in a garbage can along the way. The men looked nervous as Patrick stood in front of them, speaking directly with the girl, then he said something to the men. They backed off, and Patrick picked up the girl's bag. She looked bewildered and scared as she followed him back to where John was waiting.

"Stay here while I get a security guard," Patrick told the girl as he set her bag down at John's feet, then turned on his heel and went in the other direction.

"Hi, my name is John," John said with a friendly smile.

"I'm Marla," the girl said. She sat down on one of the chairs. John noticed that her face was pale under all her makeup, and her eyes looked frightened.

"Where are you from?" John asked, sitting down beside her, careful to leave an empty chair between them. He wasn't sure what had just happened, but he could tell she was scared.

"Leduc."

"Do you know Patrick?"

"No." Marla looked puzzled. "He just told those men he was a youth pastor and was sent to pick me up. I've never seen him before."

"What happened?" John asked of Patrick when he came back.

"That's what I want to find out," Patrick answered. Turning to Marla, he shook her hand. "I'm sorry I didn't introduce myself properly. My name is Patrick, and I am a youth pastor. It looked to me like those men were giving you trouble so I thought I'd check it out. Are you meeting someone here?"

Marla shook her head. "Who sent you to pick me up?"

Patrick chuckled. "I guess you could say God did. Actually, I'm here to pick up my friend John." He motioned toward his friend. "I saw those men talking to you. It looked suspicious, so I thought I'd check it out."

"I thought my dad called you." Marla looked down at her feet.

"No, that was just to throw those guys off. Where are you from?" Patrick asked gently, sitting down on the chair across from Marla.

"Leduc."

"Where are you going?"

"I don't know. I guess I should have thought of that."

"Did you run away from home?" Patrick asked, his voice sincere but friendly.

"Yes. My folks have too many rules." She looked embarrassed. "I thought I was old enough to make it on my own."

"Do your parents love you?"

"Yes, but they are suffocating me. They treat me like a little kid with all the curfews and wanting to know exactly where I am all the time." She lifted her hands in exasperation.

"It sounds to me like they are only trying to protect you. You are very blessed to have parents who care for you that much."

"I suppose," Marla said, some of the defiance leaving her voice.

"Do you want to go back home?"

"Yes."

Patrick took Marla to a pay phone and gave her a quarter to call home. After the phone call, the security guard stopped them to question Marla.

"Marla's dad is coming to get her," Patrick told John when they rejoined him. "I thought we could wait in the restaurant until he arrives."

"Sounds good to me," John said, picking up his bags.

Patrick picked up Marla's bag. They entered the restaurant, seated themselves, and ordered drinks—coffees for the guys and a root beer for Marla.

"I don't want to lecture you," Patrick told Marla after they had received their drinks. "But I hope this experience has shown you that running away from home can be very dangerous. All kinds of awful things can happen to girls that get picked up by bad men."

"I didn't think of that," Marla said simply, sipping on the straw.

"How old are you?" John asked.

"Fourteen."

John tried not to show his surprise. He could tell she was young, but she could easily pass for sixteen.

Patrick turned his attention to John, giving Marla a chance to collect her thoughts. "So how's your family?"

"They're doing well. Still farming. My youngest sister got married this summer."

"Does that leave you the only unmarried member of the family?"

"Yes, it does." John frowned into his coffee. "They keep reminding me of that, too."

"I bet." Patrick chuckled. "So you run away to the mission field."

"You're a missionary?" Marla asked, surprise showing on her face.

"I am," John answered. "I'm on my way to Mexico to work in a teenage shelter for street kids."

"Cool."

"Are you a Christian?" John asked Marla.

"My parents are."

"But you aren't?"

"I don't know." She shrugged. "That's kind of old-fashioned stuff."

"I suppose you're right," John agreed readily. "Jesus died on a cross around two thousand years ago, so I suppose that makes it old fashioned. Do you think it would be more relevant if he died a year ago? Ten years ago?"

"I don't know," Marla said. "I haven't thought of it that way."

"You see, Jesus is God," John continued, keeping his voice light. "He took the sin of all the world—past, present, and future—upon himself when he went to the cross. He died for every single person from Adam and Eve to the end of time. It doesn't matter at what point in history he did that—what matters is that he did. Tell me Marla, do you believe God is real?"

"I suppose so."

"Do you believe that Jesus is Christ and that he died on the cross for the sins of the world?"

"I'm not sure." Marla shrugged her shoulders and sipped on her straw.

"You're honest. I appreciate that." John rummaged in his bag and held out a couple of gospel tracts to the young girl. "These tracts explain a bunch of things in pretty clear terms. Can I give them to you? Maybe they will clarify some of your uncertainties."

Marla took the tracts from John's outstretched hand.

"Marla, there you are!" Marla turned around and was immediately engulfed in the arms of a tall, husky man. A multitude of emotions crossed the burly man's face as he crushed his daughter to his chest. "Praise the Lord you are safe!"

Keeping his left arm around his daughter's shoulders, he straightened up, holding his hand out to Patrick. "I'm Jack, Marla's father. I am deeply grateful to you young men for persuading Marla to call home."

"I'm Patrick," Patrick said, shaking Jack's hand. "I'm glad we could help her. I think Marla was ready to go home by the time we noticed her."

"I'm John," John said, taking Jack's proffered hand. He turned to Marla with a kind smile. "I'm glad we were able to help you tonight. I hope those tracts help you find answers to your questions."

After Jack and Marla left, John and Patrick gathered up John's luggage and walked out through the double glass doors to Patrick's black Chevy pickup. Throwing the luggage onto the truck box, they both climbed into the front seat.

"How did you figure out that Marla was in trouble back there?" John asked as Patrick eased the Chevy into the late afternoon traffic.

"It's not the first time that's happened," Patrick answered. "I keep an eye out for people who might be easy pickups when I go to the bus terminal. You'd be surprised how often it happens. Sometimes in the building—like today—and sometimes outside on the sidewalk."

"I've never thought of that."

"I remember the first time it happened to me," Patrick said, stopping at a red light. "I was coming back from the oilfield on the Greyhound and shared a seat with a pretty, young girl. As we talked, I got the impression that she was very nervous. Probably her first time travelling alone. Francis picked me up at the bus station, and we were about ready to leave, when we noticed a couple of sketchy looking men eyeing the girl. She noticed them too and bolted, almost falling over someone's luggage. I was already on my way to talk to her, so I was able to catch her before she did a face plant on the floor. Turned out the girl didn't have anybody picking her up. Francis offered to take her wherever she wanted to go." Patrick eased his foot off the brake as the light turned green. "Anyways, the long and short of it is that she ended up staying at Francis' place and babysitting her kids."

"Wow!" John exclaimed. "Didn't she have family or friends to go to?"

"Guess she had run away from home to have an abortion. Francis talked her into giving the baby up for adoption instead. I went back to the oilfield after a couple of days. When I started Bible school that fall—a good seven or eight months later—she was still babysitting for Francis."

"Do you know what became of her?" John was intrigued. Francis was a close friend of Patrick's parents, but John had never heard this story before.

"She went home eventually." Patrick's forehead creased, trying to remember the details as he pulled his Chevy into the driveway. "I think her dad got sick or something."

"Wow man, this is nice!" John exclaimed, letting out a slow whistle as he jumped out of the truck. A cemented walkway ran all the way from the paved driveway to the front door of the two-storey townhouse that Patrick had recently purchased.

"Thanks, man." Patrick couldn't totally conceal the pride in his voice as he unlocked the front door and led the way into his house.

John's gaze took in the entrance that gave way to an open-style kitchen and living room area.

"This is really nice." John said again as Patrick showed him the rest of the house. "I can see that you and Janelle will be very happy here." He turned to Patrick. "I am really disappointed that I can't attend the wedding."

"Me too," Patrick said as they returned to the kitchen. "Too bad your mission trip got pushed up."

"Yeah, I have mixed feelings about that," John admitted. "I was looking forward to being at home this winter."

"Do I hear a bit of wistfulness?" Patrick studied his friend closely. "Something happened that you're not telling me?"

John ran his hand through his hair as he lowered himself onto a high-backed kitchen chair. "Not really."

"Did I tell you Janelle is stopping by?" Patrick asked, opening a cupboard door. "She's picking up Chinese food on her way over." He set a couple of glasses of iced tea on the table and pulled out a chair for himself. John chuckled. Janelle's name always wormed its way into every conversation with Patrick these days.

As a youth pastor, Patrick devoted some of his time at a youth centre for street kids where Janelle was a counsellor. Over the years, their relationship had slowly blossomed into a beautiful romance. Their pending wedding was just a month away. John was truly sorry that he would have to miss it.

Janelle arrived half an hour later, laden down with the promised Chinese food. They caught each other up on the happenings in their lives as they enjoyed supper and afterward cleaned up the kitchen together. After supper, as they played cribbage, John and Patrick told Janelle about Marla.

"Patrick tells me this isn't the first time he's helped teenage runaways," John told Janelle, looking up from the cards in his hand.

Janelle's gentle eyes rested lovingly on Patrick. "God has given him a heart for troubled teens," she said proudly.

"I told John about that girl I met on the bus coming back from the oilfield years ago. The one who ended up babysitting for Francis." Patrick counted his cards as he lay them down and moved his pegs forward.

"Hey, slow down there." Janelle's green eyes flashed at Patrick as he moved his peg past hers. Patrick chuckled.

"Yeah, you told me about her." Janelle turned her attention back to the conversation as she finished her turn. "Her name was Mary, right?"

Mary.

A sucker-punch to his midsection couldn't have felt worse. Colour drained from John's face as a vice gripped his heart. It was hard to breathe. He felt sick to his stomach. *No, it can't be.*

"That's right," Patrick answered, looking down at his cards. "That was a long time ago."

"It's always a good thing whenever a teenager is snatched out of the claws of evil men," Janelle said, nodding.

"Your move, John," Patrick lifted his eyes to his friend. John sat bent over, clutching his chest. "John, what's wrong?" Instantly Patrick was on his feet, coming around the table to John's side.

"Put your head down between your knees," Janelle called as she rushed to the kitchen for a glass of water.

John's brain scrambled to recall what Patrick had told him, as his heart thumped wildly in his chest. "Guess she had run away from home to have an abortion. Francis talked her into giving the baby up for adoption instead."

"The girl who babysat for Francis—the one from the bus station—where was she from?" John's eyes burned holes into Patrick as he squeezed the words past the tight knot in his chest. He couldn't bring himself to say her name.

"I don't know. I remember asking her on the bus, but she wouldn't tell me." Patrick had never seen such a wild look in John's eyes. "What's the matter, John? What are you thinking?"

John shook his head, trying to clear his brain. *What am I thinking?* But he had to know. "Has any other girl babysat for Francis?"

"Not that I know of," Patrick answered. "John, what's gotten into you?"

John clutched Patrick's arm. "She had a baby?"

Janelle handed John a glass of water. "Here, drink some water."

John took the glass and drank. His head was spinning. Were they really talking about his Mary? He set the glass down and covered his face with his hands. *No, it can't be. She's not that kind of girl. She's sweet, innocent, and pure—what am I thinking? Of course it's not her. It can't be!*

"Why is this so important to you? Do you know her?" Patrick pulled up a chair next to John and sat down.

John took a deep breath as he raised tortured eyes to Patrick. He slumped back in his chair, feeling suddenly very tired. "I can't believe I'm actually thinking it's possible."

Patrick watched as John struggled with his emotions. John had never been interested in girls as far as he knew; his only passion was living for Jesus Christ and spreading the gospel.

"Remember I told you about my friend David?" John asked, lifting tortured brown eyes to meet Patrick's clear blue ones. His voice sounded defeated.

"Yes," Patrick said. "He was your friend that was killed in an accident."

"He has a sister Mary. When I was in Bible college, she ran away from home and for months all her parents knew was that she was somewhere in Edmonton. Then her father had a stroke and, by the grace of God, I ran into Mary on the college campus. I took her to her parents at the hospital." John swallowed hard, trying to dislodge the lump in his throat. "She was babysitting for Francis."

"Wow!" Patrick exclaimed. "You think she's the same girl we rescued at the bus station?"

"I can't believe it—but my mind tells me it has to be."

CHAPTER 6

Mike rubbed his sweaty palms over his jeans before stepping out of his car. *I haven't felt this nervous since...since I can't remember when,* he thought to himself as he crossed the paved parking lot. The sign assured him that everyone was welcome. The large brown cross on the front of the stucco-finished building beckoned him. He wondered what Francis had told her pastor.

I imagine it won't be good, but it's time to man-up and face my past. After what I've done, it's only fair that Francis is calling the shots now. Pushing the church door open, he took a moment to allow his eyes to adjust to the indoor lighting. Straightening his shoulders, he walked across the carpeted foyer to the door that read *Pastor* and knocked on the open door. The dark haired, middle-aged man behind the desk looked up.

"Come on in." The man motioned for Mike to enter as he removed his reading glasses and set them down. He stood up and walked around his paper-covered office desk. His face broke into a welcoming grin as he shook Mike's hand. "I'm Bob Browning."

"Mike Webber." Mike liked the pastor's firm handshake and friendly demeanour.

"I'm happy to meet you," Bob said, waving his hand toward a faded leather easy chair in the corner of the room. "Please sit down. Do you care for coffee or a glass of water?"

"I'll have coffee, please," Mike replied, relaxing slightly in the casual atmosphere. Bob walked over to a side cupboard where he retrieved two cups and poured coffee into both from the carafe on the counter.

"Cream or sugar?" Bob asked.

"A little cream, please."

Bob handed one of the cups to Mike and sat down in a matching easy chair across from him. Placing his ankle across his knee, Bob took a sip and smiled. "I was ready to take a break."

Mike felt some of the tension release from his shoulders as he sipped his coffee. Bob made him feel like a friend who had stopped in for a visit.

"So tell me, Mike, what's on your mind?"

Mike set his cup down on the small round coffee table between them. "I know I've been gone way too long, and I don't deserve a second chance, but the bottom line is I need Francis and the kids back in my life." *There. I said it.* Hanging his head, Mike tensed at the onslaught of verbiage the pastor would direct at him. He was, after all, Francis' pastor. *I deserve every bit of it. He will tell me I don't deserve to be back in their lives, that they're better off without me. I know that. How often have I told myself the same thing?* Silence. Mike slowly lifted his head and met Bob's eyes. There was no condemnation there.

Mike leaned slightly forward in his chair. "I have no excuse for what I did. For years after I left, my life spiralled downhill. I worked until I got paid and then went on an alcoholic binge that got me fired. The story kept repeating itself until I met Dan. He helped me clean up my life and introduced me to Jesus."

"Tell me about it," Bob said. Mike searched the pastor's face. Wrinkles appeared at the sides of soft-grey eyes as the pastor smiled encouragingly, giving Mike the impression that—although he was sincere and trustworthy—he could laugh just as easily. The tanned face spoke of time spent out of doors. Mike nodded as he plunged in.

"I first met Francis when I pulled into an A&W drive-in, and she was the carhop who took my order." Mike's voice softened, and his eyes took on a faraway look as he relived his past life with Francis. He talked about their engagement and wedding, the early years of their marriage, his spiral into alcoholism, and the ensuing abuse he inflicted on his wife. He didn't hold anything back.

When he finished talking, silence filled the room as both men reflected on their own thoughts.

"You realize that it will take a lot of hard work and counselling if you want to get back with your family," Bob said, breaking the silence.

"I'm prepared to do whatever it takes," Mike said, sincerely.

An hour later, Mike slid his long frame back into his black Mustang. Before putting the key in the ignition, he laid his head on the steering wheel. "Lord, you have brought me this far. Please reunite me with my family."

He felt emotionally exhausted. He had told Pastor Bob his entire story, from the time he had met Francis until today. He wanted no sympathy, but he wanted the pastor to understand how sincere he was about getting his family back. Pastor Bob assured him that Francis and the kids were doing well. That's all the information he passed on. He did promise to discuss Mike's wishes with Francis.

I'll do whatever it takes. But will Francis be willing? That was the question he wrestled with day and night. He inserted the keys in the ignition and started the car.

"We are now starting general boarding for Air Canada flight 1639, non-stop to Houston. All passengers please make your way to Gate 12 at this time."

John picked up his bag and—passport and boarding pass in hand—joined other passengers lining up at Gate 12 for the first leg of his flight. He handed his boarding pass and passport to the blue uniformed lady at the gate. She checked his passport, then smiled and wished him a good flight as she handed the paperwork back.

He followed the passengers ahead of him through the tunnel to the door of the Boeing 737. The stewardess greeted him with a smile, checking his boarding pass before he proceeded down the narrow aisle to seat 11F. Swinging into the cloth window seat, he stuffed his small carry-on bag beneath the seat in front of him, buckled himself in, and turned to the window where ground crews were scurrying about.

John's heart felt heavy in his chest. For the hundredth time he told himself it couldn't be true. *How could Mary have a baby and give it up for adoption?* There must be some mistake. He wanted to talk to her. He wanted to hear her say it wasn't true. *But it makes sense. Why did she leave home for months on end? Why does she refuse to acknowledge her love for me?* Part of him wanted to get off the plane, go back home, and confront Mary with the questions that were reeling through his mind. *How can I go to Mexico when I have all these questions?*

John felt the aircraft being pushed back as he wracked his brain for answers. He and Patrick had talked late into the night, trying to make sense of it. John had gone away to college right after high school. He hadn't seen much of Mary after that until her papa got sick a year and a half later. On trips back home, he had heard rumours that Mary was hanging out with the partying crowd. He had visited her family that Christmas Eve before she ran away. They had all been happy to see him, so he had chalked the rumours up as gossip. He'd known she was suffering after David's death. *But a baby?*

John was sucked back into his seat as the aircraft sped down the runway and lifted off, rising quickly above the treetops and into the clear blue sky. He leaned his head back on the seat and closed his eyes. He was on his way to Chihuahua, Mexico. How could he go so far away for an undetermined amount of time without answers? He got his Bible out of his bag. Maybe that would calm his anxieties.

"*Trust in the Lord with all thine heart; and lean not unto thine own understanding. In all thy ways acknowledge him, and he shall direct thy paths.*" He put his finger on the verse in Proverbs as he closed his eyes and prayed.

Lord I want to trust you. Mary has always been such a sweet girl. How can this be true? Lord, there must be some misunderstanding. He had trouble focusing on prayer. All he could see was the host of emotions crossing Mary's face when he had told her he loved her. *What had she said?* "*You don't know me.*" *Is this what she had meant? How old would Mary's child be?* John's mind went back through the years. *Probably seven or eight years. My goodness, the child would be in school already!* He shook his head—there must be some mistake.

Patrick had promised to do some investigating—find out what information he could get from his mom or Francis. He would let John know what he found.

In Houston, John boarded the connecting flight to Chihuahua without incident. The short hop over to Chihuahua would only take two hours. For the first time that day, he felt himself getting excited about the work that awaited him at the shelter.

"Mister." John turned to look at the little black-haired, black-eyed girl in the seat next to him. "Mister," the little girl said again, her eyes on his face. She had a strong Spanish accent. "Are you very old?"

"I wouldn't call myself very old." John smiled down at her, smothering the chuckle that threatened to escape his lips. "Do I look very old to you?"

"Not very old," the girl said, shrugging her little shoulders. She motioned to the Bible in his hand. "Is that a Bible?"

"Yes, it is." John lifted the Bible for her to see.

"Grandma reads me stories from the Bible, but Mama says Bibles are for old people."

"Do you like listening to the stories your grandma reads to you?" John studied the little girl. She was probably around six years old. The seat beside her was empty, so he assumed her mama had gone to the lavatory.

"I love the stories Grandma reads to me." Her dark curls bounced on her head as she nodded.

"Does she read you stories about Jesus?"

"Yes, and David and the giant, and Jonah and the big fish, and Noah and the animals in the big boat."

"Jesus loves children."

"Yes, Grandma told me. I love Jesus, too!"

"I'm glad you do," John told her. "I also love Jesus. That's why I read my Bible."

An older version of the little girl sat down on the other side of her. "Has my daughter been bothering you?" The mother's Spanish accent was heavier than the little girl's.

"Not at all." John smiled down at the little girl again. "We had a very nice chat."

"Sometimes she talks too much." The Hispanic lady retrieved some books from a bag underneath the seat in front of her. The girl lowered the tray from the seat-back and set the books on it.

"Your daughter noticed my Bible and told me stories her grandma reads to her."

"Ah, yes. Mother." The lady reached back into her bag and brought out a box of crayons, setting them beside the books. The girl started colouring, and the lady turned to John. "Mother doesn't always live in reality."

"You don't believe in the Bible?" John asked.

The lady dug into her bag again, this time pulling out a book for herself. "A loving God would not allow people to hurt and destroy each other."

"I have to agree there's lots of sorrow in the world." John was reminded of his own heavy heart. "We live in a fallen world where sin has tainted God's beautiful creation. Jesus tells us: *In the world ye shall have tribulation: but be of good cheer; I have overcome the world.*"

"Are you a preacher?" The lady raised her eyebrows.

"I'm a missionary," John said. "I'm on my way to Mexico to work in a teenage shelter for street kids."

"Really?" The lady looked surprised. "I wish you well." She looked like she was going to add to that, then changed her mind.

"Thank you." John smiled at her. "I appreciate that."

The lady opened her book, and John turned to the window. He said a silent prayer for the little girl and her mother.

"Mama, I'm going for a drive," Mary told her mama as she pulled the plug from the sink and let the dishwater drain.

"Where are you going?" Anna asked, putting dishes into the cupboard.

"Down to the river." Mary smiled. How many twenty-four-year-olds had to tell their mama where they were going? Not that she blamed her mother for being anxious. She'd had a hard life with her son being killed and her husband having a stroke, not to mention what Mary herself had put her through.

"That's a good idea. It'll be good for you to do something relaxing after a hot day at work."

Mary grabbed the car keys, her bag, and a blanket. All day, she'd been waiting to go down to the river. It had become a ritual. She turned the car windows down before she turned onto the gravel road.

Anna watched her daughter drive off the yard. *I wish I could see into her head,* she thought as she watched her turn onto the road, the dust kicking up behind the car. *Today is her little girl's birthday.* Anna sensed a yearning in her daughter that was never far from the surface. She had told them about the baby months after she came home from Edmonton, but it was not a subject that she discussed easily. *She's always willing to help wherever needed, never complains about the extra responsibilities placed on her young shoulders, but there's a wistfulness—a longing—in her eyes and a maturity that belies her age.* Anna's eyes followed the car until it was out of sight, her mind going back in time.

Those were difficult years. Poor Mary was devastated when her brother died. She sank into depression, rejected her friends, and then one day she disappeared. How could we know she was pregnant? Anna felt the familiar pain pierce her chest. She would never admit it to anyone, but inwardly she struggled to forgive her daughter. *Lord, why did she give her baby up for adoption? We would have raised her, loved her.*

What was she thinking? I love Mary, Anna told herself, staring off into the distant yesteryear. *But how can my child give away her own flesh and blood? Where did Jacob and I go wrong in raising her that she would think that was okay? If only she had told us she was pregnant! We would have helped her.* Yes, there would have been a lot of gossip, but they would have overcome that. Anna rehashed all the what-ifs in her mind; half praying, half thinking. *But she didn't tell us, and now our only grandchild is growing up somewhere with strangers, without her rightful mother and without her rightful grandparents.*

Anna's heart broke for the little granddaughter she would never know. Only she and the Lord knew of her struggle to forgive. She couldn't burden Jacob with her selfish yearnings, and she dared not reveal her struggles to Mary. *She wouldn't understand that I love her, even though in my heart I struggle to forgive.* Anna sighed heavily as she turned from the window. She didn't want to remember. It was too painful.

Anna went into the living room where Jacob was sitting in his easy chair. "Mary went for a drive to the river," she told him, doing her best to sound cheerful. "Benny and his friends are throwing a ball around outside. Do you want me to read to you?"

"*Jo,*" Jacob said, reaching for the book on the coffee table. Anna read to him most evenings. It had started in the hospital and had become a daily routine that they both enjoyed.

Mary turned the car onto the narrow trail, leading to the river through tall evergreens and poplar trees that formed a canopy overhead. She breathed in deeply of the pungent smell of the dark green summer foliage as she slowly made her way down the winding trail. At the edge of the tree line, she parked the car, grabbed her bag and blanket from the back seat, and headed out to her favourite secluded spot.

The almost unbearable heat of the day had given way to a slightly cooler evening, even though the sun was still high in the sky. A couple of families were on the beach, having a wiener roast. Their children played in the sand, while a group of teenagers enjoyed a game of beach volleyball. They waved at her as she walked by, and she waved back at them, but didn't stop to talk. Not today. She walked along the river bank to where a stand of tall spruce trees provided a secluded spot behind a large boulder. She climbed the sharp embankment where, every year for the last eight years, she had come on this day to remember.

Mary brushed the fallen acorns aside with her hand before spreading the blanket on a grassy spot. She lay back on the blanket, covering her eyes with her arm. The birds sang to each other in the trees as she allowed her mind to rewind to that day eight years ago—to the moment she heard the first lusty cry of her newborn baby girl. She relived the pain and exhaustion of giving birth, which was quickly replaced with the incredible joy of hearing her baby cry. The nurse had placed the tiny bundle on Mary's chest. She could almost feel the weight of the baby in her arms—against her breast. Once again she saw the perfect little round face, the tiny nose, the little pink mouth, and the tiny fingers that curled around her own. Then she was gone. One glimpse to last a lifetime. The nurse took the infant and whisked her out of the room and forever away from Mary.

"God, I miss her so much!" Tears ran unheeded down her face as she allowed herself to feel the pain of separation. She spread the broken pieces of her heart out before her Saviour. "Lord, today my baby is eight years old. Where is she? Is she happy? Does she have a loving mommy and daddy? Does she know about me?" Mary's shoulders heaved as her body shook with sobs. "Does my baby girl know I love her? Does she know how sorry I am that I gave her away? Lord, please give me the chance to hold her again. Please bring her back to me."

Mary turned over onto her stomach as she released the hidden darkness in her soul and permitted it to surface. She relived each painful memory from that awful day when David was killed. She had hurt so badly. Day after day and night after night. *I couldn't cope, and I blamed God.* Then Annie and her friends had befriended her, and she had started going to parties with them. Alcohol had become her escape from reality.

That's where she met Melvin—the tall, handsome boy from the city. *I thought he was cool and sophisticated. He was the life of the party, and he made me feel special.* It wasn't until after she was pregnant that she realized he had used her. She hadn't dared tell her parents. *The only person I told was Melvin, and he put me on a Greyhound bus to Edmonton to have an abortion.* God had intervened by sending Francis to the bus terminal. She rescued Mary when Mary had nowhere to go. Francis had given her a place to stay and an alternative to abortion.

"I know now that your hand was in it, Lord. You put Francis there to save me from killing my unborn baby." Mary shuddered as guilt washed through her being. *I was desperately lonely. The only thing that kept me going through those long months was the knowledge that after the baby was born, I could go back home. Back to Mama, Papa, and Benny, and no one would ever know about my baby.*

It hadn't worked out that way. A fresh stream of tears flowed freely as she cried out to God. "How could I be so stupid, Lord? Why didn't I realize I couldn't live without my dear baby? I love my family but no one can ever make up for the love I have for my baby girl!"

Mary didn't receive any answers, but calmness stole over her heart. Slowly the spring of tears ebbed. Wiping the back of her hand across her wet face, she sat up. She dug into her bag and retrieved a pen and her special journal—the one she kept solely for the purpose of writing letters to her little girl.

My dear little sweetheart,

Today is your eighth birthday! Even though I can't be there physically for you, my spirit is always with you. I love you more than words can tell, and I pray that somewhere—someday—we will meet again...

Mary kept a journal of letters she had started on the baby's first birthday. She wrote in it periodically, but especially on birthdays. It gave her a sense of closeness to her little girl. If God would allow them to meet again, she would give her the letters. Then her baby would know that she had always been loved. So Mary poured her mother's heart out onto the pages, telling her baby all the things she yearned to tell her in person.

The sun was sinking into the western horizon when she carefully placed the journal into her bag, gathered up her blanket, and headed home.

CHAPTER 7

John's eyes roamed the crowded room as he waited in a long line-up of people. He swept the back of his hand across his damp brow—the heat and humidity was suffocating. Through the glass, he saw a man dressed in a camouflage uniform, carrying what looked like a machine gun. *Must be a guard*, he thought to himself. *I was told Mexico would be different, but I didn't expect this!* Except for pictures, he'd never even seen a machine gun before.

He could only catch snatches of conversation around him and hoped his Spanish would be adequate.

"Next." The lady behind the custom desk looked at him. He stepped up to the desk and handed her his papers. "How long are you staying in Mexico?" She had a heavy accent and was difficult to understand.

"Three months." Since this was an unexpected trip, he couldn't get his paperwork in place for longer than three months. Hopefully by the time the three months were up, he'd have the necessary documents in place to stay longer.

"What are you going to do here for three months?" she asked, looking at his papers.

"I'm a missionary. I'll be working at the teenage shelter for street kids."

She stamped his passport and handed it back to him.

John went through the door into the next room. After picking his luggage up from the carousel, he waited in another line-up to go through security. A somber-looking security guard, dressed in a dull green uniform, waved him forward. He set his suitcase on the conveyor belt and walked through the metal detector where another uniformed guard asked if he had anything to declare.

"No," he answered.

The man motioned for him to keep going. He picked up his luggage and went through double glass doors into the hustle and bustle of people scurrying about. John blinked at the bright sunlight, allowing his pupils to adjust. His eyes came to rest on a stocky, grey-haired, middle-aged man who was holding a sign that read: *John Hepner*. A sigh of relief escaped his lips as he walked over and reached out his hand.

"Good day, I'm John Hepner."

"Cornelio Friesen," the man said in familiar Plautdietsch as he pumped John's hand heartily, a big smile on his round face. "Let me help you with your bags." He took one of John's suitcases, and they walked across the paved parking lot to Cornelio's car.

Cornelio kept up a steady stream of conversation as he navigated the car through busy streets, pointing out the places of interest. John tried to process the sights and sounds of a foreign land. The car's open windows created a welcome breeze, and John ran his fingers through his damp hair. Colourful brick buildings, with barred windows and doors, contained small shops open to the streets. Groups of people haggled with street vendors who were selling everything from soup to nuts. Brightly coloured fenced and gated brick homes were visible down the side roads. Further down the road, the homes were a cluster of small adobe huts with children and dogs playing in the front yards or on the dusty streets.

When they reached the outskirts of the city, the land gave way to a rolling countryside. *Similar to the foothills of Alberta,* John thought. Long rows of evenly spaced apple trees encompassed miles of land.

"What's that?" John pointed to what looked like netting rolled up in intervals just above the orchard trees.

"That's netting used to cover the trees so the birds don't damage the apples," Cornelio said.

"Do you have apple trees at the shelter?" John asked.

"We have a couple of apple trees and orange trees. We also have a garden," Cornelio said with a smile. "We have chickens, cows, horses, and pigs. The kids all have chores to do. It's part of their education plus it cuts down on our grocery bill." He chuckled. "It can be interesting when we introduce new kids to our farm. Many of them come from the inner city and have never worked with animals before."

"What ages are the kids?" John asked. He had read up on the shelter that the Mission had built as an outreach to disadvantaged kids—namely street kids. It was designed to remove them from the streets and provide a safe place for them. Many of the kids had been abandoned and had never known a parent's love. Some were runaways from abusive family situations, while others were sent to the city by their families to earn a living. When they were unable to find a job, they often ended up in the streets.

"Right now we have boys from eight to seventeen years old," Cornelio said, turning the car off of the main highway onto a narrower, paved road. "They have to do their chores first thing in the morning and just before supper. After breakfast, they go to the school located on our compound."

Cornelio turned onto a gated driveway. He pushed a button, and the gate opened automatically. They proceeded to a low yellow brick building set well back from the gate.

"This is where you'll live," Cornelio said as he parked the car.

"Is the entire compound fenced in?" John asked, getting out of the car. It felt good to stretch his legs after a long day of travelling. He looked around this place that would be home to him for at least three months—probably longer. There were a number of buildings scattered around the compound, whose purpose he was sure to find out soon. The tall fence ran behind the buildings toward the rear of the property.

"Yes, it is all fenced for security reasons," Cornelio said, walking towards the back of the car. He opened the trunk and helped John carry his luggage down the cement sidewalk towards the house.

"*Goondach.*" A couple of men greeted him in Plautdietsch and shook his hand, welcoming him.

"*Hola.* I'm Pedro." A Hispanic man came forward, his smile friendly and inviting. "We are so glad you could come."

"I'm Jorge." A tall, brown-haired man stepped forward and shook John's hand. Towering above the others, he was clearly not of Hispanic descent although his name attested otherwise. "We've been looking forward to meeting you. You must be hungry and exhausted. Supper is ready if you want to join us at the table."

A couple of women bearing food platters, entered through a door at the far side of the room. They were introduced as the wives of some of the men.

John felt immediately drawn to the men, who were so different in appearance from one another, but had the same infectious air of friendliness about them. He felt himself relaxing as he took his place at the table. *Yes, I think I'll like working with these guys,* John thought to himself as they bowed their heads and Cornelio asked the blessing.

Francis' mind went in a hundred different directions as she drove to Gloria's house to pick up Chantel and Emily. "Lord, please show me what you want me to do," she prayed as she drove.

"Forgive us our debts, as we forgive our debtors."

She turned down Gloria's street and stopped in front of her house. *How can I forgive Mike?* She asked herself. *How does a person forgive what he did?*

The afternoon sun beat down on her as she ran up the front steps. *Good thing Gloria's husband left her with enough money to buy a house like this,* Francis thought. It was a nice house in a good neighbourhood. Flowers nodded cheerfully at her from a well-manicured front lawn. Gloria had told her that Richard had good life insurance, which had helped her manage financially after his sudden death. *At least they were established financially. Not like how Mike left me. I think it would have been easier for me to deal with death than rejection.* She felt a twinge of guilt as she rang the doorbell.

"Hello, come on in," Gloria said, greeting her cheerfully. "I'll call the girls. They're playing in the backyard."

"I smell cookies," Francis said as she entered the house. On the marble counter was the evidence that her sense of smell was accurate. The house was spacious with modern décor; the spacious entryway gave way to a fairly large, open-concept kitchen and dining area.

"Yes, the girls and I did some baking. Emily loves to bake, and I think Chantel had fun as well." She opened the back door and called the girls.

Francis laughed. "Chantel loves baking, but I don't, so we don't bake much. Gladys used to let the kids help her bake when she babysat them. They loved it."

Gloria was beautiful in her red dress, her raven curls cascading over her shoulders and down her back. Francis felt a memory rise to the surface—that notion that she had met Gloria somewhere before. The girls came barrelling through the door, and the hint of memory faded into the recesses of her mind.

"Mom, will you take us to the swimming pool?" Chantel asked. "It's super hot today, and Emily and I would like to go swimming."

"Do you mind?" Francis asked Gloria.

"Not at all," Gloria said, turning to Emily, "You'll have to get your bathing suit then."

The women laughed as both girls scrambled to get Emily's bag packed. Francis turned her attention to Gloria. "Are you nervous for the appointment?" Gloria was starting her radiation treatments. Her dad was going to take her to her appointment.

"I'd be lying if I said I wasn't," Gloria admitted, the smile on her face quickly fading. "It's all I can think about these days. What happens to Emily if they can't remove all the cancer? I'm so afraid of dying and leaving her all by herself."

"Have you told her yet?"

"About the cancer? No. I don't want her to worry about me," Gloria said, turning to Francis. "I don't want to tell her as long as there is a chance I'll get well."

"Get some rest before Emily comes home," Francis said. She could tell Gloria was trying to hide her pallor with makeup, but Francis was not fooled.

"I will. Thanks for taking her." Her eyes shimmered with unshed tears. "I thank God he gave me such a good friend."

"I'll race you to the car," Emily called over her shoulder to Chantel as the girls re-appeared, then disappeared out the front door.

"Don't you worry about Emily. She'll have lots of fun at the pool," Francis said, going to the door.

"I don't doubt that," Gloria said with a chuckle. "That girl would live in a pool if she could."

"All the best at your appointment. I'll be praying for you." Francis hugged Gloria, who had followed her to the door. "I'll bring Emily back tonight. If you're up to it, I can stay a while and talk."

"That sounds wonderful," Gloria said, hugging Francis back. "I'll need someone to talk to. That's one of the things I miss most about not having Richard around."

"Yes, I know," Francis said, turning to the door. "See you later then." She opened the door and went to her car, leaving Gloria looking after her thoughtfully as she realized Francis had never told her how she had gotten to be a single mom with two kids. She'd have to ask her someday.

John hadn't realized working with troubled teenagers would be so emotionally and psychologically draining. The boys that came to the shelter had problems he had never encountered before. Many of them had grown up with physical, mental, emotional, or sexual abuse. As a means of escape, they had turned to sniffing glue at a young age then later to alcohol—some had even turned to hard drugs before they were rescued. Their stories varied, and John's heart broke for all of them. Some boys had an earnest desire to make the best of the opportunity they had been given, while others were tough characters who fought against everything the shelter did for them.

Somewhere beneath that rough and tough exterior there is a soul that needs saving, John told himself, *but sometimes it's all I can do not to take the next flight out of here.* At times he had to work hard not to allow negative feelings to defeat him.

John wiped the perspiration from his face. Cornelio told him it would cool off in the winter—even be cold—but right now he found it hard to believe. The sun was unrelenting; there was no reprieve from the heat. It was siesta time, when everyone at the shelter napped, but John found it too hot to nap. He took Patrick's letter, which Cornelio had given him that morning, and went outside to read it in the shade of a huge Mexican oak tree at the far end of the courtyard.

He nervously ran his fingers through his damp hair before he opened the envelope, his hands trembling. Removing the single sheet of paper, he looked off into the distance for a moment.

"What did Patrick find out? Do I want to know?" he asked himself. Taking a deep breath, he unfolded the letter.

> *Dear John,*
> *How are you adjusting to life in Mexico? Are you acclimatized yet? I imagine it's pretty warm out there. Janelle wanted to go to Mexico for a honeymoon, but I told her then we would have to postpone our wedding until winter. There's no way I'm going out there in the summer! So we decided to go to Niagara Falls instead. That'll be far enough south for me at this time of year.*

John's eyes quickly skimmed down through the wedding details until he came to the part of the letter that would answer his burning question.

I talked to Francis about the girl we picked up at the bus station years ago. Just as I thought, her name was Mary, and she stayed with Francis from January until sometime in the fall. Apparently, after she had her baby she suffered from depression. Then her dad got sick— he was hospitalized here in the city—and when he was released she went home to Springwater. Oh, and she had a brother who was killed in an accident. So it sounds to me like she's your friend's sister, alright.

His chest tightened. He couldn't breathe. *This can't be true. It can't be. Not Mary!* He crumpled the letter in his hand. "Lord, please, it can't be true," he pleaded. Yet the pieces fit together. What had Mary said to him?

"You can't love me, John. You don't really know me." John's breath came in short gasps as air squeezed past the tightness in his chest. Dazed, he rose to his feet and stumbled forward.

"No, it can't be true!" Mary's face swam before his eyes. *I love you, Mary. I thought you loved me, too.* He kept walking.

"What a fool I've been!"

What had Patrick told him? "Guess she had run away from home to have an abortion, but Francis talked her into giving the baby up for adoption instead." *Mary considered having an abortion?*

As his heart shattered within him, John fell to his knees. He tried to pray, but all he could say was, "No, God, no! How could this happen? Why?" Hot tears streamed down his tanned face as his heart fought against the very thing his mind knew to be true. *Who is the father?* The thought was unbearable.

CHAPTER 8

Francis watched the tea swirling around in her cup as she pushed the spoon around and around. *Why is Mike calling me after all this time?* The question kept repeating itself in her mind. *Why now?* A knock on the door startled her out of her reverie. She opened the door, and a smile spread across her face.

"Maggie!" She opened the door wide. "Come on in. What a pleasant surprise!" It wasn't unusual for her matronly friend to pop in since her daily walk took her past Francis' apartment.

"I told Dale I had to stop by to see how you were doing." Maggie hugged Francis before entering the apartment. "You've been on my mind since we talked the other day."

"I was just having a cup of tea," Francis said, leading the way into her kitchen. "Will you join me?"

"Absolutely," Maggie said, sitting down at the kitchen table. Francis poured a second cup of tea and set it in front of her.

"Mom, can I go play with Carmel?" Chantel bounded into the room, dressed in her favourite pink shorts and Barbie T-shirt. "Hi, Grandma Maggie!"

"Hi Chantel." Maggie's face broke into a tender smile. Francis' children had adopted her as a grandma when they were little.

"If it's alright with her mom," Francis told her daughter. "Be home by six."

"I will," Chantel said, heading for the door.

"Those children are growing up way too fast," Maggie said, her eyes following Chantel to the door. "I saw Brad outside, shooting baskets with some boys. Looked like they were having fun." The creases around her eyes deepened as she smiled at Francis. "You have good kids. You're doing a good job raising them."

"They are good kids, and I love them so much," Francis said, sinking back into the chair across from Maggie. "I don't want them to get hurt again."

"You mean Mike," Maggie said, concerned eyes resting on her young friend. "Have you heard from him again?"

"He called the other night. I told him to call Pastor Bob." Francis watched the tea swirling around in her cup for a minute before she raised her eyes to Maggie's concerned face. "All these years, I've fantasized about Mike coming home. I imagined we would be together like we were at the beginning of our marriage—in love. I've missed that part of my life terribly." She lowered her eyes and swirled the tea around in her cup again. "Then he called and I realized we can't go back—the past can't be undone. Too much has happened." She raised her tortured eyes to her friend. "Maggie, he asked if the baby was a boy or girl!"

Maggie's sharp intake of breath was audible.

"Of course," Maggie exclaimed, realization dawning on her. "It makes sense that he doesn't know what happened to the baby."

"It hurt so badly." Francis wiped at the tears that threatened to spill onto her cheeks. "He killed our baby. How can I forgive him for that? Not to mention that he walked out on Brad and

Chantel. Even if I could forgive him for what he did to me, I can't forgive him for what he did to the kids."

Silence stretched out between them, as they were lost in their own thoughts. *Lord, what are you asking of Francis? Mike has hurt her so much. It was so hard for her to raise the children on her own. She has done well. She has made a good life for them. Why are you allowing Mike to come back now? What will that do to Francis? To Brad and Chantel?* Maggie sighed heavily.

"I don't have answers," Maggie said, her kind eyes glistening. "I don't understand what the Lord has in store for you or why he would bring Mike back into your life."

"How can I explain to Brad and Chantel that their dad wants to see them? They don't even know him. How would that affect them? I don't want them to have to go through that."

"I know, my dear." Maggie was at a loss for words. "It doesn't seem right. You mentioned last time that Mike said he had changed. Do you know what he meant?"

"He said he had cleaned up his life, but I don't know what he meant by that. He wants to see me to explain. I don't think I can do that."

"Do you feel unsafe?" Maggie asked.

"No," Francis said, shaking her head slowly. "I feel like I've changed a lot since then. I'm not the same woman. When our marriage began struggling, I thought I had to fix it, that somehow I was responsible. If only I was a better wife, things would get better. I let Mike get away with drinking and carousing because I couldn't bear the thought of being alone. Even when he started hitting me, I told myself that as long as he didn't hurt the children, we could work it out. I know now that it was him—not me—so there was no way I could fix things. I don't have that guilt anymore and that has given me freedom. It was Mike's decision to do what he did, and he has to live with the consequences of his actions. One of those consequences is not seeing his children. That was his choice."

Maggie bit her lip. Francis had a point, but she didn't like the hardness that had crept into her voice. "I've always admired how you handled your situation. You did what you had to do for yourself and the children without complaint. Don't get bitter now. Whatever happens, you can be assured that God is still in control."

"You sound like Pastor Bob." Francis grimaced at her friend. "I had a meeting with him. Remember I told you I gave Mike his phone number?"

Maggie nodded.

"Guess he followed through on that. He went to see Pastor Bob."

"That's interesting," Maggie said, raising her eyebrows. "How did that go?"

"Pastor Bob is convinced that Mike is sincere." Francis finished her tea and poured some more for herself. She lifted the teapot toward Maggie, who pushed her cup toward Francis for a refill. "Apparently, Mike has a good Christian friend that can vouch for his sobriety. Pastor Bob corroborated Mike's story with him. The friend assured the pastor that Mike is a changed person in Christ. Pastor Bob recommends marriage counselling. He says he knows a good counsellor who could help us."

"What do you think of that?" Maggie asked.

Francis' shoulders slumped. "'Forgive us our debts, as we forgive our debtors.' I can't get that line out of my head. But right now, I can't see past the hurt. I thought I'd forgiven Mike, but now that he's back, I have all this hurt and anger boiling up inside me."

"Keep praying." Maggie reached across the table and took Francis' hands in her own. "Dale and I are praying for you as well. Trust the Lord to work things out."

"I've been trying to pray, but it feels like my prayers don't even reach the ceiling. I can't feel the Lord's presence." Francis' eyes grew misty. "Now when I need the Lord the most, He's not there."

"Please don't give up. Jesus loves you; you are his daughter. He won't leave you even though it may feel like it at the moment. *Can a woman forget her sucking child, that she should not have compassion on the son of her womb? Yea, they may forget, yet will I not forget thee.*' Isaiah 49:15. That's God's promise to his children."

"Yes, I know." Francis sighed. "I just have more questions than answers right now."

"Can I pray with you?" Maggie asked.

"Yes, please."

They bowed their heads, and Maggie prayed. "Father God, Francis and I come before your throne of grace, knowing that you love us. We know that you are in control of our lives and that you are in control of this situation. We don't understand why Mike is calling Francis after all these years or what he wants from her. Lord, you say in the Bible that you will give wisdom to those who ask for it, so Lord we are asking. Please give Francis wisdom and direction. Give her peace and calmness in her heart. Help her to feel your presence and your love for her. Protect her and the children. May your will be done. In Jesus' name we pray. Amen."

"Amen." Francis echoed.

"Have you talked to Gloria lately? How's she doing?" Maggie asked when they finished praying.

"She's always tired, but other than that, she seems to be doing alright."

"I've heard that radiation therapy makes a person very fatigued. Has she told Emily what's wrong with her?"

Francis gazed out the window. She could see across the parking lot to the playground where children were playing without a care in the world. Every child should have a carefree childhood. Emily had already lost her daddy. What would happen if she also lost her mommy? Francis turned back to face Maggie.

"She didn't tell Emily that she had cancer—only that she's not feeling well and that the doctors are fixing her up." Francis understood why Gloria wasn't telling Emily, even though she wasn't convinced that it was the right thing to do. "Did you know that they moved in with Gloria's parents?"

"No, I hadn't heard. That will be so much better for them."

"Yes, it is," Francis agreed. "They'll stay there until after Gloria's surgery. It will make it so much easier for them."

"Homesick?" Cornelio had asked John to join him in his office after supper. They'd had a hard day with one of the older boys, a newcomer in the throes of heroin withdrawal. John had spent all day with the boy, wiping his face when he vomited and talking to him through his pain and agitation.

The question took John by surprise. "I hadn't thought of it."

"You're doing a good job with the boys, but I get the feeling that you are struggling with something." The man's kind eyes studied John intently. "You are young and far from home, so I thought you might be homesick. I just want you to know that I'm here for you."

John stood up and paced to the window. His gaze went beyond the parched grass, the brightly coloured brick buildings, and the eight-foot fence that enclosed their compound to the majestic peaks of the Sierra Madre Mountains in the distance. It was a very different landscape from the flatlands of his home in northern Alberta.

Should I tell Cornelio about Mary? He let the thought bounce around in his head. He had received a letter from Mary the other day. It was filled with little anecdotes from work, how her family was doing, and news about neighbours and the community. There was no mention that she was the mother of a child she had put up for adoption. He had not written back—he wasn't sure he would.

John turned back to face Cornelio. "No sir, I'm not particularly homesick. I miss my family—I won't deny that—but no more than when I was away at school."

"Glad to hear that. I just want you to know that I'm here if you need to talk."

"I appreciate it, sir." John crossed the room and sat down in the chair.

Cornelio shuffled some papers on his desk then sat back in his chair and studied John. "I promised Hugo I'd go talk to his mother. It will take a couple of hours to get to the village in the mountains. I'd like you to come with me."

John was surprised Cornelio had asked him, since he was the newest member of the staff. Hugo was doing very well after spending a few years at the shelter. His eighteenth birthday was coming up, and he wanted to go home. He needed to know that his mother was ready to receive him. His father had left them when Hugo was twelve. When he was fifteen, Hugo had gone to the city to find a job—only to end up working for a drug cartel. When the mission people found him, he had escaped the cartel and was hiding in the streets, begging and stealing to feed himself. From what John had heard, Hugo had been a mess when he first came. He was paranoid the cartel would catch up to him and he'd be in big trouble. After almost two years,

105

Cornelio thought he'd be safe to go home—that no one was looking for him anymore. In the meantime, Hugo had given his life to the Lord and was excited to go home. Cornelio needed to discuss the homecoming details with the boy's mother.

"If you'd rather not, that's alright," Cornelio said, mistaking the pause for hesitancy on John's part. "I thought it would be a good experience for you."

"Yes, I'd love to come," John said quickly, reigning in his thoughts.

"Good. We'll leave right after breakfast. I want to be back before dark."

"Yes, sir."

John was excited the following morning as he got into the passenger seat of Cornelio's older model car. He had promised himself he would leave his worries behind and enjoy this new adventure. *A drive to the mountains will be good for me,* he thought to himself, setting the container of sandwiches that the cook had prepared onto the backseat.

Cornelio got into the driver's seat and turned the key in the ignition.

"Have you ever been to the mountains?" Cornelio asked as he shifted the car into gear and eased it forward.

"Not these mountains," John said. "I've been to the Rocky Mountains in Canada. Went there with friends when I was in school in Edmonton."

Green cornfields stretched out on either side of the road when they left the village street behind. The majestic Sierra Madre loomed in the distance. The morning sun was already promising another sweltering day, but Cornelio assured him that the mountain village would be cooler than the flatlands.

"For some reason I didn't expect Mexico would have such nicely paved roads," John commented. "They're much better than the gravel roads in my community back home." He chuckled softly. "Mexico is different from what I expected. It's like being in a different world altogether."

"Yes, I know what you mean," Cornelio said, nodding his greying head. "I grew up here, so to me this is what the world should look like. When I go to Canada or to the United States, it all looks very different to me."

Cornelio pointed out the various sights from cornfields to apple orchards to rolling hills of cactus and tumbleweed. John took it all in. It was so different from the flat farmlands and miles of wooded areas in northern Alberta. After about an hour of driving, the landscape shifted to mountains towering up above them. John was amazed and a little apprehensive of the steep hills and hairpin turns.

"Don't they have any guard rails?" John asked, after a series of turns where he was almost certain he'd be able to see their tail lights if it was dark.

"What's that?" Cornelio chuckled. "No, you won't see too many guardrails on this road. Hang on—we're almost at our destination." He shifted down as he began the descent into the little village.

Cornelio turned off of the paved road onto a dirt street, being careful of the children and dogs playing on the side of the road. Pedestrians carried heavy loads on their backs or on their heads. He stopped in front of a small hut that had a brightly coloured blanket for a door.

A woman in a faded yellow dress appeared in the doorway. John was surprised to see the woman who sat beside him on the plane.

"*Hola.*" Cornelio greeted the woman in Spanish as he climbed out of the car. "Are you Sofia?"

"*Si,*" the woman answered.

107

"My name is Cornelio and this is John." Cornelio waved his arm towards John.

"*Hola*," John said. Then continued in English. "You sat beside me in the plane." He looked around. "Where's your little girl?"

"She's in school," Sofia answered in heavily accented English, eyeing them warily.

"We have come from the mission shelter," Cornelio continued in Spanish. He took a picture from his pocket and showed it to the woman. "We have a young man named Hugo living there. I believe he is your son."

"*Si, si,*" Sofia said, taking the picture. She looked at it for a long time, then motioned for them to follow her around the outside of her hut to the shade of an orange tree in the back where she invited them to sit on the parched grass. She sat down as well.

"My Hugo, he wanted to earn money to send to me but I never heard from him again." Her voice was low, as if she was afraid someone was eavesdropping.

"Hugo was in bad shape when we found him," Cornelio told her. "He had started working for the drug cartel. Things got a little out of hand there, and he escaped."

"That was probably his father's doing!" Sofia blurted out angrily. Then caught herself and lowered her voice. "Hernandez has been involved with the cartel for many years. I was afraid for Hugo when he went to the city, but what can you say to a young boy who thinks he knows it all?" she wiped at her eyes angrily.

John had a hard time following the rapid conversation in Spanish. He understood enough to know that Cornelio told Sofia how Hugo had escaped the cartel. He was on the run when they rescued him.

"It is not safe for him to come home," Sofia told them emphatically, although she had lowered her voice considerably. "His father would find out, and he would take him back.

"Hugo didn't know his father was involved with the cartel?" Cornelio asked, lowering his voice as well.

"No. Who would tell him?" she asked. "Hernandez wouldn't admit it, and I didn't want him to know. I wanted a better life for him."

Things were obviously more complicated than Cornelio had realized. Hugo couldn't have known that his own father was his demise.

"I agree it wouldn't be safe for Hugo to move back here if that's the situation," Cornelio admitted reluctantly, rubbing his chin. He looked around at the meagre living conditions. "How many children do you have?"

"Just Hugo and Gracia," Sofia said.

"I thought by now it would be safe for Hugo to come home," Cornelio said thoughtfully. "I thought after almost two years at the shelter the cartel would have forgotten about him."

"You are wrong, *Señor*," Sofia said in her expressive way. "The cartel will watch my house and know when Hugo returns, and they will take him back." Her voice rose in panic as she talked.

"Do you have anywhere else you could move too?" Cornelio asked.

"My mother lives in Texas," Sofia said, bending closer to Cornelio.

John looked over his shoulder; their conversation was making him uneasy. Were they being watched?

The sun continued its trek towards the western peaks of the Sierra Madre, but the three sitting in the shade of the orange tree paid no heed. They had to make a plan that would keep Sofia and her children out of the clutches of the cartel, which would be hard to do if Hugo's father was involved.

"I didn't want to leave this late," Cornelio said later that afternoon as he started the car. The sun was threatening to sink behind the mountain peaks. He opened the glove compartment and retrieved his documents. "Better stuff your passport and any other identification in your socks in case we get stopped." Cornelio lifted his pant leg and proceeded to do that very thing.

John felt a sense of foreboding settle in his chest at the strange behaviour but followed instructions. Cornelio shifted the car into gear, and they started their journey back.

"I don't mean to scare you, John. It's not advisable to drive through these mountains after dark. If we hurry, we might get through most of it before it's completely dark."

"So the rumours about kidnapping are true then?" John asked, holding onto the dashboard with his right hand as Cornelio turned into a sharp corner. The hairpin turns that had been an exhilarating experience in daylight hours were sure to be intimidating after dark.

"It's definitely a danger," Cornelio answered, manoeuvring the car around the curve and up an incline. "If Sofia is right that her house is being watched, then we could be in real danger. You pray while I drive."

Fear clutched its vicious tentacles around John's insides. He glanced at Cornelio—the man had never looked more serious—and began to pray.

CHAPTER 9

Mary stopped in at the post office after work, her heart beating a little faster as she quickly checked through the mail for a letter from John. There was none. She had been waiting for a letter from John for weeks now. She quickly rifled through the envelopes again, her heart sinking. Nothing. *He's been gone for weeks,* she told herself. *He's probably very busy getting adjusted to his work and new lifestyle. It's probably a huge change from everything he's used to.* All the same, she couldn't deny her disappointment.

"Hi Mary." Mary turned to see Lena step out of her car.

"Hi Lena." Mary smiled at her friend. "How have you been? You're looking really good!"

Lena laughed as she leaned against Mary's car. "I'm doing well. When are you coming over to visit?"

"I thought I'd let you settle into your new home first," Mary said. It was good to see her friend so happy. She hadn't seen her since right after they'd come back from their honeymoon. Mary had gone to help Lena find a place for all their wedding gifts.

"Oh, we're all settled in." Lena waved that excuse off with the back of her hand. "Why don't you stop in after supper tonight? Henry works on the farm in the evenings, so it would give us a good time to catch up."

"That sounds perfect," Mary said. "I'll be there."

"Alright. See you later!" Lena turned away, and Mary got into her car.

"He said he'd write to me," Mary muttered to herself as she reversed out of the parking stall. "It was his idea that we write to each other, so why isn't he writing?" When she didn't hear from him within the first couple of weeks, she had taken the initiative and written him a letter. "Is John that busy that he doesn't have time to write? Or did he change his mind about corresponding with me? Maybe he met someone else." Her thoughts chased each other around in her head as she drove her car down the gravel road.

She waved to Annie, who was working in her garden, as she passed her house.

"I should stop in and visit her one of these days," she told herself as she drove by. Annie could probably use some help canning. The heat was practically unbearable this summer—being heavily pregnant must make it so much worse.

Arriving at home, she dumped the mail on the kitchen table on her way to the living room. "Hi," she said with a smile as she sank into the overstuffed chair next to Papa. She patted his hand where it lay on the armrest.

"Hello," Papa responded, a smile lighting up his face.

"Hi Mary." Mama looked up from where she was sewing a new dress on her treadle sewing machine close to the window. "How was work?"

"Work was good," Mary said. "Hectic, but good. I ran into Lena at the post office. She asked me to come over after supper. Henry is working long days, so she's home alone quite a bit. Where's Benny?"

"He's doing chores." Mama held up the partly finished dress. "What do you think?"

"It's very nice." Mary walked over and took a closer look. "It will look good on you."

"Well, I don't know about that." Mama would never admit anything looked good on her, which was customary in the Mennonite culture. To admit to looking good was considered a form of pride, and pride was unacceptable. Since childhood they were drilled to be humble. "But it has been a long time since I sewed myself a new dress."

"Too long," Mary said, fingering the soft material. "You're always too busy taking care of everyone else. I'm glad you're doing something for yourself."

Anna lowered her eyes as she blinked back sudden tears. *Mary has such a compassionate nature. How could she give up her own child?* No one knew the silent battle raging within Anna's soul. They couldn't see the beating her faith had received. Countless times she had questioned God on why he had allowed all these sorrows to come upon their family. Her heart ached from the loss of David. Yes, the pain had lessened over the years, but she still missed him so much. If only she could tell Jacob how she felt, but she couldn't burden him with her struggles. It wasn't fair to tell him what was on her heart when he couldn't even express himself. No, he had more than enough to deal with as it was.

Every day, Anna longed to see her granddaughter. *If only Mary had told us she was having a baby instead of running away and giving her daughter up for adoption. We could have raised her. I could sew her little dresses. It would do my heart good to have a child in the house.* Of all the things that had happened to them as a family, not being able to be a grandma to her little granddaughter broke her heart the most.

"Should I make supper?" Mary's question startled Anna out of her reverie.

"If you want to," she said, laying her partially finished dress down, "but you've worked all day already."

"I don't mind," Mary said, heading towards the kitchen. "Then you can sew a little longer."

Benny came in with a pail of fresh milk just as Mary put the potatoes on to boil.

"Are you making supper?" Benny asked, setting the pail on the floor beside the cream separator. "You want me to put the milk through the separator?"

"If you don't mind. Did you get the chores done already?" Mary asked, putting thick slices of ham into the frying pan.

"Yes, I did." Benny headed to the bathroom. "I'll just wash up first."

Mary was proud of how Benny was taking up the responsibilities of doing chores. He enjoyed working with animals and that took a load off of her shoulders. *Funny how God works things out,* she thought as the cream separator hummed in the background. *David would have left to be a missionary in a distant land but Benny is looking forward to taking over the farm.* She got four plates from the cupboard and set them on the table. *I wonder if David would have gone to Mexico with John.* She retrieved four glasses and cutlery and set them on the table as well.

Mary jumped as Benny jabbed her in the side in passing. She spun around and swatted at him, but he ducked and ran behind the table, laughing at her. She ran after him, picking up the wet dishrag on the cupboard. He evaded her—keeping just out of her reach.

"What's going on in there?" their mama called from the living room.

"Benny's being a pest," Mary said, laughing as she ran around the table trying to get at him. Benny pulled out chairs behind him to slow her down.

"Don't let supper burn," her mama warned.

"I owe you," Mary told Benny, waving the dishrag in his direction. She turned back to the stove to turn the slices of ham over in the pan.

"You were so deep in thought I couldn't resist." Benny chuckled. He turned back to the cream separator and put the milk and cream into the fridge.

"Supper's ready," Mary announced as she put the last dish on the table. Benny led Papa to his chair at the table and Mama followed. They bowed their heads to say grace before dishing up.

"How was work?" Mama asked Benny as she fixed Papa a plate of potatoes, ham, and peas.

"Good," Benny answered, passing the peas to Mary without taking any. Mary hid a smile as she remembered Benny's aversion to peas. Mama had finally given up on making him eat them. "I'm going fishing with Danny and Fred after supper."

Mama set Papa's plate in front of him. Papa stabbed his fork into his potatoes and slowly brought it to his mouth.

"Cows?" Papa asked, eyeing Benny across the table.

Benny gave a detailed report on the animals and the crops. Papa nodded his head, listening intently as he ate. Mary's heart went out to him. She knew Papa would love to be out there tending to his farm but that wasn't possible anymore. Benny took him out to the barn occasionally. It made him feel involved.

When Mary arrived at Lena's house, her friend threw the door open before Mary could knock.

"I'm so glad you came," Lena said, stepping aside so Mary could enter.

Mary stepped past her friend into the small house that Henry had built. As expected, it was immaculate. Not a thing was out of place except a new electric sewing machine in the far corner of the kitchen.

"Grab a chair." Lena waved a hand towards her kitchen table. "Do you want some coffee?" she asked, heading to her dark mahogany cupboards.

"Yes, please, I'd love some. What are you sewing?" Mary asked, wandering over to the sewing machine.

Lena took two coffee mugs off of the mug tree on the counter and poured coffee in each. Her auburn curls bounced cheerily as she set the steaming cups on the table and practically floated to her sewing machine.

"I'll show you." She picked up a stack of folded white flannel and handed it to Mary.

Mary gasped as she realized she was holding soft flannel diapers.

"Are you pregnant?" Mary gaped at her friend.

"Yes!" Lena laughed excitedly, her eyes dancing.

Mary had never seen her friend this excited. She set down the diapers and pulled Lena into a hug. "That's wonderful! I'm so happy for you!" She needed a moment to push down the jealousy that welled up in her heart and put a smile on her face. "When did you find out? When's the baby due?"

"We just found out this week, but I couldn't help myself—I started sewing right away." Lena giggled as she pulled herself free from Mary's arms. Mary picked up the yellow and green flannel beside the sewing machine, avoiding her friend's eyes. *This is Lena's moment, and I won't spoil it,* she told herself sternly.

"What's this for?"

"Receiving blankets."

Mary laughed at her friend. "You'll have this house full of baby stuff if you keep this up!"

"That's what Henry tells me." Lena giggled again. "But he's just as excited as I am."

"You're going to be a great mama," Mary said as they went back to the table and sat down. "You've always loved children—and Henry. It just took Henry a long time to realize he loved you too."

"What about you and John?" Lena asked, searching her friend's face. "You've always loved him." Lena didn't often question her friend, but she had noticed how Mary and John looked at each other at her wedding. Anyone with half a brain could see they had feelings for each other.

"Oh, that was just childhood puppy love," Mary said, waving her hand in dismissal. She raised the coffee cup to her mouth and took a sip.

"I don't think so," Lena said. "I think you have feelings for each other. I just can't understand why you don't get together."

The door burst open and Henry barged in. His face was ashen.

"Henry! What happened?" Lena jumped out of her chair and went to her husband. "What's wrong? Here, sit down." She pulled at his arm.

"John is missing," Henry blurted. "They think he's been kidnapped!"

"No!" Mary didn't recognize her own voice.

"What?" Lena asked, stunned. "Are you sure? How do you know? Surely, this can't be true!"

"Mr. Wieler got a phone call from the mission board." He took Lena's arm and led her to a chair. "Here, you sit down." He sat down beside her. "Apparently John and Mr. Friesen went to a village in the mountains to talk to the mother of one of the boys at the shelter. They didn't come back."

"Mary, are you alright?" Henry looked at Mary in alarm. Her face was devoid of colour.

Henry and Lena's faces swam in front of her. Mary felt incredibly hot, and her eyes wouldn't focus. Lena grabbed a wet washcloth and placed it on Mary's forehead while pushing Mary's head down between her knees.

"It'll be alright," she said in a soothing voice while Henry got her a glass of water. "I'm sure there's more to it. They'll find John. I'm sure he's fine." She used the same tone of voice she used on her younger siblings when they got hurt. Mary's world stopped spinning, and her eyes cleared up. She lifted her head.

"Thanks," she said to both of them. "I'm sorry." She took a sip of ice-cold water.

"No, I'm sorry," Henry said, resuming his seat. "I should have broken it to you more gently."

"Do you know anything else?" Lena asked as she sat back down and took Henry's hand in hers.

Henry eyed Mary cautiously. "That's all I know. Mr. Wieler just said to pray for John and Mr. Friesen."

John's brain was foggy with exhaustion. He had lost all track of time. They had trekked through the jungle all night, over steep and uneven terrain. The evasive moon sent occasional snippets of silvery beams through the dark canopy of age-old trees. His hands were tied behind his back, making it impossible for him to protect himself from the branches lashing at his face and body—his feet screamed for relief. The incessant, ferocious, howling monkeys overhead spooked his frayed nerves, paralyzing his mind with the fear that at any moment a wild animal could pounce on him or he might step on a sleeping snake.

God have mercy was all he could think to pray. John stumbled and fell over one of the many vines snaking their way across the jungle floor. Searing pain shot through his thigh as a sharp branch ripped through his pants and pierced his leg as his head slammed against a tree trunk. His captor swore in Spanish and yanked him upright.

"*Vamonos!*" the harsh voice barked at him, pushing John forward with the barrel of his massive gun. "Hurry up or I'll shoot you right here!" He swore again then mumbled derogatory comments about gringos.

John placed one aching foot ahead of the other as quickly as he could. He had no idea where they were or where they were going. The jungle had swallowed them up. The few words their captors spoke were barked out in Spanish at him or Cornelio.

John almost stumbled into the side of a grimy brick hut overgrown with camouflaging vines. The barrel of a gun prodded John towards the black hole that he quickly realized was an open door. Cornelio stumbled in right behind him. John winced as one of the masked captors grabbed his aching arms behind his back and removed the rope that was tightly wound around his wrists. Without another word, the masked men backed away through the door. Darkness swallowed them up. The metal door clanged shut behind them with finality. Their captors spoke in low tones that quickly faded away as they left.

John collapsed onto the bare wooden floor from sheer exhaustion.

"What's happening?" he whispered to Cornelio, fighting hard against the panic in his chest. He couldn't see Cornelio in the blackness that surrounded them.

"I don't know," Cornelio whispered. "I think it might be one of two things: Either they took us for ransom or they were watching Sofia's place and were waiting for us."

"So you think it was a setup?"

"I don't know," Cornelio whispered. "Hugo has never let on that he knew his father was involved with the drug cartel. He never mentioned his father except to say he had left the family. I hate to think that he knows more than he's told us, but when it comes to the cartel operations, you never know. I think it's more likely that his father knows where Hugo is and is taking this opportunity to get Hugo back."

"You mean they'll keep us hostage until Hugo leaves the shelter?" John's exhausted mind struggled to comprehend what Cornelio was saying.

"I don't know. It's possible." John heard Cornelio shifting his weight on the hard floor. "Let's not worry about that now. We have to get some sleep before they come back. There's no knowing what they'll do next. We must sleep when we can, but first let's commit this whole situation to God."

John closed his eyes as Cornelio prayed. "Heavenly Father, John and I don't know where we are or what will befall us, but you know exactly where we are. We pray for our safety, Lord, and we pray for our captors—that they will turn from their evil ways and will turn to you. We pray that you will undertake for us and set us free. Be close to our families and help them not to be anxious about us. Father, give us peace and calmness so we can sleep as your Word says, 'I will both lay me down in peace, and sleep: for thou, Lord, only makest me dwell in safety.' Help us not to be anxious. In Jesus' name we pray. Amen."

"Amen," John echoed, finding comfort in the prayer.

CHAPTER 10

"Maggie, I don't know if I can do this," Francis told Maggie over a cup of coffee that morning.

"You don't have to, Francis," Maggie said. "You have to do this your own way, in your own time." Her heart ached for Francis. The girl had been through so much, and now she was feeling pressure to meet with Mike.

"I've gone over a hundred different scenarios in my mind. I don't know what to do or say. What do you say to a husband you haven't seen in ten years? What do you say to a husband who has beaten you, killed your baby, and left you to fend for yourself and your children?" Francis couldn't hide the bitterness in her voice as she got up and walked over to the window that overlooked the parking lot. "What if this is a ploy to take the children away from me?" An unbidden tear slipped over her eyelid and trickled down her cheek. "I can't bear the thought."

"Francis, do you think Pastor Bob would encourage you to have this meeting if he thought that's what Mike had in mind?" Maggie joined her at the window and put her arm around Francis' shoulders. "Do you think the courts would give the children to Mike after he's been out of their lives for this long?"

"Yeah, probably not. I hadn't thought of it that way."

"What does God want you to do?"

Francis shrugged. "I don't know. I can't feel God anymore." She sighed heavily. "I've never felt so alone."

"Why do you think that is?" Maggie asked tenderly.

"Oh, I don't know." Francis shrugged her shoulders. "The only thing that keeps running through my head is 'forgive us our debts as we forgive our debtors'." Francis turned to look at Maggie. "How can I forgive him?"

Maggie's heart broke at the anguish in Francis' eyes. *Lord give me wisdom.* "Do you think that's what the Lord is asking of you?"

"How could he? Maggie, he killed my baby!" She grabbed a tissue from the box on the cupboard and sat down at the table, wiping her eyes.

"I know," Maggie said softly, resuming her place at the table, "I found you—remember? I know what he did to you. Oh Francis, if I could make this all go away, I would. Can I pray with you?"

Francis nodded, "Yes, please. Maybe God will listen to your prayers."

"My dear," Maggie reached over and took Francis' hand. "God hears your prayers as well. He's working on answering them. Have faith, my girl. Remember the words of our Lord in Jeremiah 29:11 'For I know the thoughts that I think toward you, saith the Lord, thoughts of peace, and not of evil.' Let's pray."

They bowed their heads and Maggie prayed. "Lord please keep your hand over Francis. I bring her before your throne of grace. Almighty God, please fill her with your peace. Give her wisdom. Give her direction. As she meets with Mike this afternoon, please fill her with your spirit and speak to her heart that she will know what you would have her do and say. May your will be done. Thank you, Jesus. Amen."

"Amen," Francis echoed.

Maggie picked up her empty coffee cup and carried it to the sink. "I have to go, but I'll keep praying for you. Please don't feel anxious. The Lord will be with you."

"Thank you." Francis gave Maggie a hug. "What would I do without you? I so appreciate being able to confide in you."

"Just don't give up. You'll get through this!"

A ray of light shone through a small opening at the top of the cabin wall when John woke up the next morning. It took a few seconds for him before the events of yesterday tripped over each other as they bombarded his mind.

The road that saw little traffic in the morning had been busy after dark. John had felt Cornelio's tension mount as he manoeuvred the car up the steep inclines and around the hairpin curves. Rounding one of those curves—a ragged rock wall to their left and a sharp cliff to their right—Cornelio hit the brakes to avoid the vehicles parked on either side of the road. Masked figures loomed in their headlights, machine guns pointed at their windshield. Cornelio had no option but to stop the car.

"Get out! Get out!" The gunmen had yelled at them in Spanish, yanking the doors open. John was dragged out of the car and slammed face down onto the asphalt. The cold barrel of a gun pressed into the back of his head as his arms were jerked behind him and tightly tied together. They had been dumped into the back of a covered truck and driven away. Sometime afterward, they had stopped at the side of the road, and they had started their trek down a path and deep into the heart of the jungle.

John sat up abruptly, every muscle in his body groaning. His right thigh throbbed with pain. His blood stained jeans were ripped, revealing an ugly gash in his thigh. He moved his jaw, trying to work up enough spittle in his mouth to soothe his parched throat.

"Good morning." Cornelio's face was scratched and swollen with a streak of dried blood on the left side. The side of his shirt was ripped.

"You're hurt." John said.

"Nothing major." Cornelio moved his arms and legs. "Still works. Are you injured?"

John looked down at his scratched-up arms. They bore cuts and bruises from their long trek through the jungle.

"I think I'm alright," John replied, flexing his arms. They felt stiff and sore but that was expected.

Cornelio gestured to the far corner of the room. "Look what I found."

In the dimness, John could tell that the room was bare except for one small jug standing in a corner. "Water?"

"Yes," Cornelio answered. "I smelled it before I tasted it, and it is water."

"Is it safe to drink?" John asked; his throat was parched.

"I have no idea," Cornelio said. "We don't have to drink it yet, but if we're here too much longer we'll have to chance it. At least there don't seem to be any snakes in here."

"Snakes!" John exclaimed. "I was so exhausted last night, I didn't even think of snakes or rodents!" He shuddered at the thought of all the unwelcome critters that could have made their home in this abandoned hut in the middle of the jungle.

"I thought of it, but we couldn't do anything about it in the dark so I didn't mention it."

John shuddered. "I'm not sure I would have slept at all if I had thought there might be snakes or rats hiding in here. I was too tired to think."

"Do you still have your documents?" Cornelio asked, holding up his own. "I still have mine."

John hiked up his pant leg and groaned at the soreness the movement caused. He checked his sock and pulled out his passport. "Yes, it's all here."

Francis nervously drummed her fingers on the steering wheel as she stopped at the red light. Pastor Bob had met with Mike a couple of times and was convinced that Mike's change was sincere.

"Good old Pastor Bob," Francis muttered to herself, taking her foot off the brake as the light turned green. "He's so thorough; meeting with Mike's friend and the pastor of Mike's church."

So she had agreed to meet Mike in a public place of her choice. She had purposely chosen a park in a different neighbourhood so Mike wouldn't find out where she lived. Cars whizzed by on either side of her as she accelerated. *Might as well get this meeting over with,* she thought as she turned at the next intersection, slowing down as she entered the sleepy neighbourhood of cookie-cutter houses set back from the street. *Goodness, don't people have an imagination anymore?* She decided to park the car a block from the park and walk from there.

A gentle breeze kept the bright sun from feeling too hot on her shoulders. Her flowery shift dress complimented her slim figure, the skirt swishing softly just above her knees with each step. She met a young couple pushing a baby stroller. Down the street an elderly man mowed his front lawn, teasing her nostrils with the scent of freshly mowed grass. Any other day Francis would have enjoyed the walk, but today she had to work hard to calm the anxiety mounting in her chest. Her heart beat erratically as she quickly scanned the park.

"He's not here yet," she muttered, breathing a sigh of relief. She had given herself lots of time, hoping to arrive first. Other than a young woman swinging a child in a baby swing, the park looked vacant. Francis chose a park bench farthest away from the playground equipment. A stand of oak trees provided a sense of shade and privacy. She sat down on the faded brown wooden bench. *Lord, help me,* she pleaded silently as her eyes anxiously scanned the park. *I can't do this on my own.*

A sleek black Mustang pulled up to the curb, and Francis' heart caught in her throat as she watched the tall, blond man unfolding himself from the driver's seat. Ten years seemed like two seconds as she watched his eyes scan the park—then light up in recognition as they came to rest on her. She struggled to breathe as she watched those long legs close the distance between them. His blond curls were cut shorter, but the royal blue T-shirt and blue jeans left no doubt that the muscular body they covered was the one she remembered.

"Francis, you look stunning," Mike said, sitting down beside her. "Thanks for coming."

Reality came crashing down around her at the sound of his voice. Ten years. Ten long years of struggling to make ends meet, raising two children. Ten years of loneliness. The baby who should be almost ten years old. Francis lowered her eyes in shame and frustration. *How could my body betray me like that? Remember what he did!*

"Why, Mike?" Francis asked, her voice catching in her throat.

"I'm sorry, Francis." Mike's voice turned serious, his eyes pleading. "I'm so sorry. I have no excuse."

Francis gazed across the park—across the years—to a time when she had loved this man. She remembered the night he proposed. It was the night of her graduation from high school. She remembered their wedding day and the birth of their firstborn. They had been so in love. Life became harder as their little family grew to include a second child and taxed their meagre earnings.

"I would like a second chance." Mike's voice interrupted her thoughts. "I want a fresh start with you and the children."

Francis turned her haunted eyes to Mike. "How can you even ask that?" Her voice sounded strangled.

"I know I've done you wrong." Mike reached out and took her hands in his. *How I've missed these soft hands,* he thought to himself. He prayed silently for the right words. "I've straightened my life out. I don't drink anymore. It's a long story, but I'm living my life for the Lord now. I miss you and the kids. I'd do anything to have you back in my life."

Francis pulled her hands from his and laid them in her lap. *Take him back? He wants to come live with us?* "The kids don't remember you."

Mike recoiled as if she had slapped him. "It's been a long time," he admitted. "Too long. I've missed them terribly. I knew I had to clean up my own life before I could even think of coming back. It took years, but I finally met a man who pointed me in the right direction. He gave me a job, cleaned me up, and took me to church. After I asked Jesus to forgive me and be a part of my life, I knew I needed to ask your forgiveness as well." He cupped her chin in his hand, lifting her face to meet his eyes. "I love you. I never stopped loving you." His sky-blue eyes held hers. "I know that is hard for you to believe. I just want the chance to prove myself to you."

Francis struggled with the emotions in her heart. Anger, resentment, confusion—love? She broke eye contact, and he dropped his hand.

"I'm willing to take it as slow as you want," Mike said. He paused, taking a deep breath. She hadn't answered his question when they spoke on the phone, but he needed to know. "The night I left you told me you were pregnant. Was it a boy or girl?"

"I don't know."

"You don't know?" Mike's eyebrows shot up. *What is she saying? That doesn't make sense.* "What do you mean?"

"You didn't want another baby."

"I was drunk. I wasn't in my right mind when I said that—what do you mean you don't know?" A thought sucker-punched him in the gut. "Did you give the child up for adoption?" He was horrified. "Oh no, Francis, you didn't give the child away, did you? Is that what I forced you to do?" He had never considered that she would resort to giving the child up. But what else could she have done? They had hardly been able to get by with two children, never mind trying to raise three by herself. "I'm so sorry, Francis. I never even considered that. I should have been there for you."

"No, I didn't give it away. You took care of that." Francis' body trembled as her mind took her back to that horrible night. "The baby didn't survive your beating."

Colour drained from Mike's ruddy face and for a moment Francis feared he might faint. "No!" The single, strangled, word ripped out of his heart. "No." He shook his head—his mind trying desperately to process the information. *That can't be!* his whole being screamed. *She's lying!* But no—she had never lied to him before.

Francis watched a myriad of emotions wash over his face. Disbelief. Shock. Horror. Sorrow? He seemed to crumble before her eyes as his head dropped into his hands. She had never seen him cry before. He was always macho—the tough one. Mike's shoulders shook as his soul confronted him with the depth of the brutality he was capable of.

Francis searched her purse for tissue and pressed it into Mike's hand. The spark that swept through her as her hand brushed his took her by surprise. Suddenly she wanted to console him with every fibre of her being. She wanted to put her arms around him and fix everything that was broken between them. Abruptly, she stood up and hurried back to her car—back to her life.

She sat in the car for a long time until the pounding in her chest subsided. "What was I thinking? I can't fix things. I'm way past that," she muttered to herself. "I just never expected Mike to break down. It took me by surprise."

When she finally started her car and pulled out from the curb, the black Mustang was gone.

"Mary, you need to start eating more," Anna said in her gentle voice. She had saved this conversation until the two of them were alone in the kitchen doing dishes. "You love *Wareniki en Warscht*." She had prepared Mary's favourite Mennonite dish—hoping the girl would find her appetite—but she hadn't had more than a few bites.

"I am eating, Mama," Mary said, sinking her hands into the sudsy water.

"What you're eating wouldn't keep a bird alive." Anna's voice was laced with deep concern.

"I'm sorry, Mama. Food just doesn't agree with me these days."

"You can't worry yourself sick like this, Mary," Anna said, drying the dishes Mary placed in the dish rack. "We have to trust God to take care of John."

"It doesn't make any sense," Mary said. "Why would God call John to be a missionary only to be kidnapped and possibly killed? It seems like wanting to be a missionary is a curse. First David, now John."

"I don't have answers, Mary. God's ways are not our ways, and his thoughts are not our thoughts. We have to pray that God's will be done and trust that it will all work out."

"I can't bring myself to pray that God's will be done. What if his will is that John is never found? Or he's killed?"

"We must pray that whatever happens will be to God's honour and glory. Maybe John and Cornelio's disappearance will cause a great breakthrough among the people and many will accept Jesus as their Saviour."

Mary fell silent. *I can't pray God's will be done. What if his will is for John to die? I just can't.*

Mother and daughter worked in silence for a while, each lost in their own thoughts.

"Would it help you to write John a letter?"

"I have written to him, but he hasn't responded. Anyways, what good would it do to write now?"

"Isn't there something you should tell him?"

"What would I tell him?"

"That you love him."

"I don't..."

Anna held up her hand. "Mary, listen to me." She laid her hand firmly on Mary's arm. "I'm not blind. I know you care about him and not just as a friend either."

"He would never understand." Mary's shoulders slumped as she washed the dishes.

"About the baby?" her mama prodded. "You won't know until you tell him. You know you love him, and he loves you too. I can see it in his face as much as I can see it in yours. Come clean with him. Yes, you chance rejection. But if you never tell him and keep spurning his love you're not happy anyways."

"It's too late now. Nobody knows where he is." It broke Anna's heart to hear her daughter so dejected. Mary pulled the plug in the sink and let the water drain. "When I gave my baby up for adoption, I vowed I would never tell anyone. I also vowed I would never marry because it wouldn't be fair to my husband."

"Oh Mary, you are not being fair to John. Let him make up his own mind. Rejection is hard, but what you are doing is hard for both of you. It is time for you to put your stubbornness aside and come clean with John. Please tell me you'll at least pray about it."

The phone rang, interrupting their conversation. Mary quickly went to pick up the receiver. "Hello."

"Hello, Mary." Lena's voice came over the line. "Have you heard about John?"

Mary's heart stopped as she clutched the receiver. *Please, Lord, let him be found!* "No. What is it?"

"They know for sure now that he was kidnapped. The kidnappers have asked for a ransom of half a million dollars and the release of one of the boys at the youth shelter."

"Nobody has that kind of money!" Mary exclaimed, as her heart pounded and her spirit sank to the floor. "What happens if they don't get it?"

"His captors are threatening to kill them if they don't have the money in a week from today. Henry's papa talked with Mr. Wieler. There's a prayer meeting at our church tonight. Will you come? We can pick you up."

"Yes, of course. Oh Lena, do they know for sure he's still alive? Did they talk to him?" Mary felt like flying to Mexico herself and looking for John.

"No, they just got a phone call from the kidnappers."

When they hung up, Mary sank into a chair and buried her face in her hands.

"What happened?" her mama asked anxiously. "Who was that?"

"Lena. John and that other man were kidnapped. The kidnappers have asked for half a million dollars ransom and the release of one of the boys at the youth shelter." Mary swallowed a sob.

Anna slowly lowered herself into a chair. "Nobody has that kind of money! Why would they ask for a boy at the shelter? I thought they were there of their own free will."

"I don't know." Mary's body started shaking uncontrollably—like it did when David died. "The kidnappers are threatening to kill John and Mr. Friesen if they don't get the money by a week from today." Silent tears slipped down her cheeks—she didn't bother to wipe them away.

"We must pray." There was an urgency in Anna's voice as she wiped at her eyes. "Pray that somehow God will save them."

"How will they ever get that much money?" Mary asked, dejectedly. "There's no way."

"With God all things are possible," her mama insisted. "And all things, whatsoever ye shall ask in prayer, believing, ye shall receive," Anna quoted scripture. She laid a hand on Mary's arm reassuringly. "We must believe that."

CHAPTER 11

John winced as he moved his swollen right leg. The pain was getting harder to bear, and his leg was hot to the touch. He didn't dare examine the puncture wound too closely for fear Cornelio would notice. He didn't want Cornelio to worry about him. Poor guy had enough to think about, having a wife and children back home who he knew would be worried sick about him. John knew his family would be worried as well, but that was different than having a wife and children.

The lock on the door rattled then creaked as it swung open. A heavily armed gunman wearing a balaclava entered the hut. John's stomach growled as he eyed the dented pot the guard set on the floor. Everyday a gunman entered the hut and brought them a little food and filled their water jug. It wasn't much, but the men were thankful for each morsel they received.

"*Gracias*," Cornelio said, standing up. "God bless you for bringing us food."

"I take your pictures," the gunman said, stepping between Cornelio and the pot on the floor. He motioned the two of them to move closer together.

"What is happening?" Cornelio asked the gunman quietly as John struggled to his feet. "When are we going to be released?"

"I don't make the decisions." The gunman shrugged and snapped the picture.

He backed out of the door, and the clang of metal on metal signified it was barred shut again. Voices faded away as the gunmen left. There were always two. One would come into the cabin while the other remained outside. Cornelio and John dug into the small pot of tortillas and drank from the jug of water the gunman had left. It was just enough food to still the hunger pangs for a while. They rationed both food and water, not knowing when they would come again.

"Why do you think he took our picture?" John asked, setting the water jug on the floor.

"There's only one reason," Cornelio answered. "Our captors are asking for a ransom and want to assure the mission board that we are alive. My guess is that the mission board will keep asking for more proof to give them time to decide what to do."

"Have you dealt with ransoms before?"

"Not me personally, but it has happened before."

"Did the hostages survive?"

"Not always." Cornelio sighed. "You ask too many questions. We must pray and leave it in God's hands. He can get us out of here if it's his will."

John groaned as he moved his leg. He coughed to cover his groan. "Your family must be very worried."

"Yes, I'm sure they are—as yours will be."

"I don't want to think of how stressful it will be for my parents. But I don't have a wife and children worrying about me, like you do."

"A girlfriend?"

John shook his head. "No girlfriend."

Cornelio cocked his head to one side at the sadness in John's voice. "You want to tell me about her?"

"What do you mean?" John asked, raising an eyebrow. "I said no girlfriend."

Cornelio leaned forward. "Something has bothered you ever since you came to the shelter. The sadness in your voice tells me there's probably a girl involved. Am I wrong?" He fixed a steady gaze on John.

John closed his eyes. Mary's image appeared as clearly as if she was standing in front of him. Pain coursed through his chest. *Maybe Cornelio can help me make sense of it all.* With a sigh, he opened his eyes. "No, you're not wrong."

"You want to tell me about it?" Cornelio asked. "Sometimes it helps to talk, and I have time to listen."

"There's not much to say." John's eyes were a sea of pain as he struggled with the words. "She told me she doesn't love me."

"You don't believe her?" Cornelio asked, raising his bushy eyebrows.

"I didn't believe her." John brushed his hand through his hair in agitation. "Now I don't know. I'm so confused."

Cornelio shifted his weight but remained silent, his eyes encouraging John to get it off his chest.

"I've loved her since grade school." John's voice grew soft as his mind wandered back over the years. "I always thought I'd marry her someday. Her brother, David, was my best friend, so I was at their house often. Then her brother died in a car accident when he was seventeen, and Mary was crushed. I finished high school and left for Bible College within the year. Whenever I went home—which wasn't often—I heard rumours that she was spending her time with a questionable group of kids. I was in my second year when I heard that Mary had disappeared. Her parents were beside themselves. She had left them a note that she would come home soon, but she didn't. They searched for her and found out she had caught a bus to Edmonton.

Months later, her father had a stroke and was flown to a hospital in Edmonton, where I was going to school. One day when I came back from visiting her papa at the hospital, I stumbled across Mary sitting beneath a tree on the campus grounds. She hadn't heard that her father was sick, so I took her to the hospital and she was reunited with her parents. We spent some time together, but weeks later, when her papa was released, she went home with them." John fell silent.

Mary ran away from home. No one knew where she was for the better part of a year.

Why didn't I question her about that?

Heartbreak and desperation choked John's voice as he continued. "Just before I came to Mexico I found out the reason Mary had disappeared all those years ago. She had a baby whom she gave up for adoption."

"Do you know that for sure?" Cornelio asked gently, automatically reverting to his counsellor voice.

"Yes." John's answer rode on a wave of pain that swept through his inner core.

"Have you talked to Mary about it?"

"No. I was already in the city on my way here when I found out."

"You could write to her." Since he looked after the mail, Cornelio knew John had not mailed a letter to the girl who had written to him.

"What would I write? She already told me she only loved me as a friend. I should have gotten the hint. I kept pursuing her because I thought I saw love in her eyes." He groaned. "I didn't know she hadn't stayed true to me."

"Did you ask her to?"

"No. She was too young. I thought we had an understanding."

"Why don't you ask her about it?"

"What's the use?" John sounded defeated. "I can't marry her now."

"Why is that?" Cornelio persisted. "Is she involved with another man?"

"No. At least I don't think so. That happened years ago, and I never heard that she was seeing anyone."

"Then why don't you talk to her? Ask her about it?"

"What difference would that make? She's been with someone else. She has a daughter."

"Oh, I get it," Cornelio said, nodding his head knowingly. "She's not pure. She has sinned, so now she's not good enough for you."

John's head jerked up. "No," he exclaimed a little too quickly. He hadn't thought of it that way. Not consciously. "I always thought I'd marry a girl who had kept herself pure for her husband."

"Of course. I understand. That's what most young men think," Cornelio said thoughtfully. "Is Mary a Christian?"

"Yes." John studied Cornelio. *What's he getting at now?*

"Do you think Jesus has forgiven her?"

John closed his eyes as he struggled with his emotions. *What is Cornelio implying? Of course Jesus has forgiven her if she has asked him. If Jesus forgave her, can I do any less?*

Cornelio prayed silently as he watched John wrestle with the concept.

"For if ye forgive men their trespasses, your heavenly Father will also forgive you: but if ye forgive not men their trespasses, neither will your Father forgive your trespasses." The verses from Matthew 6:14-15 ran through his mind. They had always been easy verses for him. How often had he used those same verses to counsel others?

But Lord, John's heart cried silently, *Mary has ruined my life—our life together. How can I forgive her?*

The phone rang. Mike let it ring. Maybe they'd hang up. Finally, when he couldn't stand the incessant ringing any longer, he got up from the couch and lifted the receiver to his ear. "Hello."

"Hi. Mike, are you alright? You don't sound good." Dan's voice came across the line.

"I need you." Mike said, wadding up the tissue in his hand. His sinuses were stuffy from crying. He wanted a drink. Badly.

"I'll be right there," Dan said. He knew the desperation in Mike's voice. He had felt it himself. "Give me five minutes." He didn't bother to say goodbye. He slammed the receiver down on its cradle.

Dan recognized the cry for help. He prayed he wasn't too late. Grabbing his car keys he ran out of his house, taking the stairs two at a time. He jumped into his car, revving the motor as he turned into the street. *Jesus, please keep Mike safe. He didn't sound good. Lord, be right there with him. Help me get there in time.* Dan prayed all the way to Mike's apartment.

Mike let the receiver fall back into its cradle. The craving was bad. A drink would help him forget. He tried to pray, but all he could say was, "Please Jesus, help me!" There was a knock on the door and Mike got up to unlock it. Dan stepped through the door and grabbed Mike in a bear hug.

"What happened?" Dan's eyes quickly scanned what he could see of the rooms. *No bottles. Good.*

"No, I haven't been drinking," Mike said, recognizing Dan's look. He plopped down on the couch. "But I have a bad craving."

"Things didn't go well?" Dan asked, sitting down on the couch beside Mike.

"It's way beyond that." His voice was listless. His eyes were red and swollen. Tissues littered the floor.

"What happened?"

"Remember I told you I beat her up just before I left?" Mike's voice was filled with self-loathing. He had always despised himself for that, never realizing the full extent of the damage his rage had caused.

"I remember," Dan said. "She told you she was pregnant."

"I asked her about the baby—was it a boy or girl—and she said she didn't know," Mike choked up. Dan grabbed a tissue and handed it to Mike. The anguish in the eyes that met his reminded Dan of his own torment after the accident. "The baby didn't survive the beating."

Dan swallowed the gasp that rose in his throat. So many emotions from the past overwhelmed him. He knew Mike was feeling those same emotions now. "I'm so sorry." They sat in silence, each lost in their own regrets.

"Francis said she can't forgive me. I don't blame her—I can't forgive myself." Dejection saturated Mike's voice. He had worked hard to get his life back on track. Now all he had worked for was slipping through his fingers.

"Believe me, I have a pretty good idea what you're feeling right now." Dan prayed for the right words. "For years I struggled to forgive myself. I think that's the hardest thing to do. Paul says in Philippians 3:13-14: 'Brethren, I count not myself to have apprehended: but this one thing I do, forgetting those things which are behind, and reaching forth unto those things which are before, I press toward the mark for the prize of the high calling of God in Christ Jesus.' Paul was a great man of God. In fact, God inspired him to write a large portion of the New

139

Testament. But before Paul met Jesus, he sentenced Christians to death, even going out of his way to cities beyond Jerusalem to gather Christians and bring them to judgement. He stood by and watched as the first martyr, Stephen, was stoned.

Then one day on his way to Damascus, Paul met Jesus and his life changed. He realized that Jesus was the Way and that he, Paul, was wrong. Don't you think Paul carried a lot of guilt?" Dan paused, letting the words sink in before he continued. "God can't use a person burdened down with guilt. We have to ask God's forgiveness, ask forgiveness of those we have hurt, and we must grant forgiveness to ourselves. Paul says, 'Forgetting those things which are behind, and reaching forth unto those things which are before, I press toward the mark for the prize of the high calling of God in Christ Jesus.'"

"All these years, I have wondered if that baby was a boy or a girl," Mike said. "I pictured the child growing up alongside Brad and Chantel. Never once did it cross my mind that I might have killed it." The hurt, the regret, the shame, and the horror, spilled over and flowed down his cheeks.

"Jesus cried to God the Father while they nailed him to the cross, 'Father, forgive them; for they know not what they do,'" Dan said. "Jesus wasn't only crying out for those people who were physically nailing him to the cross. He cried out for me and for you, 'Father, forgive them; for they know not what they do.' My sins and your sins nailed Jesus to the cross, but still he cried out to the Father to forgive us. If God the Father can forgive you, then you must forgive yourself."

"Oh, God, please forgive me." Mike wept, his shoulders shaking under the heavy burden of guilt, shame, and remorse. "Please forgive me."

Dan waited for Mike to continue, but when he didn't, Dan softly started praying for him. "Lord, heavenly Father, please relieve Mike of this heavy burden of guilt that he is carrying. Look at his heart and see his remorse and repentance. Lift him up, Lord, and help him to walk again. Forgive him, please Jesus, and give him the grace to forgive himself. Please give Francis and the children the grace to forgive him as well. Amen."

"I felt sorry for him," Francis admitted to Maggie over a cup of tea in Maggie's kitchen. "He seemed genuinely sorry." Francis tried to make sense of the array of emotions that had gripped her since the meeting with Mike. "I'd never seen him cry before."

Maggie studied her friend anxiously. *Lord, keep Francis safe. She's lonely and vulnerable. Give her wisdom.* Francis looked up and met Maggie's thoughtful eyes.

"I feel like I'm on a giant merry-go-round. My emotions are all over the place. One minute, I hate Mike for all he did to me and the kids—all he put us through. The next minute, I get a glimmer of how wonderful it would be if he's truly changed, and we could be a family again." Francis sighed.

"My advice is to take this very slowly—and with much prayer—if you are considering a future with Mike. Be very sure the change in him is real. Ten years is a long time, and a lot of things have happened since then." Maggie was glad that the bitter edge she had heard in Francis' voice had softened a little, but she couldn't help but be anxious for her.

"Trust me, I'll be careful," Francis said with a rueful smile. "I'm not a teenager anymore." She grimaced at the thought of how willful she had been as a teenager. Maybe if she had listened to her parents and not jumped into marriage so soon, her life might have turned out different. *Even if we had just waited a couple of years before we got married.* "My heart feels lighter now that Mike knows the truth about that night. I feel like I'm not alone in this anymore. He can finally take responsibility for his actions. I don't know if I can ever totally forgive him." Francis finished her tea and deposited the cup on the cupboard. "I really should be going. I have to pick Chantel up from her piano lesson, then go home and make supper. I invited Gloria and Emily over."

"How is Gloria?" Maggie asked, putting her own teacup on the counter and following Francis to the door.

Francis sighed, her hand on the doorknob. "I worry about her. She's lost weight, and she doesn't look well."

"Poor girl has already lost her husband so suddenly and has that little girl to care for." Maggie's caring heart ached for the two of them.

Francis sighed, her own heart heavy for Gloria and Emily. How quickly they had become an important part of her life. "Yes. Gloria is meeting with the surgeon today."

"We must keep praying for both of them."

"Yes, we must," Francis said as she hugged Maggie. "You're so caring. I don't know what I'd do without you. I know Gloria can count on you to give her strong spiritual support, just like you've always given me."

Maggie's eyes were misty as she waved goodbye to Francis. *There's too much heartache in this world.*

Later that afternoon, Francis was putting lasagna in the oven when Gloria knocked on her door.

"I'll get it," Chantel said. Sprinting to the door, she flung it open. "Hi Emily, Mrs. Simpson, come on in. I have the Barbie's all set up," she told Emily, and the two girls disappeared into Chantel's bedroom.

"Those girls are going to pick up playing right where they left off," Gloria said with a chuckle, as she came into the kitchen, pulled out a chair, and sat down at the table. "Where's Brad?"

"Brad's at baseball practice," Francis said, setting the teapot and cups on the table. "You want to tell me about it?" she asked, pouring the tea before sitting down.

Gloria sighed heavily. "The surgeon confirmed what my doctor already told me," Gloria said, spooning honey into her tea and stirring it. "I need a mastectomy. Then there'll be chemotherapy treatments after that."

"I'm sorry." Francis covered Gloria's hand with her own. "You know I'll be happy to keep Emily here while you're in hospital and however long you need me to."

"You don't know how much I appreciate that." Gloria looked up to meet Francis' eyes. "Emily will stay with my parents while I'm in the hospital. They don't have the energy to keep up with an active eight year old anymore. Emily would love it if she could come here sometimes, just for the day." She smiled. "She absolutely loves spending time with Chantel."

"They really hit it off." Francis nodded her agreement. "I'm glad they're getting along so well. It's good for both of them since neither one has a sister. Emily can spend as much time here as she wants to."

"There's something else that I need advice on," Gloria said. Laying her teaspoon aside, she sipped her tea, looking over the cup at Francis. "I don't like talking about it because Emily is as much my daughter as if she were my flesh and blood." She set the cup on the table. "Richard and I weren't able to have children of our own. After years of yearning for a child and subjecting ourselves to medical examinations and testing, we adopted Emily." She hesitated, gauging Francis' response.

Francis surprised Gloria by clapping her hands together, a big smile on her face. "Now I know why you look so familiar!" she exclaimed. "You were the lady I met in the park one day. You had just heard from the doctor that you wouldn't have your own children."

Gloria was surprised. "That was you?"

"You remember?" Francis asked excitedly. "From the first time I saw you in church, you looked familiar but I couldn't place you."

"Yes, I remember." Gloria smiled ruefully. "Guess it is a small world! I was so upset that day. I didn't remember what you looked like—I only remembered how kind you were to listen to me." She sipped her tea. "After that appointment, we decided to get serious about adoption, and about a year later, we got Emily." Her eyes sparkled at the memory and her voice turned soft. "We were ecstatic. Little Emily was ours from the moment we saw her. We couldn't have loved her more if we had borne her ourselves. She was truly the apple of her daddy's eye." Her eyes grew misty. "Then suddenly Richard was gone, and we were alone—just the two of us." Francis reached over and squeezed Gloria's hand. "Now what frightens me most is what will happen to Emily if I can't beat this cancer?"

"You have to stay positive," Francis said.

"Yes, I know—and I am—but I still have to be realistic." Gloria set her cup down and looked at Francis with serious eyes. "I want to find Emily's birth mother."

Francis gasped. "Why would you do that? That could be very risky."

"I know," Gloria said, "and it scares me. But I need to know the birth mother's situation. Maybe she would take Emily if something happens to me."

Francis stared at Gloria as she processed this information. "What if she wants Emily back and you get well?"

"I've thought of that," Gloria said. "I would like to find her without her knowing and stay anonymous until I know her circumstances." She searched Francis' face. "Am I being unreasonable?"

"Maybe," Francis said, her mind going in a hundred different directions. "I think I understand why you're thinking about it, but you'd be playing with fire. You could get burned." She mulled it over in her mind. "Then again, it might work. I do agree that you should be very discreet if you do find the birth mother—at least until you know what kind of person she is."

The door opened and Brad came in. He dumped his glove in the corner of the entrance before he entered the kitchen.

"I'm starved," he said. "Hi, Mrs. Simpson," he added when he noticed her sitting at the table.

"Hi Brad," Gloria said.

"You're always starved," Francis said, laughing at him. "How was practice?"

"It was good," he said, opening the fridge. "Do we have anything to eat?"

"Not right now," Francis said. She went to the stove to check on the lasagna. "Supper will be ready in fifteen minutes." She got out the lettuce and other ingredients for a salad.

"Can I help?" Gloria asked, coming around the counter.

"Here," Francis said, handing Gloria the bread, "you can make garlic toast."

CHAPTER 12

Mary packed her book bag with paper and pen and headed down the dusty path to the cabin. Her heart was heavy. She didn't notice the birds twittering to each other in the trees or the squirrels scurrying around in the branches. She didn't even notice the warm summer sun bathing her in its loving rays. The mission board had received the requested photos verifying the two men were still alive—or at least had been when the photos were taken. The Board remained adamant that no ransom would be provided, fearing it would only increase the number of kidnappings. Mary understood their reasoning but desperately wanted them to provide whatever the kidnappers demanded so John would be released.

"Mama is right," she told herself, kicking at a small stick in her path. "I should have told John how I feel. I should have told him about the baby." Fear of rejection had ruled her decision, but the fact that John's life was in jeopardy gave her cause to rethink her motives. Was she afraid of rejection or was she afraid of the blemish an illegitimate child—given to adoption or not—would be on their family name? Was she so afraid of what people would say that she was willing to throw away her only chance of happiness? Was she being dishonest to John and to her friends by not revealing the truth?

"*Confess your faults one to another.*" The verse echoed in her mind.

"Lord, what have I done?" She lifted her eyes to the heavens. "What do you want me to do?"

The sun slid behind a cloud as Mary entered the cabin. Closing the door behind her, she leaned against it as she took it all in. Precious memories tugged at her heart of happy, carefree days when David and John had worked so hard all summer to build this cabin. They had laughed and joked while they worked, caring for nothing but the thought of having their own place to hang out. Mary had been right there alongside them, helping wherever she could, trying hard to prove her worthiness. Amid lifting logs and pounding nails, she had fallen in love with John. She ran her fingertips lightly over the smoothly sanded wood table where David had told her of his conversion. Tears filled her eyes—she missed him so much. She sank into a chair. Crossing her arms on the table in front of her, she put her head down in dejection and defeat.

Forcing herself to look into the depths of her heart—the way Jesus would—she was appalled at what she saw. She had told John he didn't really know her. That was true. Nobody truly knew her because she had kept the most important part of her life—her little girl—a secret. Why had she never told anyone—not even her best friends? Was it because she feared rejection? Yes, she admitted to herself, she feared rejection. She feared what people would think of her.

"Jesus, please forgive me," Mary cried, taking the first tentative step to redemption. "I am a hypocrite—covering my sin—because of pride. I have caused John to suffer by not telling him the truth. Please give me the chance to come clean with him."

What had he said to her before he left? "I don't have anything keeping me here." If she had told him her true feelings, maybe he would have stayed. Then he wouldn't be in the predicament he was in now.

She removed pen and paper from her book bag. She would write a letter to John as Mama suggested.

"Funny how Mama is so certain that John loves me." She had not told Mama of John's declaration of love. Her dear mama couldn't understand why she didn't confess her past to him—sure John would forgive her. Mary wasn't so certain but she owed him the opportunity to make that decision.

She put pen to paper. "Dear John."

"What do I say?" she asked herself. "How do I tell John that the girl he loved all these years isn't the girl he thought she was? How can I tell him the truth?" She wrote a few lines, reread them, and crumpled up the paper. She tried again. It didn't sound right so she crumpled it up again.

"Dear John,

As I write this letter, I don't know where you are. I don't know if I'll ever see you again, but I have to write, believing that God will answer my prayers, and that you will make it through this ordeal alive. I'm sorry that I didn't trust you enough to tell you that I love you…"

Mary lifted her pen from the paper. She wouldn't tell John about the baby. It wouldn't be proper to do that in a letter. She'd wait until she could tell him face-to-face. She lowered her pen once more and continued writing.

The wind whipped at Mary's skirt when she finally stepped out of the cabin; the completed letter stowed safely in her bag. Mary looked up at the angry sky. Ominous dark clouds rolled overhead. She picked up her pace.

"I should have paid attention to the changing weather," she told herself as she hurried along. Large raindrops stung her face and she shivered, wishing she'd brought a coat. Lightning flashed in a zigzag across the blackened sky. Mary felt the ground tremble beneath her as thunder crackled overhead. The clouds opened up and relinquished rain in a downpour that drenched her in seconds. Keeping her head down, she broke into a run. Ice pellets stung her arms as she reached for the door. Slamming the door behind her, she leaned on it for a moment, catching her breath.

"Mary!" her mama exclaimed, coming from the living room. "I was so worried about you. Look at you. You're soaked!" She grabbed a towel out of the closet and threw it to Mary.

"Thanks, Mama," Mary said, wrapping herself in the warm towel. "The storm caught me by surprise. Where's Benny?"

"He's in the living room with Papa," Anna said, looking out the window. Lightning lit up the western sky. Thunder crackled, rattling the windowpanes. "I was expecting a big storm after all that hot weather we've had."

"Look at that hail!" Benny called excitedly from where he was watching the storm in the next room. "Have you ever seen hail that size?"

Mary shivered, thankful she'd made it before the hail came.

Minutes later, Mary came out of her bedroom after changing into dry clothes. The phone rang, and she picked up the receiver.

"Hello," she said.

"Mary, is that you?" There was panic in the voice that came across the line.

"Yes." Mary's heart leapt into her throat. What had happened? "Annie, what's wrong?"

"Mary, can you come over?" Annie asked, her voice rising anxiously. "I need to go to the hospital, and I'm home alone with the kids. Isaac is working." Annie's husband was a truck driver.

"What happened?" Mary asked. Then realization dawned. "Is the baby coming?"

"Yes. Can you come please? I'm so scared." It sounded like she was crying.

Mary glanced out the window and cringed. "I'll leave right away," she said into the receiver. "Please calm down. I'll be there shortly."

"Please hurry."

"I will. See you soon." Mary hung up the receiver and grabbed her jacket, pulling it over her shoulders as she peeked into the living room. "I'm going to Annie's. She called. She's at home alone with the children, and she needs a ride to the hospital."

"Now?" her mama asked, alarmed. "In this weather?"

"Babies don't wait." Mary grabbed her car keys.

Her mama followed her to the door. "Be very careful, the roads are bound to be treacherous."

"I will," Mary promised. She opened the door and made a mad dash to the car across the hail-covered ground, rain pelting down on her. *At least it's not hailing anymore,* she thought as she put the key in the ignition. She turned the car around and headed down the driveway.

Turning onto the road, her heart sank at the size of the mud puddles she would have to navigate. The road was worse than she had anticipated. Turning the wipers on high, she leaned forward over the steering wheel. The gravel road, that minutes before had been dry and dusty, had turned slick and muddy. Mary's fingers clenched the steering wheel, fighting for control as strong winds pushed the skidding car dangerously near the ditch. Lightning zigzagged across the darkened sky, lighting up the road ahead like an eerie movie, as thunder crashed all around her. She swerved to avoid a fallen tree.

"Lord, please help me," she prayed. "Annie needs me."

A tree crashed down onto the road just ahead of her. Startled, she slammed on the brake, sliding to a stop within inches of the tree. Heart pounding in her chest, she reversed. Then inch by inch, she manoeuvred her car around the fallen tree. The wipers couldn't keep up as she squinted through her rain-blasted windshield.

"How far to Annie's house? Lord, don't let me miss it." She felt disoriented.

Driving at a snail's pace, she breathed a sigh of relief when she finally spotted Annie's driveway.

Parking the car as close to the house as possible, Mary pulled her jacket up over her head and made a dash for the door. She knocked as she opened the door—not waiting in the rain.

"Annie?" she called, closing the door behind her. Annie's two little children looked up at her from where they were playing on the floor. "Where is your Mama?" Mary asked, pasting a smile on her face. *I don't want to scare the children.*

"In here."

She followed Annie's voice and found her sitting on the edge of a double-sized bed in a small bedroom at the back of the house.

"I'm so glad you came. I didn't know what else to do. You live the closest," Annie explained. "The baby's coming early."

"When did your contractions begin?" Mary asked, trying to keep her voice calm. She sat on the bed next to Annie, her heart still racing from the nail-biting drive—not to mention how much the situation at hand scared her.

"My water broke right before I called you. I couldn't go to the hospital on my own and take the children." Annie motioned to some bags on the bed. "I packed for us. My parents will pick the children up at the hospital."

"Okay. You'll need jackets, it's pretty stormy out there."

Annie got the children ready, picked up the bags, and followed Mary to her car. With a child on each arm, Mary was extra careful not to slip in the pouring rain. She opened the car door and deposited the children. Annie climbed in after them.

Mary turned the car around and carefully headed back down the driveway. When she got to the road, her heart stopped. A giant spruce tree had fallen across the road—successfully blocking it off completely. For a moment, she panicked at the realization of what that meant for them.

"Can we get around it?" Annie asked, fear lacing her voice. The children started crying. Annie gathered them in her arms.

Mary took a deep breath. *Lord, help us.* "There's no way we can get around that tree. We can't make it to the hospital. We'll have to go back to the house." A flash of lightning followed by crackling thunder accented her words. She put the car in reverse and carefully backed it up along the muddy driveway.

Annie turned frightened eyes on Mary. "What will we do? I can't have the baby here!"

"Don't panic, Annie, you're scaring the children." Mary kept her voice as calm as possible, although her thoughts ran wild. *Lord, help us.* "I'll call my brother Benny. Maybe he can come get rid of the tree."

Annie took a deep breath as she looked down at her children. "You're right. I shouldn't panic." Her breath caught as her abdomen contracted. They waited until Annie was able to walk before going back into the house.

Mary picked up the receiver from the wall phone and pushed the button to open the party line. Nothing. *We're not going anywhere tonight.* She replaced the receiver and turned to Annie. "The line is dead."

Annie's eyes filled with fear as she grabbed onto the side of the cupboard and concentrated on her breathing. Mary went to her and rubbed the small of her back.

"Don't worry, Annie. You'll be fine. Women have babies all the time." Her voice belied the terror she felt inside. "Have the children had supper?"

"Yes, we had just finished eating when I called you." Annie looked at the clock on the wall. "They should be going to bed soon."

Annie explained to the children that Mary would spend the night. Little Fritz had some questions but was soon put at ease. Two-year-old Greta allowed Mary to help her into her pajamas. Trying to make everything as normal as possible, the two women worked together to get the children into their beds.

While Annie tucked the children in, Mary went to the kitchen. *Lord, help us,* she prayed. She poured water into a pot and put it on the stove to heat. Opening drawers and cupboards, she collected items she thought they would need. Arms laden with clean towels and sheets, Mary walked back into the bedroom to find Annie in the throes of another contraction. She set her supplies down and went to Annie's side.

"You'll be okay, Annie," she spoke soothingly, putting her arm around Annie's shoulders. "You can do this." Outside the wind howled and the thunder crackled. "Why don't you get into your nightgown and make yourself as comfortable as you can. I'll go check on your little ones."

Mary left the room and found both children fast asleep in their shared bedroom. She stood there a moment—collecting her thoughts and praying. *Lord give Annie and me strength and courage.*

Annie was in bed when Mary entered her bedroom. She pulled a chair up to the side of the bed and sat down to wait. The wind and rain beat down on the small house as the hours ticked by and Annie's pains increased. Mary tried hard to be encouraging and not let her rising anxiety show. She wiped the beads of perspiration from Annie's forehead with a cloth and rubbed the small of Annie's back. She changed the soggy pillowcase with a clean, fresh one, and plumped the pillow up to make her more comfortable—still the baby didn't come.

"I'm going to die," Annie said, clenching Mary's hand. Sheer terror emanated from her eyes. A chill ran down Mary's spine.

"You won't die, Annie. You can do this," Mary encouraged, praying her words were true.

"It's taking too long." Tears slid down Annie's cheeks. "I'm not ready to die."

"You believe in God don't you, Annie?" Mary asked, tenderly smoothing Annie's damp red hair back from her face. *Lord give me words,* she prayed silently.

"Yes, but I haven't lived right. I have so many sins," Annie said, her words came in short sentences drenched in pain.

"Jesus says, 'Let not your heart be troubled: ye believe in God, believe also in me.' Would it help if I read to you from the Bible?" Mary asked.

"Yes," Annie said, nodding her head.

Mary retrieved the small Bible she kept in her bag and opened it to the third chapter of John. "I'll read to you from Jesus' own words, starting at John 3:16. 'For God so loved the world, that he gave his only begotten Son, that whosoever believeth in him should not perish, but have everlasting life.'"

"Yes, I know that verse." Annie said. "But I haven't lived right. I thought I had lots of time."

Mary continued reading. "The next verses say, 'For God sent not his Son into the world to condemn the world; but that the world through him might be saved. He that believeth on him is not condemned: but he that believeth not is condemned already, because he hath not believed in the name of the only begotten

Son of God.'" Mary looked up to find Annie hanging onto every word she read. "Do you believe Jesus is the Son of God?"

"Yes, of course," Annie said. Even though church was not an important part of her life, she'd still been taught that Jesus was God's son. "But how do I know I'll go to heaven?" She groaned as the pains got stronger. Mary prayed silently until the pains subsided. She wiped Annie's face with a cool cloth.

"That's what people asked the apostle Peter." Mary turned some pages. "Here, I'll read it to you. It's in Acts chapter two. Peter was preaching to the Jews, explaining that the man Jesus—whom they had killed—was the Messiah whom they had been waiting for. I'll read starting at verse 37: 'Now when they heard this, they were pricked in their heart, and said unto Peter and to the rest of the apostles, Men and brethren, what shall we do?'" She met Annie's eyes. "Now listen to Peter's answer: 'Then Peter said unto them, Repent, and be baptized every one of you in the name of Jesus Christ for the remission of sins, and ye shall receive the gift of the Holy Ghost. For the promise is unto you, and to your children, and to all that are afar off, even as many as the Lord our God shall call.'" Mary looked up to see comprehension dawning in Annie's eyes.

"I got baptized before I got married," Annie said. Getting baptized was a prerequisite to getting married in their church. Mary was well aware that this custom sometimes resulted in couples getting baptized without accepting Jesus as their Saviour. Their focus was on getting married more than on Jesus Christ.

"Have you repented? Have you been truly sorry for your sins and asked Jesus to forgive you?" Mary's eyes met Annie's troubled ones.

Annie slowly shook her head. "I thought all I had to do was get baptized. I thought I'd be different then, but nothing happened. At first, after I got baptized, I tried to live right but it didn't last long."

Annie's breathing became heavy as she sank into a world of pain once again. Mary coached her and encouraged her until she was able to relax a little. Mary could tell Annie was exhausted as she wiped her face and gave her a drink of water. She continued explaining scripture to her partly because Annie needed Jesus and partly to keep her mind occupied.

"You can't live a righteous life on your own. The Bible says all our righteousness is as filthy rags to God. That's why God sent Jesus to die on the cross to pay for our sins." Mary sat down and looked at her open Bible. "It says here that when you repent and are baptized, then you will receive the Holy Ghost. The key is to repent. You have to be truly sorry for your sins and ask Jesus to forgive you. Then the Holy Spirit will come and live within you. It's the Holy Spirit living inside of you that will help you live for God." Mary took Annie's hand in hers, her eyes locking with Annie's. "Do you want to ask Jesus to forgive you now?"

Annie's breathing was coming hard and fast so Mary waited, rubbing her hand gently and praying silently, *Lord, please don't take her before she's accepted you as her own personal Saviour.*

Annie opened her eyes and said in a weakened voice, "Isn't it cowardly to ask God to forgive me when I'm dying?"

"Remember when Jesus was crucified there were two others crucified with him?" Mary asked. She was amazed at the words coming out of her mouth. The Spirit surely was using her.

Annie nodded.

"Those other two men were robbers and murderers. Yet when one of them said to Jesus, 'Lord, remember me when thou comest into thy kingdom,' Jesus said to him, 'Today shalt thou be with me in paradise.' Jesus will forgive if you repent."

Tears ran down Annie's cheeks as she responded to the prompting of the Holy Spirit and asked the Lord to forgive her sins. When she finished praying, Mary added, "Thank you, Lord, for the miracle of this new birth in Annie. Thank you for calling her, for drawing her to yourself, and for saving her. Please help Annie give birth to a healthy baby."

As the dawn broke in the eastern sky, a baby's cry broke through the stillness of the night. In awe of the miracle of new birth, Mary wrapped the newborn baby girl in a warm towel and handed her to her mother. Annie's exhausted eyes thanked Mary silently as she hugged the tiny bundle close. A few minutes later, Annie's eyelids closed in exhausted, restful sleep. Mary gently took the baby from her mother's arms.

The young lady walking towards him had a familiarity about her. Her long chestnut-brown hair hung down her back like a glorious mane. There was a skip in her step and a smile on her face like it was years ago when he first realized he loved her. Mary! She was coming to him at last! John's heart overflowed with joy. She broke into a run as she came closer. He reached out his arms to catch her. She stopped just short of his reach. Her face turned sad. A tear trickled down her cheek.

"Mary." John said. Desperately he reached for her, but she stayed just beyond his grasp. His heart thumped in panic. Mary took a step back. Her eyes averted to something in the distance. John followed her gaze. A little girl was playing amidst the flowers of the fields. Mary turned slowly and headed towards her.

"Mary, come back!" John called. Tears flowed down his cheeks. He moved to follow her, but his feet were stuck to the ground.

"John. John, wake up." John woke up to find Cornelio shaking him. "You were yelling in your sleep," Cornelio said. He tore a corner off of his shirt, poured a little water over it, and mopped John's face. "You are running a fever." Cornelio didn't mask the concern in his voice.

John couldn't help the tears that trickled from his eyes. It was just a dream, but it felt so real. *How can I let a little girl come between me and the woman I love?* His pain had been so excruciating when Mary turned away from him. It lingered on now that he was awake. *How can I love a woman who hasn't been true to me?* He was so confused.

"*Dankschoen,*" he said, thanking Cornelio for wiping his face. He met Cornelio's eyes. "What did I say?"

"Mary, come back." John turned his face to the wall, embarrassed that Cornelio had heard that.

"John, let me tell you a story," Cornelio said. He folded the piece of material he had torn from his shirt, poured a little more water on it, and laid it on John's forehead to cool his fever. "There was a man who went to fight in the army during the war. He was gone for years, and his wife had to scrape together a living for her and her two children. Then one day, two uniformed men came to her door and told the wife that her husband was missing in action. She was devastated. Times got worse as the war progressed, and the wife and her children were starving. One of the army officials stationed in her town had taken a liking to her and pressured the woman to be his mistress. He would take care of her, give her and the children food, and repair her house. She was totally against it—she would rather die than have anything to do with him—but she had two children who were starving. For a long time she refused. As the children got weaker she finally consented. After a couple of years, the war ended. The army official went back home, and she never heard from him again. About a year later, her husband came home. He had been taken captive and spent the last years of the war in the enemy's prison." Cornelio paused and let his eyes rest on John. "Do you think the husband should forgive his wife for what she did?"

John mulled the story over in his mind. "That's a hard question," he finally said. "Did he know what she had done?"

"Yes. She told him."

"I don't know," John said. "It would be a hard thing to forgive."

"I agree," Cornelio said. "Sometimes life gets hard, and there's a lot of grey between the black and white. When we are faced with grave decisions, we have to ask ourselves: 'What would Jesus have me do?' This woman had a difficult decision to make but—right or wrong—there were reasons why she did what she did. I'm sure it was extremely difficult for her husband, but he forgave her. They ended up growing old together."

"Is that a true story?" John asked, curious.

"Yes, it is," Cornelio answered. He had a sad look in his eyes. "They were my grandparents' neighbours." Cornelio bent forward to rest his elbows on his knees. "I told you this story so you know that sometimes people have to make hard decisions to find true happiness. We live in a fallen world where people will let us down, and we will let others down. That's just the way it is. How often did Jesus tell Peter to forgive his brother?"

"Seventy times seven." John knew why Cornelio told him the story. *He thinks I should forgive Mary.*

"If Jesus forgives, then who are we to withhold forgiveness?" Cornelio asked. He turned serious eyes on John. "Son, I want to give you a little advice. Be forgiving and don't hold grudges. Grudges will eat you up from the inside out and make you bitter. Best to forgive and make the best of what you have. Life is short."

"Hi Gloria, how are you doing?" Francis asked as she entered the dimly lit hospital room. She deposited a bouquet of flowers on Gloria's nightstand and bent over to give her friend a hug.

"Hi. Thanks for the flowers," Gloria said, her black hair spread out over the stark white pillowcase.

"You're welcome," Francis said, straightening up. "How are you doing?"

Gloria sighed, her hand nervously picking at the sheet. "The cancer has spread to my lymph nodes. I start chemotherapy next week."

"I'm sorry." Francis tried hard to hide the emotions that swept over her. *As if a mastectomy isn't trauma enough!* She didn't know much about cancer, but it didn't sound good if it had spread.

"How's Emily?" Gloria asked.

"She's fine. The girls are busy making cookies at Maggie's." Francis pulled up a chair close to Gloria's bed and sat down.

"That sounds nice," Gloria said, a smile hovering over her lips. "I hope that won't be too much for Maggie."

"I think Maggie was looking forward to it as much as the girls were," Francis said with a smile. Then she grew serious. "Have you decided what you're going to tell Emily?"

"No." Gloria sighed heavily as she leaned back on her pillow. "I'll have to tell her something; I'm just not sure what. I don't want to scare her."

"I think you should be truthful with her," Francis said. "I know you don't want to scare her, but she knows you're sick.

You keep having to go back to the hospital for treatments, for surgery, and now more treatments. Kids are a lot smarter then we give them credit for. You need to tell her, or she'll lose trust in you." Francis didn't want to tell her that Emily had already confided to Chantel that she was afraid her mommy was going to die.

A tear slipped from the corner of Gloria's eye. "That's what my mom says. I was hoping the mastectomy would get rid of all the cancer, and she wouldn't need to know. At least not until she's older."

Francis reached for Gloria's hand. "I'm here for you and for Emily."

"I know and I'm grateful," Gloria said. She squeezed Francis' hand. "You've been so good to me. I couldn't have asked for a better friend when I moved here—and I'm thankful Emily has Chantel."

CHAPTER 13

John moaned as he moved his leg. Beads of perspiration broke out on his forehead. Cornelio bent over him, examining the infected gash in John's thigh.

"You need a doctor," Cornelio said, his voice edged with concern. "This gash in your leg looks infected, and you have a fever." Cornelio reached for the jug of water the guard had left and lifted it to John's lips. "Here. Drink a little." John lifted his head and took a sip, then let his head drop back to the hard floor.

Cornelio prayed, his hands on John's wound. "Lord God, we know and believe that you can heal John right here and now if you so choose. You say that we have not because we ask not, so Lord we ask that you heal this wound. You are the great physician. Deliver us from this situation we are in—if it is your will. Lord, we long to return to our loved ones. If that is not your plan for us then I pray that you will keep us strong in the faith until the end. May your will be done and your name be honoured and glorified…"

The door crashed open, and two masked gunmen burst into the hut, waving their rifles and yelling.

"*Vamanoos! Vamanoos!*" Cornelio scrambled to his feet, pulling John up with him. The men yelled at them to get out of the hut. Cornelio wrapped John's left arm around his shoulder as he encircled John's waist with his right arm, helping him along. They were herded out of the hut and down a path into the blackness of the jungle.

Monkeys screamed at them from the trees overhead as Cornelio half carried John over the uneven jungle terrain—the barrel of a gun stuck in the small of his back. John tried hard to keep up with the pace—desperately fighting against pain and dizziness. Nausea mounted up in his chest. He clutched Cornelio's shoulder for support as he concentrated on putting one foot in front of the other.

"*Vamanoos!*" yelled the masked man close behind them, nudging the gun barrel sharply into Cornelio's back.

"I'll shoot the sick one. He's slowing us down." The man in the lead turned and pointed his machine gun at John's head. Cornelio and John froze in their tracks.

"No!" the man behind them shouted. "Hernandez wants them both alive."

"We'll tell him he was already dead."

"Hernandez will decide what's to happen with him," the man behind them snarled. "I tell you—keep going." The man in front of them grunted something unintelligible but lowered his gun and kept going.

"Thank you, Jesus," Cornelio whispered softly so only John could hear. Then he prayed silently. *Lord, help us. They won't let John live once we get to where they're taking us—if they let him live that long. Either they'll let him die from his injuries or they'll kill him. They have no use—and no mercy—for sickness.*

Mary was restless. She hadn't slept well last night, and she hadn't been able to keep her mind on her work all day. She checked the clock on the wall, slipped the file she was working on into the filing cabinet, and bent down to get her purse from the bottom drawer.

"Goodnight," she called out to whoever was still left in the office as she walked through the reception area to the front door.

"Goodnight," her boss called from his office. Mary turned off the light in the main area and walked out the door, locking it behind her. She got in her car, rolled down her window partway, and started the engine. She decided not to check the mail but to go straight home. She didn't feel like running into anyone that would want to stop and chat.

After the supper dishes were done, Mary put her Bible and journal into her book bag and headed down the path to the cabin. She needed some time alone with God. *Lord, I am anxious today, and I need to come into your presence and find peace. It's been days since John went missing without any word on how he's doing.* She walked along the dusty path leading to the cabin. She was too engrossed in her thoughts to appreciate the smell of the canola fields waving in the breeze to her right and the tall poplar and spruce trees to her left. *What if I never see John again, Lord? I never told him the truth. Never told him I loved him. I've been deceiving him. You want me to ask for forgiveness. You want me to be truthful.*

Mary sighed heavily as she opened the cabin door. She dropped her book bag on the wooden table. Her heart aching, she knelt on the floor beside what was once David's bed. "Please, Lord, keep John safe. I cannot bear to think I might never see him again. Oh, how foolish I have been! Forgive me, Lord, I have been selfish. Please give me another chance."

"*Commit thy way unto the Lord; trust also in him; and he shall bring it to pass.*" The verse flowed through her heart like a caress.

"Lord, give me the peace that passeth all understanding. Increase my faith." Mary rose from her knees and sat down at the table, opening her Bible.

The door burst open and Benny rushed in. "Mary, come quick. John has been rescued!"

Startled, Mary jumped up, tipping the chair in the process. "Are you sure? When? How do you know?"

"Mr. Wieler called. Mama said to come get you."

"What happened? How were they rescued?" Mary's questions tumbled over each other as she stuffed her Bible into her book bag and followed Benny out of the cabin.

"I don't know the details." Benny said excitedly as they ran back to the house.

Unspeakable joy flooded Mary's heart. *Thank you, Jesus!* Her heart cried.

Anna looked up from her knitting when Mary and Benny entered the living room.

"Is it true?" Mary asked, her voice just above a whisper.

Anna lowered her knitting to her lap and looked at her daughter. *Mary tries so hard to hide her feelings, but this thing with John is extremely difficult for her.* How long had she been praying for Mary to be honest with John?

"The Mission Board called Mr. Wieler," she said. Mary's heart beat frantically in her chest. "John and Cornelio have been rescued," Anna confirmed. "John is in hospital. He's been injured and they think the infection may have entered his blood stream. He's very sick."

"He's alive and safe!" Mary exclaimed. Her heart was overwhelmed. *John has been rescued!* God had answered her prayers.

"Mary, he's very sick," Anna repeated, trying to make her daughter understand the severity of the situation. "The doctor's don't hold out much hope that he'll survive."

Mary gasped as her heart jumped into her throat. "Why? What happened?" Her voice sounded strangled. She massaged her throat and tried to swallow her tears. Her knees buckled, and she sank into the chair next to her papa.

"He has a gash in his thigh that got infected. The infection has entered his blood stream, and he is in critical condition in hospital."

"No! Mama, he'll get better." Mary frantically denied the possibility of never seeing John again. "He's been rescued. Why would God allow him to be rescued just to let him die?" *What about David?* Her thoughts reminded her. *He dedicated his life to the Lord and God took him away.* Mary shook her head. *No, God, please no!*

Jacob slowly reached his hand out and patted Mary's arm. Tears glistened in his eyes. John was special to all of them. As David's friend, he had practically grown up in their house.

"I'm sorry, Mary." Anna reached out and took Mary's hand, her own eyes swimming in tears. She felt Mary's pain. "We'll pray that John will get well. God can—and does—work miracles. But you need to know that it could go the other way."

Cornelio prayed as he sat beside John's hospital bed. *Lord, please heal him. He's just a kid who's on fire for you. He has his life ahead of him.* Cornelio thought of the girl who was waiting for John in Canada. *It sounds like she's been through a lot and too ashamed to confess to the man she loves. Lord, if John survives, please put it in his heart to forgive her. You know John's heart, and you know Mary's heart.*

His mind went back to the events of the night they were rescued. He hadn't realized how sick John was until he had to half carry him through the jungle. After about a half hour trek, they had come upon a truck with a covered box, parked at the side of the road. Both men were handcuffed and forced into the back while the two gunmen got in the front.

Cornelio suspected the police had been tipped off because they had been caught in a check stop before they made it to the next town. Heavily armed federal police had swarmed their vehicle. He had heard shouting and doors being ripped open as their captors were yanked from the truck. The officers had not seemed surprised to find Cornelio and John stowed away in the back.

John and Cornelio had both been put in an ambulance and taken to hospital. Cornelio was assessed, had his wounds treated, and was released. The police had taken Cornelio back to the station to be interviewed before he was free to go. He had gone right back to the hospital.

John had been diagnosed with septicemia and was in critical condition in the Intensive Care Unit. He was fighting for his life as the infection raged through his body. John's parents had been notified. They were on their way. Cornelio had vowed to stay by John's bedside until they got there.

A doctor and nurse came in to examine John, so Cornelio got up from his chair and went over to the window. He looked out on the crowded streets of Chihuahua City. Cornelio had insisted that he be allowed to remain with John. They had gone through this ordeal together—he couldn't abandon him now. *I talked him into coming with me on that trip into the mountains, so it's my responsibility to be here for him.* He was glad his wife understood. *Thank you, Lord, for rescuing us and thank you for the informant—if there was one.*

"How is he, doctor?" Cornelio asked in Spanish when the doctor straightened up and took the chart from the nurse.

The doctor shook his head. "It doesn't look good. So far he isn't responding to the antibiotics we're giving him. Maybe it is too soon. We'll have to wait and see."

Mary was slow getting undressed. She had spent the evening at a hastily called prayer meeting at the church. She had been careful not to give people cause to wonder at the depth of her feelings and now she was exhausted. She pulled a soft, pink, cotton nightgown over her head and knelt by her bed. *Heavenly Father, please hear our prayers and heal John.* She didn't know what else to say. All evening, groups of people had gathered in the church to pray. Everything had been said, but she remained on her knees—silent before God. Her mind wandered back over memories stored in her heart. Tears flowed down her cheeks. She was helpless to do anything for John except to lay her heart's petition before the Almighty God of creation.

"*Likewise the Spirit also helpeth our infirmities: for we know not what we should pray for as we ought: but the Spirit itself maketh intercession for us with groanings which cannot be uttered.*" The verse ran through her mind as the tears flowed. *Thank you, Lord, that the Spirit makes intercession for me when I don't have the words.*

Her heart had leapt for joy that John and his friend were rescued—God had answered prayer—only to find out he was critically ill. *Jesus, would you take John after letting him be found? That would be unbearable.* Her thoughts went back to her brother—he had been on fire for the Lord—yet God had taken him away. *Why? I prayed that David would survive—but he didn't. Now I'm praying that John will be healed—but your answer to prayer isn't always yes—and I'm scared. I'm afraid you'll take him. Lord, help my unbelief!*

Trust me, the voice whispered to her heart.

"Brad, Chantel, are you ready to go?" Francis called to her children as she glanced at her watch. She pulled her hair back into a ponytail at the nape of her neck. "We don't want to be late." They were going to help Patrick and Janelle at the soup kitchen.

"Shotgun!" Chantel called, coming out of her bedroom. She was wearing a pair of knee-length navy shorts and a pink T-shirt. Her hair was done up in two ponytails—one on either side of her head.

"Only if you get there first." Brad burst out of his bedroom, and the kids raced out the door.

"Kids!" Francis exclaimed, grabbing her purse and following them. They joined Patrick and Janelle at the soup kitchen downtown once a month to help out. She wanted to teach her children to care for others. Brad was starting to have some interaction with the clients, but she didn't allow Chantel to come out of the kitchen. There was lots of time for that in the future.

They arrived in plenty of time to set up tables and bring the food out. When the doors opened, Brad and Chantel went to help in the kitchen. Francis positioned herself behind a pot of stew, ready to ladle it onto the plates of their hungry clients. People came in at a steady pace once the doors opened. Francis smiled at each one she served, ladled stew onto their plate, and added a bun. Some thanked her, others didn't.

Francis lifted her eyes to smile at the next bedraggled person in line but stopped short—ladle poised in mid-air. The dark eyes looking back at her could only belong to one person. She leaned closer. "Jason?"

Startled, the man squinted at her. "How do you know who I am?"

"I'm Francis. You worked with my husband, Mike, at the service station. I met you at your wife's birthday party."

Jason shuffled his feet, obviously embarrassed to be recognized. "Oh, yeah. How's Mike?"

It was Francis' turn to be embarrassed. She ladled the food onto Jason's plate as she answered in a tight voice. "He left me." Memories flooded over her. *I should have kept my mouth shut. Of course, he knows Mike left me. He probably took Jason's wife with him.*

Jason mumbled something and moved down the line. Francis had a hard time being cheerful to the rest of the patrons. She was surprised to find Jason still occupying a place at the far end of the tables when they were finished serving.

"Pray for me," she said to Patrick, nodding her head in the direction of the lone man sitting at the far end of the room. "I need to talk to him."

Patrick nodded as she poured two cups of coffee and walked over to where Jason sat.

"What brought you here?" Francis placed one cup in front of him and sat down across the table with the other. Most of the patrons had already gone. Just a few stragglers were left behind.

"Thanks." Jason brought the cup of coffee to his lips. His bedraggled beard and long hair showed hints of grey. It looked like it hadn't been combed in days—maybe weeks. Francis was reminded of a children's story she had read about birds making their nest in a beard. Deep lines etched his forehead. His black eyes looked vacant.

"I haven't seen a friendly face in a long time." Jason sighed heavily, setting his cup on the table.

He's a far cry from the man who came on to me that night at Cheryl's party, Francis thought as she waited for him to continue. *Lord, give me the right words. If this is where he has ended up, he needs help. He needs you.*

"So Mike left you, huh? That's stupid," Jason said. "When?"

"It's been ten years."

"Is that when he left the service station?"

"I don't know. I never checked if he was still there." Francis bit her lip. "How's Cheryl?"

Jason's laugh was bitter. "No idea."

Francis took a deep breath. She hated to ask, but she had to know. "Did she leave with Mike?" She held her breath waiting for the answer.

Jason gave a curt laugh. "No. Mike was a toy. Just one more of a string of men she left behind." He brought the cup up to his lips and took a drink.

Francis heard the bitterness in his voice. "What happened?"

"She ran off with a guy who could give her the lifestyle she craved."

"Are you still at the service station?"

"Nah," Jason said. "Got fired for not being reliable. We lived off of Cheryl's father for a while. When she left, my livelihood disappeared. Life has been going downhill since." His voice sounded so dejected that Francis felt genuinely bad for him.

"I know a place that takes people in when they're down on their luck. They help them find work and a place to live." Francis removed a pen and paper from her pocket and scribbled an address and phone number on it, then pushed it across the table to Jason. "Give them a call. Maybe they can help you."

Jason stared at the paper for a second before stuffing it into his pocket. He got up.

"Thanks," he said before turning his back and walking away. Francis watched him as he crossed the room and disappeared through the front door.

Mike didn't take Cheryl with him when he left, she thought to herself. *I always assumed he ran off with her. Oh Mike, you ruined our marriage for nothing. All your cheating landed you exactly nowhere!*

John walked down the cobblestone path between gorgeous flower arrangements of every kind. He had never seen such serene beauty before. Hues of red, purple, orange, yellow, and pink dispersed amongst a variety of green shrubs and trees, surrounded him. A gently flowing river wound its way through the garden. The crystal clear water rippled over rocks of gold, diamonds, sapphires, and rubies. Here and there, pristine waterfalls cascaded over the edges of precipices. The path grew more beautiful the farther he went. He inhaled deeply, allowing the fragrance to become one with him. A deep peace flooded through him. His feet moved effortlessly, as if he was walking on air—nothing weighed him down.

Someone was sitting on a white park bench up ahead. John squinted his eyes but couldn't tell who it was. As he got closer, recognition dawned on him like the soft rays of a rising sun. *David!* John started running—unable to contain his excitement at seeing his friend.

"David!" John exclaimed as David caught him in his arms. "I have missed you so much!"

David laughed. "You have always been my best friend, John."

They hooked their arms together as they continued down the path. David pointed out the delicate intricacies woven into the peaceful splendour surrounding them. John reached out and touched an exquisite blossom here—a unique gem there.

John felt a small tug backward, and he grasped David's arm. "I want to stay here with you."

"Someday, John, you will be here with me, but it's not your time yet. God still has work for you to do." David turned to face John, his face the definition of peace. "Mary needs you. She was devastated when I left. Satan took that opportunity to control her life for a season, but Jesus never left her. He extended his forgiveness to her and in due time she accepted his gift." The love that shone through David's eyes enveloped John. "She needs you John."

Unfathomable sadness welled up in John's heart as he realized he must tell David the truth about his sister. He had a right to know. "David, Mary has a daughter."

"I know," David said with great tenderness. "She's a beautiful little girl who loves Jesus with all her heart."

"Mary gave her up for adoption," John continued, trying to convey the seriousness of her offence. "I don't understand how she could do that."

"Judge not, that ye be not judged," David said gently. "Do you know the dark valleys she goes through? Do you know the pain she carries in her heart every day? Do you know that angels directed you to find her in the park at your campus? John," David said earnestly, laying his hand on John's shoulder, "Mary is the girl God has for you—marry her."

"How can I marry her—knowing she's been with someone else? How can I trust her to bear my children when she gave her daughter away?" His voice grew urgent as he felt another tug—like someone pulling him away from this glorious place.

"Jesus looks on the heart." David reminded him. His hazel eyes sparkled with love and compassion. "Remember the grace Jesus extended towards you when he forgave you and washed you clean of all unrighteousness. While he hung on the cross, Jesus cried out, 'Father, forgive them; for they know not what they do.' That included me. That included you. That included Mary. Just like he extends his unending grace and mercy to us, 'in that, while we were yet sinners, Christ died for us.' Jesus will give you the grace to forgive as well. You only need to ask him. 'Freely ye have received, freely give.'"

Melodious strains of music wafted through the air as David turned away.

"David, please don't leave me!" Desperation welled up in John's heart and spilled across his lips as he felt himself being drawn away from his friend. "Please take me with you!"

David turned back to face John. His eyes shone with love. "Your work is not finished. Jesus bought you with a price—it cost him his life—now go and extend that same grace to Mary."

"John! John!" John faintly heard someone calling his name—drawing him back to earth. Desperation turned to sorrow as he watched David disappear through the golden arch into the brilliant light beyond. More than anything he longed to follow David through that arch, but he was unable to move his feet.

"John!" The call was more distinct as the vision faded from sight. John struggled to open his eyes.

"Lie still, John," an unfamiliar voice told him. "You're safe in the hospital, and your parents are right here beside you. You can't talk because of a tube going down your throat."

John's eyes focused on the white coat of the man standing over him. His eyes wandered beyond him to the hazy images of his parents. His mama came close to the bed and took his hand.

"Oh, John, you're finally waking up! Can you hear me?" she asked. Bending over, she kissed his forehead as a tear trickled down her cheek.

"You'll be fine," John's papa said, looking over his wife's shoulder. "You have a bad infection in your leg, and you've been very sick, but you're getting better now."

John closed his eyes. He was so tired. All he wanted to do was to go back and join David. As he drifted off into a restful sleep, he tried to hold onto the incredible peace that had enfolded him in that place.

"Hello, Francis." Mike's voice came across the line. "Please don't hang up. I need to talk to you. Can we meet in that park again?" His voice was gentler than she had ever heard it before. Her heart skipped a beat.

"What do you want to talk about?" She still wasn't sure what to make of him. She was glad she had run into Jason. At least now she knew Mike and Cheryl hadn't run away together.

"Us. The kids. Life. Anything and everything." A deep longing ran through the undertones of his voice.

Lord, show me what to do. Francis prayed silently.

"*I am with you always.*" The scripture spoke to her heart. She smiled. The Lord was speaking to her again!

"I promise I will not hurt you or the kids. Please believe me."

"I wish I could." Francis sighed into the receiver she held in her hand. "It's not that easy."

"I know. I want to say 'trust me' but I know you have no reason to trust me."

Francis sighed. *Lord, why did you bring Mike back into my life? Everything was going well. I have a good job, the kids are happy—why now?*

"My thoughts are not your thoughts, neither are your ways my ways."

"Okay," she said into the receiver. "I'll meet you at the park." They arranged a time for the next day and hung up.

The following day, Francis parked her car next to the park and bowed her head over her steering wheel. *Lord, be my guide. I have no idea where to go from here.* She got out of the car, locked the door, and dropped the keys into her purse. Mike was already sitting on a park bench—away from the playground equipment—waiting for her. He stood up as she approached.

"Hi Francis. I'm glad you came." A tender smile lit his ruggedly handsome face. "This park looks like it has some nice trails, so I thought we could take a walk, if that's okay with you."

"Yes, of course," Francis said. *I would much rather be walking than sitting on a bench trying to make conversation.* They started off down a paved path that took them through the trees.

"How have you been, Francis? How are Brad and Chantel?" Mike asked. There was so much he needed to catch up on.

"We're doing alright," Francis said. *What do I say? How much should I tell him?* "Brad and Chantel are both doing well in school. Brad likes to play sports. Chantel likes to play with Barbie dolls. They both love A&W."

Mike laughed, releasing some of the tension between them. "Do you have pictures?"

Francis stopped walking as she fumbled in her purse for her wallet. She showed him the small school pictures she carried with her. *Are those tears? His eyes are tearing up!* Francis thought. She studied Mike's face as they stood in the middle of the path while Mike feasted his eyes on the children's photos.

"They're beautiful!" His heart was overwhelmed. A tender look shone in the sky-blue eyes that met hers. "Just like their mother."

Francis blushed and Mike grinned. "I've missed them terribly. I've missed all of you something terrible." He handed the pictures back, and she dropped them into her purse. They started walking again.

"I did you wrong." Mike's voice was low and serious. "I pray that someday you'll find it in your heart to forgive me. I'm willing to do whatever it takes to win your trust back." He told her his story, starting from the night he left. He told her of the nights spent in his car, his life spiralling downward into hopelessness. He told of the jobs he got only to be fired when he showed up drunk, or with a hangover, or failed to show up at all. Then he told her about Dan and Alcoholics Anonymous and his way back to sobriety and Jesus. Mike talked about the later years when he took counselling to work through his issues while working his way up in Dan's construction company.

"I am very open to marriage counselling if you would agree to go."

Francis mulled that over in her mind. "I'll have to pray about it. You've given me much to think about."

Mike put his hands on her shoulders and turned her to face him. He waited until she raised her eyes to meet his. "We can take this as slow as you want." His voice was gentle and serious. "I want you and the kids back in my life—but you call the shots."

"I don't know what to say."

"Let's start with—can I see you again? Here or somewhere else it doesn't matter. I'd like to see the kids too."

"I don't want the kids to be hurt. They don't remember you."

Mike felt the familiar pain pierce his heart. "I know. I promise I won't hurt them. I understand that it's just my word, and you have no way of knowing that you can count on that. Can I call you?"

Francis hesitated for a moment. "Yes, you can call me. Maybe I'll have it figured out by then."

He walked her to her car. She unlocked the door and got in. Mike pushed the door closed behind her. Lifting his hand in a wave he turned and walked to his Mustang. He watched her drive away before getting into his car.

"What are you going to do?" Maggie asked Francis. They were sitting on Maggie's backyard patio watching Brad and Chantel help Dale weed his small garden.

Francis sighed. "I don't know." She felt like she couldn't make decisions anymore. "The children don't remember their dad, and it scares me to bring him back into their lives."

"Why is that?" Maggie asked, rubbing her arthritic leg. Francis squinted her eyes at Maggie. "What is it that scares you, exactly?"

Francis leaned back in the thickly padded patio chair and inhaled deeply of the scents Maggie's roses sent her way. *What doesn't scare me?* She let her breath out slowly.

"The children were young when Mike left. They've adjusted. What if he comes back only to find out he can't do it and leaves again? At the ages they are now, they would be devastated. What if he wants visitation and goes into a rage when the kids are alone with him? There are so many 'what ifs'."

Maggie remained silent, mulling Francis' questions over in her mind.

"What if he really has changed, and I don't give him a second chance?" Francis continued, bringing her hands up to either side of her head in frustration. "I'm so confused. I keep going back and forth. My brain is spinning."

"What does the Lord want you to do?" Maggie asked thoughtfully.

"That answer remains the same," Francis replied. "The Lord's Prayer keeps running through my mind. 'Forgive us our debts, as we forgive our debtors'."

"Sounds to me like the Lord is giving you the answer."

"What does forgiveness look like?" Francis asked philosophically. "Does it mean I have to take Mike back? That he can come back after all these years like nothing ever happened? Does it mean I have to trust him after what he's done?" She searched Maggie's eyes. "I don't know what to do."

"You're afraid of upsetting the proverbial apple cart," Maggie said. She picked up the pitcher of iced tea and refilled their glasses.

Francis thanked her. "I suppose that's true."

"What does God do when we come to him in repentance?" Maggie asked, and then she answered her own question. "The Bible says, 'As far as the east is from the west, so far hath he removed our transgressions from us.' If Mike is truly a changed man and is living for Christ, then maybe the Lord is giving you both a second chance. If you do decide to take him back, you would first need to forgive Mike and not let the past become a dark cloud hanging over your marriage."

"I don't know if I can do that," Francis said truthfully. "For years I thought I had forgiven him. Now that he is back I am having difficulty with it."

Maggie's heart ached for her friend. She had a strong feeling that God was at work in this situation. "The apostle Peter says in Acts: 'Repent ye therefore, and be converted, that your sins may be blotted out...' I realize we are not like God, and that we cannot blot things from our memory, but with time and effort—and putting our trust in the Lord—our memory of past wrongs does fade. If Mike has truly repented and been converted to live his life for the Lord, then God has blotted out his sins."

"Your point being if God blots out his sins and I don't, then I'm the one doing wrong," Francis said with a wry grin.

Maggie chuckled and then grew serious as she continued. "I understand that extending total forgiveness to a person who has hurt you badly is incredibly difficult—but forgiveness is not a choice. We must forgive as God forgives." Laughter from the garden caught her attention and a tender smile curved her lips. *Dale enjoys having the children around.* She got up from her chair. "I want to show you something," she said to Francis, then disappeared into the house.

Francis watched the children with Dale. *They gravitate towards Dale. They need that father figure in their lives. Can I deny them of that?*

Maggie returned with her Bible and sat down, her fingers deftly leafing through the worn pages. "Further to the part of the Lord's Prayer that you say keeps crossing your mind," she said, handing the Bible to Francis, her finger on Matthew 6:14, "read verses 14 and 15."

"For if ye forgive men their trespasses, your heavenly Father will also forgive you: but if ye forgive not men their trespasses, neither will your Father forgive your trespasses." Francis looked up from reading, her eyes moist. "That sounds like God will not forgive me if I don't extend forgiveness."

"That's the way I understand it," Maggie said. "You can forgive Mike and not take him back—that's your decision—but according to these verses, you must forgive." She took her Bible back from Francis. "I don't mind telling you that I have my own struggle to forgive Mike for what he did to you. I can't get that vision of how I found you out of my head. Not to mention your years of struggling to bring up the children without a husband and father. I wish we could blot those things out of our minds, but they will always be there. We just have to rise above it and go on, trusting the Lord to make things right."

Francis watched as the three gardeners came toward the house. She laid her hand over Maggie's hand. "Thank you for pointing me in the right direction. I'm so blessed to have such a good spiritual friend."

Maggie turned her hand over and clasped Francis' hand in hers. "I enjoy our conversations. You are as much of a blessing to me as I am to you."

CHAPTER 14

Sunday morning, Mary helped Benny get their papa into the car for the ride to church. Anna got in the back with Jacob. Benny put the wheelchair in the trunk before folding himself into the front passenger seat.

"Ouch!" Benny bumped his head getting in. "This car is too small," he said, rubbing his head. "We should get a pickup truck."

Mary laughed as she turned the key in the ignition. "I thought you'd have gotten used to it by now. You do it every time you get in!" She put the car in gear and headed down the driveway. "You know Papa can't get into a pickup."

"I know," Benny said, "but it would be nice to have a vehicle that was a bit bigger."

"You can get a pickup truck when you buy your own vehicle," their mama said from the back seat.

"I've been saving up money," Benny said, turning his head so his mama could hear him better. "I think by the end of the year I might be able to get something cheap."

"*Jo,*" their papa nodded, obviously agreeing that his son should get an inexpensive vehicle.

"I can hardly believe you're old enough to get your own vehicle." Mary cast a quick glance at Benny. "Good for you that you've saved up that much money already." Both Mary and

183

Benny contributed to household expenses so it wasn't easy to put money aside. "You're a hard worker with good money sense."

"*Oba jo*," their mama agreed, pride for her children lacing her voice. "You both are."

Mary turned the car off of the country road onto the churchyard. She was glad to see Annie and Isaac getting out of their car, as they didn't attend regularly. She helped Benny get their papa out of the car and into the wheelchair. Benny drove the wheelchair up the ramp and into the church, parking it beside a wooden pew halfway down the aisle. Benny sat down in the pew beside his father. Men and women sat on opposite sides of the church so it was up to Benny to look after him. Mary was proud that he was willing to take care of their papa and sit with him, while his friends all sat together in the back pews. *Benny is a good kid. David would be so proud of his little brother.*

Mary searched Annie out and went to sit with her. "Good morning," she whispered.

Annie smiled and returned the greeting while little Greta smiled shyly from the other side of her mother. "How are you doing and how's little Maria?" Annie had named the baby after Mary.

"We're both doing very well," Annie whispered back. They were taught from childhood to be silent in church. Any conversations were whispered. "Do you want to hold her?"

"Of course," Mary said, reaching over to take the tiny bundle. Little Greta quickly climbed onto her mama's lap. Mary settled the tiny pink bundle in the crook of her arm, cuddling her against her chest. The little rose-coloured lips puckered at being disturbed—then relaxed in sleep again. *What would have happened if I had kept my baby? Could I have managed?* The never-ending rhetorical questions! She loved the feel of the little one in her arms even though her heart was saddened by the thought of that other baby and all she had lost. *Oh, the heavy consequences of sin!*

The song leaders filed in and took their place at the front of the church. Annie reached for her *Gesangbuch*, their German songbook, sharing it with Mary. Together they sang the familiar songs. After the song leader announced the second song, the preachers filed in. Halfway down the aisle, they stopped and the bishop gave the blessing. Then they took their place at the front of the church, opposite the song leaders. The song leader announced the song a second time, and then led the congregation in singing. No musical instruments were allowed in church.

Annie closed the *Gesangbuch,* and both women settled down to listen to the sermon. Although there were those—like Lena, Henry, and John—who had taken up membership in a more liberal denomination; Mary had remained with the more traditional church she had grown up in. She understood why some of her friends had made the switch, but it was more convenient for her to stay.

Who else would take Mama and Papa to church? She believed God's church consisted of all born-again believers regardless of which church they attended. Not everyone in her congregation agreed with that concept. Mary knew there were good Christian people in her church just as there were in other churches. *Salvation comes from and through the Lord Jesus Christ—not from any particular church—it's a personal experience between me and Jesus,* Mary thought as the baby squirmed in her arms. She shifted her arms slightly, and little Maria settled down.

Mary was clearing the table after lunch when the phone rang. Benny answered it on the second ring.

"Hello." A pause. "I'll get her for you." Benny held the receiver out to Mary. "It's for you."

Mary wiped her hands on a dishrag before taking the receiver from her brother. "Hello."

"Hi Mary, have you heard?" Lena sounded a little breathless.

"Heard what?" Lena had a tendency to get overly excited about just about anything.

"John came out of his coma! They announced it in church."

Mary's knees buckled, and she sank down into a kitchen chair. "Are you sure? When?"

"Last night. Mr. Wieler got the phone call from Mexico this morning." Lena rushed on. "He only woke up for a minute, but it's a good sign. Mary, can you believe it? Our prayers are being answered!" Lena rambled on like she did when she got excited. Mary listened as relief washed over her entire being.

"Is he going to make it? Did they say?" Mary croaked, then coughed to clear her throat.

"He's still very sick. But the doctor was optimistic."

"That was Lena," Mary told her mama, who was looking at her expectantly when she hung the receiver back into its cradle. "John came out of his coma last night. It was announced in their church."

"*Oba*, that is wonderful!" Mama exclaimed, heading to the living room. "Jacob, did you hear that? John woke up."

Thank you, Lord. Thank you for answering prayer. Please heal John completely, Mary prayed silently. She couldn't bear it if John didn't have a full recovery. As happy as she was about the good news, it also revived old anxieties. John had not written to her at all since he went to Mexico. She'd still gone ahead and written a second letter after he was captured—professing her love. Then she'd sent a third letter with his parents when they went to Mexico.

What if he decided he doesn't want my friendship after all? What if he met someone in Mexico who stole his heart? What if I've waited too long? It seemed like all she ever had was questions. *Why does life have to be so complicated?*

"We should probably get these dishes done," Anna said, coming back into the kitchen, breaking Mary's reverie.

"Yes, I suppose we should," Mary said, getting up from her chair. *What's done is done, and I have to leave the results up to God. I'll keep praying that he will get well and then take it from there. I can't change what is done.*

Francis was nervous, but the children were both very excited. Their exuberant response to the news that their dad wanted to see them had caught her off guard. Brad had surprised her by telling her that he still remembered his dad a little. He had told Chantel what memories he had.

It seems I'm the only one with reservations, Francis thought to herself as she prepared the food. They were going to meet Mike for a picnic in the park down by the North Saskatchewan River. It would be the first meeting between Mike and the kids since he had left all those years ago.

I hope it goes well, she thought, trying to calm her frazzled nerves. *I'm still not sure I'm doing the right thing, Lord.* Even though Mike had not been pushy, he had told her a couple of times how much he missed the kids. Maggie had pointed out that as a father he did have a right to see his children.

So Francis had sat the children down one evening and told them that she'd heard from their father. They had both stared at her as if she was an alien who had just landed on earth. She had told them that he wanted to see them, but that it was completely up to them if they wanted to meet with him.

"You mean I could have a dad like other kids?" Chantel asked, excitement mounting in her voice as the thought took hold of her.

Francis had bitten her lip. This could turn out so bad. She did not want to set the kids up for disappointment and heartbreak.

"I don't know exactly what your father has in mind," she had told her children. "He has asked to see you, so you will have to ask him those questions."

"How do you feel about it, Mom?" Brad had looked Francis in the eye, always sensitive to her feelings.

"I haven't figured that out yet, Brad," she had told him honestly. "We could meet with him—see how it goes. What do you think?" Although trepidation filled her being, she did not want to influence her children's decision about their father. She was careful to hide her own emotions to give the children the freedom to make up their own minds.

Brad had studied her carefully, trying to gauge what she was really feeling. When he was satisfied that his mother would be happy with whatever his decision was, a smile started tugging at his lips.

"I would love to see him, Mom," he had said, his eyes misty as he told her how much he had missed not having his dad around.

"Mom, where are the lawn chairs?" Brad asked, coming into the kitchen and breaking through Francis' thoughts.

"They should be in the entrance closet," Francis said, closing the picnic basket. Brad went in search of the elusive chairs while Francis opened the fridge and retrieved cans of pop and bottles of water, which she placed in an ice cooler.

"Do you think this outfit is good enough?" Chantel entered the kitchen. She must have tried on a half dozen outfits already.

"It's fine, Chantel." She looked charming in jean cut-offs and a neon-pink tank top. "You'll have to wear sunscreen with that so you don't get roasted."

"Where is the sunscreen?" Chantel asked.

"It should be in the bathroom cabinet," Francis told her. The banging of the front door notified her that Brad was back. She handed him the picnic basket. "Here, carry this." Francis picked up the cooler just as Chantel came back with the sunscreen.

"You kids grab your jackets on your way out," Francis called after them.

"Awe, Mom, it's hot out!" Brad complained.

"There's no guarantee it will stay that way," Francis said, glad to see they both picked up their jackets without further complaint.

Most businesses were closed on Sunday so traffic was light as they drove to the park.

"Let's stop at A&W for a root beer," Brad said, as the A&W sign came into sight.

"Not today, Brad. I've packed lots of drinks in the cooler," Francis said. She glanced at her son and he shrugged.

"Worth a try," he said, his face breaking into a smile. "I'm teasing you, Mom. I know you packed drinks."

Francis stopped at the red light and playfully punched Brad's shoulder. Brad laughed, then turned serious.

"I wonder what Dad will be like." He turned to face Francis. "Do you think he'll recognize me?"

"Well, you have grown up since he saw you last." Francis glanced at her son in the passenger seat beside her. At fourteen he was taller than her. Sports had given him a muscular physique similar to his dad. "Are you feeling anxious?"

"Maybe a little," Brad admitted. "I have a little bit of a memory of me and him playing cars on the floor."

"I don't remember him at all," Chantel piped up in the back seat.

"No," Francis said, releasing the brake as the light turned green, "you wouldn't remember him. You were just a baby."

"I'm kind of excited to see him but kind of nervous too," Chantel said.

"That's understandable, Chantel." Francis glanced at Chantel in the rear-view mirror. "I think we're all a little bit nervous."

Francis turned off the street and into the parking lot, pulling into an empty space. They piled out of the car. Brad got the lawn chairs out of the trunk, while Chantel helped Francis with the food and drinks. They found a spot in the shade under a stand of maple trees that gave them a good view of the river.

"This looks like the perfect place," Francis said as she set down the cooler and picnic basket.

"Will Daddy find us here?" Chantel looked around.

"He'll find us," Francis assured her. *If he wants to find us, he will,* she thought to herself. She was having a hard time keeping the butterflies in her stomach under control. She wasn't sure she wanted Mike to show up except that she didn't want him to stand the kids up.

"Mom, is that him?" Brad pointed to a man walking in their direction, with a football tucked under one arm and a bag slung over his shoulder.

Francis turned to look in the direction Brad was pointing. "Yes, that's him," she said. She turned to look at Brad. "How did you know?"

Brad shrugged his shoulders. "The way he walks. Something familiar about him."

Francis watched Mike approach. His stride was purposeful and confident. *Can Brad really remember the way he walks?* "I thought you'd say he looks like pictures of himself."

"He's not close enough to recognize his features, Mom," Chantel said, eyeing the stranger that was her dad.

"I suppose so," Francis said. "That's incredible that you recognize his walk, Brad. Maybe you remember more than you think." She turned to look at Brad, but he wasn't at her side. He was walking towards Mike, his gait so similar to his father's. Chantel took a step closer to her mother. Francis put her arm around her as together they watched the scene unfold. Mike dropped the football and held out both arms. Brad broke into a run and flung himself into his father's embrace. Time stood still as father and son clung to each other.

"I don't remember him at all," Chantel whispered, anxiously slipping her arm around her mother's waist.

Francis' pulled her daughter close. "I know, honey, I know. You were just a baby, not even a year old."

They watched as Mike picked up the football and handed it to Brad. *Lord, please don't let Mike hurt the kids again.* Francis prayed silently. Brad had asked for his daddy for a long time after Mike left. *We can't go through that again, Lord. This time they wouldn't forget the hurt.* She felt anxiety building up in her chest. She took a deep breath.

"Trust me." The words washed over her soul like the gurgling of a gentle brook. She released her breath and relaxed her shoulders. God was in control.

"Hi Francis," Mike greeted her with a smile that lit up his eyes, then turned to Chantel. He knelt down in front of her and took both of her hands. "Chantel." He said her name softly—a caress—his eyes misty. "You're beautiful—like your mother."

"Thanks," Chantel said, a shy smile tugging at her lips.

"I brought you something," Mike said. Letting go of Chantel's hands, he tugged at the bag slung over his shoulder. He reached in to retrieve the gift and gave it to Chantel.

Chantel unwrapped a Barbie doll, complete with extra outfits. Her eyes lit up and she looked at the man that was her daddy. "Thank you," she said, and then held the doll up for her mother to see. "Mommy look! I've wanted this doll for a long time!"

"Yes, you have," Francis said, smiling at her daughter's excitement. She was glad that Mike had thought to bring gifts for the kids.

"Here, let me get that doll out of the box for you." Mike sat down on the grass and worked on the packaging.

By the time Francis spread a blanket on the ground and got the food out, Mike had released the doll from bondage.

Lunch was a pleasant affair. Mike asked the kids about school, sports, and piano lessons. They were excited to fill him in. Francis took it all in—not sure how it made her feel. She was glad they got along so well, yet at the same time she felt... betrayed? She would have to examine that emotion more closely on her own.

"Time to throw that football around," Mike said, getting to his feet after they finished eating.

"Yes!" Brad jumped up and the two of them played catch while Chantel was busy changing Barbie's clothes. Francis lay back on the blanket taking in the scene. Birds chirped in the maple trees above her. She loved the sound of Brad's laughter as he threw the football to Mike.

I'm surprised how easily the children are taking to Mike. I don't know what I expected, but it certainly wasn't that Mike would just be able to step back into our lives after all this time. Have the children been longing for him without talking about it? She heard Chantel giggle and saw she had joined Brad and Mike. Her thoughts changed from musings to prayer. *Lord, I don't know what lies ahead of us. Has Mike really changed this much? If he has, can I really accept him back into my life? Lord, you know how much he hurt me. How can I trust him to be a good husband and father? Is that what you're asking of me?*

"Mom, are you sleeping?" Francis opened her eyes to the sound of Brad's voice next to her. She stretched and looked at her watch—then looked sheepishly at Brad—embarrassed to be caught napping.

Francis sat up and stretched her legs. "I must have fallen asleep."

"Dad said he'd buy us ice cream—do you want to come?"

Dad. Francis felt like he'd kicked her in the gut. *Is it that easy for the children to accept their father? After all these years?* Suddenly she felt very lonely. *Is Mike trying to take the children away from me?* She scrambled to her feet and started throwing things into the basket. She grabbed the blanket off of the grass and started folding it blindly, fighting the panic welling up in her chest.

"Francis, what's wrong?" Mike was at her side in an instant. "What happened?" He took both of her arms, turning her to face him. He saw the panic in her eyes.

"What do you want from me—from us?" Francis pushed the words past the lump in her throat.

"I want you and the children back in my life." Mike's voice sounded husky. "I need you more than I need to breathe." His Adam's apple bobbed as he swallowed hard. "But only on your terms. You call the shots."

Francis searched those clear blue eyes she had loved so much. She saw no deviousness in them—no anger—she began to relax. Mike drew her into his arms, hugging her against his chest.

"I mean it, baby." He rested his cheek against her soft hair. "You call the shots."

Francis pulled back and searched his face again. "I'm scared."

193

"I know," he said. "You have every reason to be—but I'm not that man anymore."

With a slight nod, Francis stepped out of his embrace. "Let's get that ice cream."

The children raced ahead of them to the ice cream stand. Francis' breath caught in her throat when Mike caught her hand as they walked. She didn't pull away.

"How much have you told the kids about me?" Mike asked.

"Not much. They were so small. We ended up at a friend's house until I was able to go back to work. Then we moved into a different apartment. There was such an upheaval in our lives that the fact that you were gone sort of got lost in the shuffle. When Brad asked for you I told him you had to leave, and I didn't know when you were coming back. He eventually stopped asking. As they got older, they just accepted the fact that they didn't have a daddy." Francis looked up at Mike and recognized the pain in his eyes.

"I'm so sorry. How can I ever make it up to you?" Francis shrugged her shoulders. It was a rhetorical question. Mike went on. "I would like to talk to the kids about it—ask their forgiveness—but I don't want to do it in such a public place. Would you be willing to bring the kids to my apartment?"

Francis thought about it before she answered. "I think it would be better for you to come to our apartment so the kids are in familiar surroundings."

Mike stopped in his tracks and studied Francis' face. "Are you sure? Do you trust me enough?" He knew why Francis always arranged their meetings in a public place. He couldn't fault her for it. She was only protecting herself and the children.

Francis felt the heat rise from her neck. *Mike figured out why I always meet him in a public place.* She felt embarrassed.

"Hey," Mike said, lifting her chin so she had to look at him. "I understand. After what I did to you, you have every right to make sure I don't know where you live."

Francis searched his eyes—the eyes she had fallen in love with way back in senior high. Caring eyes. "Yes, I'm sure. I think it would be better for the kids."

CHAPTER 15

The head of John's hospital bed was raised so he could see the lush greenery outside his window. The tubes had all been removed, and he felt stronger each day. Plans were being put in place for him to return to Canada to convalesce since he was expected to have a lengthy recovery. He'd had surgery to remove the piece of tree branch that had lodged in his thigh. There was some muscle damage, so he would need physiotherapy once he got back to Canada. John reached for the letter on his nightstand. He unfolded the sheets of paper and started reading, as he had every day since his mama had given it to him.

> *Dear John,*
> *I am devastated that you are so very sick, and I continually pray that you'll get well soon. Your parents are leaving for Mexico to be with you. I wish I could go with them. I'd like to be there by your side. Since that's not possible, I'm sending this letter with them. I went with Lena and Henry to the prayer meeting they had for you at church. There were a lot of people there praying for you. We have to trust that God will answer those prayers.*

I've done a lot of thinking since you left, especially since I heard you were captured. It made me realize that life is short. I have to admit that I haven't been totally honest with you. I do have feelings for you that go beyond friendship. But there are things I haven't told you that might change how you feel about me. Those things are better said in person, so I pray God will grant me that opportunity.

I'll keep praying that you will recover and that we can talk when you come home. I miss you very much.

Love,
Mary

John tenderly ran his fingers over the writing.

"*Ach,* Mary," he said softly, as yearning for her engulfed his entire being. "Why didn't you tell me?" He closed his eyes and remembered David's words. *Jesus will give you the grace to forgive. Freely you have received, freely give.* He had been stubborn about forgiving Mary.

He called to mind a conversation he'd had with Cornelio in the hut. Cornelio had asked him if he knew the circumstances surrounding Mary's pregnancy. Was she taken advantage of? Was she drugged or raped? He'd had to admit he knew nothing.

Now as he lay in the hospital bed he had lots of time to think. He had to admit he had jumped to conclusions. He had been selfish. Not once had he thought of the trauma she must have gone through. Feeling sorry for himself, he hadn't given Mary the benefit of the doubt. It was only fair to let her speak for herself. In his self-righteousness, he had judged her without getting the facts.

No wonder she didn't tell me. John berated himself. *She knew I would judge her—that I would not accept her for who she is. The Bible teaches us not to judge, but that's exactly what I was doing until David reminded me.*

Jesus, John prayed, *give me the grace to forgive when I need to forgive. Lord, forgive my unforgiving spirit and make me the person you want me to be. Forgive me for judging Mary when I know nothing of her circumstances. Who am I to pass judgement when you forgave her?* He prayed till he fell into a peaceful sleep.

John woke up to find Cornelio seated by his bedside. He shifted his leg, and Cornelio looked up from the book in his hands.

"*Goot jeschlopen?*" Cornelio asked. He closed the book and laid it on the night table.

"Yes, I had a good nap," John said, his eyes scanning the room. "It's good to see you again. Where are my parents?"

"They went for supper," Cornelio said. He had arrived back at the hospital that afternoon after spending a couple of days at home. "They are working hard to get you back to Canada. It sounds like you might be able to go soon."

"*Jo,* that would be better all around. It's hard for my parents to be so far from home." John turned to Cornelio. "I was hoping to talk to you privately before I leave."

Cornelio slid his chair closer to the bed. "What would you like to talk about?"

"I can't remember much about the night we were rescued. I remember the gunmen barging into the hut and yelling at us to get out. After that, my memory turns hazy. How did we get to the hospital?"

"You were a very sick man," Cornelio said. "I hadn't realized how sick you were until I had to pretty much carry you through the jungle." He paused a moment, deciding not to tell John about the gunman wanting to shoot him. *Maybe someday—but it's too soon.* "They had a truck waiting for us when we got to the road, and they stuffed us in the back. I think someone must have tipped off the police because we hadn't gone far, when we ran into a check stop, and the federal police swarmed the truck."

"God provided for us," John said thoughtfully.

"He sure did," Cornelio agreed, rubbing his chin. "I don't know why this happened to us but I do believe everything happens for a reason."

"Cornelio, can I tell you something I haven't told anyone else?" John asked. They had grown close while they were captives. Cornelio had proved himself to be a loyal friend and a true man of God.

"Of course," Cornelio said, smiling at him.

"When I was in a coma I spoke with David." John watched the older man's reaction. He wanted to know what Cornelio thought of his experience. Would Cornelio think he was crazy?

"Your friend who was killed in the traffic accident?" Cornelio felt goosebumps on his arms.

"Yes. I was in an indescribably peaceful place. Words cannot explain how beautiful it was. I walked down the path and there—sitting on a park bench—was David. We talked. I wanted to stay there with him, but he told me it wasn't my time yet, that I still had work to do."

Cornelio felt an excited shiver run up and down his spine. "You were very sick, and the doctors didn't think you'd pull through."

"David told me about Mary. You know the girl I told you about?" Cornelio nodded and John continued. "He told me that I needed to forgive her as Jesus has forgiven me. He said Jesus would give me the grace to forgive if I asked him too."

John paused as he wiped at his eyes. This was harder to put into words than he had thought it would be. "He quoted scripture, he said: 'Freely you have received, freely give.'" John's voice broke, and he paused for a moment before he continued.

"I always thought that when the time was right, Mary and I would get married. It never crossed my mind that Mary wouldn't wait for me. I was busy going to school and preparing for the life we would have together. I was crushed and confused when she told me she didn't love me. When I found out she had a daughter, I was devastated. How could I marry a defiled woman? I thought a missionary needs a pure wife—otherwise my testimony would be at stake."

He took a deep breath and looked at Cornelio. "When you said something about how Mary had sinned and therefore I thought she wasn't good enough for me—that got me thinking. Was I that self-righteous? The verses from Matthew 6:14-15 kept running through my mind: 'For if ye forgive men their trespasses, your heavenly Father will also forgive you: but if ye forgive not men their trespasses, neither will your Father forgive your trespasses.' If Jesus could forgive her, then who am I not to forgive? Am I more important than Jesus?" John struggled to control his voice. It was humbling to have this conversation, yet he felt he needed to come clean with Cornelio.

"When I talked to David in that garden, I told him my doubts and struggles, and this is what he said to me," John studied Cornelio's face as he continued. "David said: 'While he hung on the cross, Jesus cried out, 'Father, forgive them; for they know not what they do.' That included me. That included you. That included Mary. Just like he extends his unending grace and mercy to us—'in that, while we were yet sinners, Christ died for us'—Jesus will give you the grace to forgive as well. You only need to ask him. 'Freely ye have received, freely give.'"

John picked at the blanket that covered his weakened body, lost in the memory for a while. He looked up and met Cornelio's eyes. "Since I woke up, it's like everything is clear to me. As a forgiven child of God, I have no choice but to forgive Mary—or anyone else that asks my forgiveness. My heart feels in tune with God again."

Cornelio sat in silence for a while after John finished talking. *God, you move in mysterious ways. Thank you for revealing true forgiveness to John.*

"You don't know how happy I am to hear that," Cornelio said, a big smile on his face and tears in his eyes. "It's a blessing when God gives you the grace to forgive someone. Thank you for sharing."

"One more thing." This time John had a smile on his face. "Mama gave me a letter Mary had asked her to deliver. In it, she tells me that she hasn't been honest with me and that she needs to tell me something that may change my mind about her. She'll be surprised when she finds out I've already forgiven her." He chuckled. "The best part is—she says she loves me."

Cornelio laughed as he patted John's shoulder. "You sure go to a lot of trouble to get the girl to say the words you want to hear."

"I hadn't thought about it like that," John said, chuckling. "Hope I'll never have to go through that much trouble ever again!"

"God uses different ways to get our attention." Cornelio grinned as he pulled an envelope from his pocket. "This was waiting for you back at the shelter." He winked at John as he handed it over. "I thought you might like to have it."

John took the letter and turned it over in his hands. It had Mary's handwriting on it and was date stamped after his kidnapping. He looked up at Cornelio with a smile. "Thanks."

"I think someone can't wait for you to come home," Cornelio said, chuckling. Then he grew serious. "Thanks for sharing your experience with me. I know God has great things in store for you and Mary. He's gone to great lengths to bring you together."

John's parents entered the room, and Cornelio rose to leave.

CHAPTER 16

Mary cuddled little Maria in the crook of her arm. *This little miracle is helping me heal,* she thought to herself. She was quite surprised by that. She had made a habit of stopping in to see the baby and visit with Annie. The experience of that stormy night had created a bond between the two young women that ran much deeper than the bond they'd had as teenagers.

"I'm so glad you were able to stop by," Annie said. She poured two cups of coffee, and brought them to the table, taking care not to trip over two-year old Greta who was happily playing on the floor. "I don't often get to just sit and visit with anyone."

"I can't keep away from this little bundle for long." Mary smiled apologetically at Annie and thanked her for the coffee. The baby squirmed, and Mary placed her finger in the palm of the baby's hand. Maria wrapped her tiny fingers around it.

"You're welcome," Annie said. She looked out the window, checking on four-year-old Fritz, before pulling a chair out from the table and sitting down. "I have been wanting to talk to you. I read my Bible every day, but I find it hard to understand. I'm not sure what God expects of me."

Mary's heart rejoiced. Annie had been the one who encouraged her to rebel as a teenager. Annie was the one who had introduced her to partying, with all its pitfalls. Now here they were—both Christians. *God moves in mysterious ways,* she thought to herself.

Mary took a sip of coffee. "The Bible can be difficult to understand at first. As you keep reading, the Lord will start revealing his truths to you."

"I have difficulty reading high-German, never mind understanding it," Annie said, stirring a little cream into her coffee.

"Don't you have an English Bible?" Mary asked. Her generation had lost a lot of the German language since the government had closed their private schools and required that all children attend public schools.

"Yes, I do. We got it as a wedding gift from my aunt. I was always taught that German is the correct version of the Bible. I wouldn't want to read something that is wrong."

Mary couldn't mask her astonishment. She was starting to realize that not all Mennonites had the same view of the Bible, God, or life in general. Until recent years she had thought they were all more or less the same.

"I always read in English," she told Annie. "I can't read German well enough to understand either."

"But how do you know that it's right?" Annie bit her bottom lip nervously.

"Well," Mary said thoughtfully, "I never really thought that they might be different. If you don't trust it, you could get a Bible that has both languages. Papa has one of those. That way, you could read in both languages and see if the meaning is the same."

Annie's eyes lit up. "They make those? I didn't know that!"

"Yes, you can get one at the book store. But if you already have a Bible in each language you could just cross-reference them to make sure they're the same."

"That's right," Annie said. "Why didn't I think of that?"

Mary laughed. "Sometimes things are so simple that we don't consider them." She cooed at the baby and watched her smile. She looked up at Annie. "What does Isaac think of your conversion?"

"He's been taught the same way I was taught—that you can't know you're saved. He's a little cautious, but that's okay. He has to find his own way to Jesus, and I know he will because I pray for him every day." Annie walked over to the window to check on Fritz. She stood there, watching him as she continued thoughtfully. "We were taught that we had to go to church and do what they tell us. We should try to be as good as we can be and hope that in the end God will take us to heaven. We were taught not to read the Bible too much, or study it, or talk about it with others because we would become confused. Just do the best we can and hope that will be enough."

She turned away from the window and came back to the table. "We tried that. When we first got married, we tried living right. It only lasted a little while before we were right back where we had been. Isaac started drinking again, and I felt like there was no purpose in life. Whenever I tried to do better, it wasn't long before I was defeated again."

"But the church teaches about Jesus." Mary was surprised at Annie's revelation. What Annie was describing was so different than what she had been taught by her parents.

"Yes, but somehow we got it all mixed up. Isaac and I both thought that if we did what was expected of us, we could hope to go to heaven when we died," Annie said, sipping her coffee. "I felt like I could never measure up. I could never be good enough or do enough good things. I felt defeated."

"We can't do it on our own," Mary explained. "The Bible says all our righteousness is as filthy rags before God, but first John says, 'These things have I written unto you that believe on the name of the Son of God; that ye may know that ye have eternal life, and that ye may believe on the name of the Son of God.'"

"I know that now," Annie said, her face lighting up in a smile. "It finally made sense to me the night Maria was born."

Maria started crying, and Mary handed her back to Annie.

"I should be going," she told Annie. "Maria's hungry, and Mama will be wondering what's taking me so long." She chuckled. "Mama always worries when I'm late." She gave Annie a hug and ran her finger over Maria's soft cheek. "Thanks for the coffee." She turned to Greta and waved. "Bye-bye, Greta." Greta waved back then resumed playing.

"I look forward to your visits," Annie said, following Mary to the door. "I enjoy our conversations."

Mary slid behind the wheel of the car with a song in her heart. It was amazing how God was using little Maria to heal her. After giving her own baby up for adoption, she had never let any baby get close to her. Then God had put her in a position where she'd had no choice, and it was doing her a world of good.

"God is so good," she told herself as she turned onto the road towards home. Taking part in Maria's birth had released something inside of her. Now she was excited for Lena's pregnancy as well and looking forward to meeting her baby.

—⋘✦⋙—

John had mixed feelings as he fastened his seatbelt in the Boeing 737 bound for Canada. His short stay in Mexico had turned out very different from what he had expected. There was a maturity about him that hadn't been there when he arrived at the shelter a few months ago. God had taken him down a difficult road to teach him a lesson he was glad he had learned.

His mother reached over and patted his hand. "How are you doing?"

John smiled down at her. "I'm doing just fine, Mama."

"Are you sad to be going back so soon?"

"No," John said, thoughtfully. "God had a reason for bringing me here. Even though my stay here was shorter than I anticipated, I know God's purpose was accomplished." Mrs. Hepner looked perplexed, and John squeezed her hand slightly. "Someday I will be at liberty to tell you all about it, Mama."

Mrs. Hepner studied her son's face before she nodded—she could wait. She drew his attention to the landscape outside their window as the force from the powerful engines sucked them back into their seats.

"I never thought that I'd take a trip to another country," Mrs. Hepner told her son as the jet lifted them off the ground and climbed up into the cloudless blue sky. "Everything about Mexico is different from Canada—the people, the language, the terrain, the vegetation—everything."

"The kidnapping," John added with a wry grin.

"That too," his mother agreed. "I'm glad we were able to make this trip to be with you while you were in the hospital."

"Me too, Mama," he said with a smile.

John was exhausted by the time the Boeing 737 touched down in Edmonton. He was relieved the ambulance was waiting for him when he got off the plane. As the paramedics buckled him onto the stretcher and stuck an intravenous needle into his arm, he breathed a silent prayer of thankfulness. In the sweltering hut in the jungle, it had seemed impossible that he would ever see freedom again. He had much to be thankful for.

"Man, it's good to see you!" Patrick said, engulfing John in an embrace when he stopped by the hospital later that evening. "We prayed for you every single day. Man, you had us scared!"

John hugged Patrick back. "It's good to be back. Thanks for praying. I'm sure that's why I'm here today, because so many people prayed. The Lord was with me every step of the way." John pushed himself up farther in his bed. "Thanks for taking care of my folks."

Patrick had picked John's parents up at the airport. They were going to spend a couple of nights with the Pitmans before making the long drive home.

"No trouble at all. Mom and Dad will love having your folks over." Patrick pulled a chair closer to the hospital bed and sat down. "You're exhausted aren't you?"

John gave Patrick a lopsided grin. "I've felt exhausted ever since I got sick." He gave a rueful chuckle. "I feel like an old man."

"You've been through a lot. I can't wait to hear the whole story, but I won't bother you with that today. Maybe tomorrow after you've had a good night's rest."

"Tomorrow sounds good."

"Looks like you're going to need some fattening up."

John grinned. "Yeah, I was on a pretty rigorous diet for a while. First in captivity and then with tube feeding in the hospital."

Patrick shuddered. "That must have been tough."

"It wasn't a walk in the park," John said with a chuckle. "I have so much to tell you. What about you? You're a happily married man now?"

John lay back and listened as Patrick brought him up to speed on what was happening in his life. Patrick told him about the wedding, the honeymoon, and getting used to sharing his life with his wife. He talked about his work, keeping his narrative humorous and positive. John felt himself relax as he listened to his friend. When he fell asleep, Patrick got up and quietly left the room, pulling the door partially closed behind him.

The following afternoon, John's parents and the Pitmans entered John's hospital room. John was relieved to see his parents looked more rested than they'd been the entire time they were in Mexico.

"It's so good to be back in Canada," Mrs. Hepner said when John commented on it. "Just to know we are in our own country makes me feel much more relaxed."

"Knowing we can go home tomorrow helps too," Mr. Hepner added ruefully. He turned to the Pitmans. "We are very grateful to you for inviting us to rest a couple of nights before heading home."

"It has been our pleasure," Maggie responded, patting Mrs. Hepner's hand. "We used to enjoy having John over when the boys were in college, and it's a privilege for us to get to know his parents."

"Knowing that both of you and Patrick will be here for John is a tremendous relief to us," John's mom said.

"You have a fine son," Dale said. Turning to John he added, "We were very concerned for you—that must have been a horrendous experience. We prayed for you every day and are very thankful that you're back and well on the way to recovery."

"Thank you, Mr. Pitman," John said. "I'm thankful as well. It's humbling to know that so many people, both here and in Mexico, prayed for me."

Mary picked up the receiver from her desk phone at work.

"Yes?"

"Mrs. Hepner is here to see you," the receptionist told her. "She says she doesn't have an appointment."

"Send her in." Mary set the receiver into its cradle, rearranged the files on her desk, and stood up. "Hello. Come on in," she said when John's mama appeared in the doorway.

"It's good to see you," Mrs. Hepner said, shaking Mary's hand.

"Please have a seat." Mary waved in the area of the chair across from her desk.

"Oh no, I don't want to take your time." Mrs. Hepner handed Mary an envelope. "John asked me to deliver this for him."

Mary reached out her hand and took the letter. She felt both deliriously happy and anxious all at the same time.

"I feel like a mailman, delivering letters back and forth between you two," Mrs. Hepner said with a chuckle. She watched Mary study her name that was scrawled across the envelope.

For months she had waited. Now with the letter in her hand Mary wondered. *Was I too late?*

"Thank you," she said. Looking across her desk, she smiled at John's mother. "How is John doing?"

"He's doing well. The recovery might be lengthy, but he's in good spirits." Mrs. Hepner smiled, her eyes kind. "Mary, I know my son. You are very important to him. I don't know what he wrote in this letter, but I do know he treasured the letter you sent him. It meant a lot to him."

"Thank you," Mary said again, swallowing her emotions. She took heart at Mrs. Hepner's words.

Mrs. Hepner left, and Mary put the unopened envelope into her purse. She would open it later in private. Maybe she'd go to the cabin after work. *Lord, please let it be good news.*

―⋘✦⋙―

John marvelled at the beautiful colours of the sunrise over the city. When he let his mind take him back to those awful days in captivity, he still found it hard to believe that he had made it through alive. *Each day is a gift from God.* He understood that now. *No more playing games. Time is too precious for that. From now on, I'll be honest and open with my feelings.*

"Hey man," Patrick said later that morning as he walked into John's hospital room. "Pitman limousine at your service."

John laughed. "You call that big truck of yours a limousine?"

Patrick did his best to look offended, then shrugged. "Oh well, you get what you pay for."

"What are your rates, sir?" John enjoyed the light banter between them. Patrick and Janelle had offered him a place to stay for the next week while John continued treatment as an outpatient.

"More than a poor missionary can afford so don't bother asking." Patrick grinned. "Are you ready to go?"

Patrick picked up John's bag and slowly the two walked down the long hall to the elevator. John blinked at the bright sunshine as they walked through the glass doors.

"It's been awhile since I've been outside," he said as Patrick helped him into his pickup. John's leg was stiff and painful.

"That leg really did you in," Patrick said when John was seated in his truck. He threw John's bag in the back and walked around to the other side.

"Yeah. I started physiotherapy a few days ago," John said as Patrick slid behind the wheel and started the pickup. "Hopefully by the end of next week it will be a lot better."

"No hockey for you this winter," Patrick said, merging the truck into traffic.

John laughed. "I suppose you're right."

"I'm going for a walk," Mary called over her shoulder to her parents as she headed out the door.

She pulled her sweater tighter around herself as she walked down the path to the cabin. The weather had cooled off considerably since that huge storm the night Maria was born. The fields were bare, and the garden vegetables were preserved for winter. If they were lucky, it would be another month or two before the snow came. Tonight she hurried to the cabin, hardly noticing the colourful leaves on the trees, the unread letter spurring her on. In another week or so, John was coming home.

"I can't wait to see him," she told herself as she hurried along the dirt path. "So much has happened since I saw him. That makes it seem even longer than it actually is."

She sat on David's bed to read John's letter—feeling as if he was smiling at her today. She opened the envelope and pulled the letter out.

> *Dear Mary,*
> *Thank you for finally being truthful about your feelings! I can't wait to hear you say those words to me in person.*

Mary smiled. It sounded so like John. She read on.

> *You won't believe how happy I was to receive your two letters while I was in the hospital in Mexico. It made my whole ordeal worthwhile! Tomorrow my parents are going home, so I'm going to get Mama to deliver this letter*

to you. I'll probably be in Edmonton for a while yet. Once I'm released from the hospital, I'll stay with Patrick and Janelle until I'm done physiotherapy.

We have so much to talk about! But then we have the rest of our lives to talk, so I guess a few more days, or weeks, don't matter too much.

Looking forward to seeing you soon.
Love always,
John

Mary clutched the letter to her chest, thankful that his feelings for her hadn't changed. Yet. She still had to tell him about her daughter.

Patrick and Janelle invited Dale and Maggie for supper the evening before John went home. John's appetite was returning, and the roast beef Janelle cooked up was delicious. He told her so as he took a second helping.

The doorbell rang as they settled themselves on various couches in the living room after supper was cleaned up.

"I invited Francis over," Patrick said on his way to the door.

John looked up to greet Francis but instead found himself face-to-face with a set of familiar hazel eyes he had thought he would never see again this side of heaven. There in the doorway stood a little girl he had never seen before. Yet she looked familiar. John felt shivers run up and down his spine.

"Emily, don't just stand there. You're blocking the door." Chantel gave the little girl a slight push into the living room.

Francis crossed the room to give John a hug, and the spell was broken.

"Where's Brad?" Maggie asked Francis.

"He went to a basketball game with Mike," Francis said. Maggie and Dale smiled at each other with a look that said, "The Lord is working in the Webber household."

Patrick looked at John and asked, "Are you tired? You look pale."

John shook his head. "No, I'm okay." His gaze followed Emily as the two girls settled at the table with colouring books and crayons. Her left cheek sported a cute dimple when she smiled at Chantel. *Where have I seen her before?*

"Have I ever met Emily at your house?" he asked Francis. "She looks familiar. I feel like I should know her from somewhere."

"I don't think so. Emily and her mom moved to Edmonton from Red Deer last summer," Francis said. "Did you meet her before you went to Mexico?"

"No. I just spent one night with Patrick before my trip," John said, searching his memory. "Patrick and Janelle were the only ones I saw."

"Your meds are messing with your mind," Patrick suggested.

"Must be," John said, settling back into his chair.

That night, John slept fitfully as a little girl with friendly hazel eyes and long, chestnut-brown hair flitted through his dreams.

CHAPTER 17

"I don't know what to do," Francis confessed to Maggie, wrapping her hands around the cup of tea in her hands. "Mike wants to come live with us. He's not pressuring me, but I know that's what he wants. I would love to step back in time and change what happened, but I can't do that." She turned her eyes on Maggie. "I'm scared."

"Honey, that is totally understandable." Maggie was thoughtful as she stirred a spoonful of honey into her tea. She asked the one question she always asked: "What is God telling you to do?"

Francis thought about that before responding. *What is God telling me?* Just this morning she had asked God that same question.

"I don't know." Francis sighed, letting her gaze rest on the colourful maple leaves in Maggie's backyard. A furry brown squirrel darted up a branch and out of sight. "I know the Lord tells us to forgive. He's pointed that out to me on numerous occasions."

"Forgiving him and living with him are not synonymous of each other," Maggie said. "The Lord does direct us to forgive each other, but that doesn't necessarily mean you have to take him back. Have you forgiven him?"

217

The squirrel peeked out from behind the tree and then disappeared again. "I think I have. He was not himself when he did those horrible things. He was under the influence of alcohol and stress. I believe he's left all that behind. He's living for Jesus now and has a good job. But can I trust him not to turn back to his old ways when things get tough? Can I trust him with Brad and Chantel's lives?"

Maggie reached across the table and put her aging hand over Francis' hand. "Sometimes we have to trust that God is looking out for us even when we're not sure which way to go. Sometimes we just have to step out in faith believing that God has our back."

"Are you saying I should take Mike back?"

"I'm saying it's your decision. I don't know Mike except what you have told me. You know who he was when you first married him. You know who he is now. Is that good enough for you? Are you willing to take the risk? I suppose the most important question is—do you love him?"

Francis watched the little squirrel darting in and out of the tree branches. If only she was as carefree as that squirrel, yet she knew he had his struggles too. Even squirrels had to prepare for winter and keep safe from predators. She had to protect her children—but she couldn't deny the feelings Mike invoked in her. *If we could only get back the love we had...*

"Francis? Are you still with me?"

Francis pulled herself back to the present with a slight chuckle. "Mike has a good heart. I think I still love him, but I don't know if I trust him."

"Once our trust is compromised, it's hard to get back. Dale and I are praying for you," Maggie said. She sipped her tea and then changed the subject. "How are Brad and Chantel doing these days? With the exception of church, I haven't seen them in a long time."

"Now that school has started again, they're keeping very busy," Francis told her friend. "Brad is in hockey again, and Chantel is taking piano lessons."

As Francis walked home, she reflected on her conversation with Maggie. *Lord, show me what you would have me do. Brad and Chantel want to have their dad around, but can I trust him not to hurt them or me?*

"Trust in the Lord with all thine heart; and lean not unto thine own understanding. In all thy ways acknowledge him, and he shall direct thy paths."

Oh Lord, are you saying you want me to trust you in this? Did you bring Mike back into our lives to restore our family? Or is that just wishful thinking on my part?

Francis turned the corner to her apartment just as Gloria's dad's car pulled up and Gloria got out.

"Hi Gloria," Francis said, waving at her. She quickened her step.

"Hi," Gloria said. Her pale, thin face was etched in worry lines. "I'm sorry I didn't call. I need to talk to you." She waved to her dad as he pulled out from the curb and back into traffic.

"No problem. I'm glad I came home when I did. I was over at Maggie's house." Francis opened the door, and together they went up the single flight of stairs to her apartment. Francis noticed Gloria's heavy breathing as she unlocked her door. "Come on in. Can I get you a cup of tea or coffee?" she asked. Pulling a chair from the table, she motioned for Gloria to take a seat.

"I'll have coffee please. Black." Gloria sat at the table while Francis opened the cupboard door. "Where are your kids?"

219

"Brad is at hockey practice, and Chantel is at piano lessons." She measured ground coffee into the coffee maker and poured the water in. "Where's Emily? How's she doing?"

"She's at my parents. My dad picked her up after school." Gloria turned and coughed into her sleeve. "I had a doctor's appointment."

Francis picked up the two steaming cups of coffee.

"Let's have our coffee in the living room," she said. "It's more comfortable seating." She had noticed how exhausted Gloria looked. Gloria followed her and sank into an overstuffed chair.

"How did the doctor's appointment go?" Francis asked, handing Gloria a cup of coffee before taking a seat on the couch.

Gloria lifted the mug up to her lips and took a sip. "That's one of the things I wanted to talk to you about."

Gloria had lost weight, and she was wearing a wig. She had lost her hair to chemotherapy.

"I'm supposed to have more tests at the hospital tomorrow." Gloria fastened her eyes on Francis. "Would you mind watching Emily again? You've done so much for me already that I hate to ask, but I know Emily loves it here."

"Absolutely! We'd love to have her," Francis said. "Chantel and Emily play so well together that it's no problem to have her over at all. You're not doing too well, are you?" Francis didn't bother trying to keep the concern out of her voice.

Gloria sighed. "I'm exhausted." She leaned her head back against the chair and closed her eyes for a moment. "I don't know how much longer I can fight this."

She looks so pale, Francis thought to herself.

Gloria opened her eyes. "I want you to help me find Emily's birth mother."

Francis raised her eyebrows. "Are you sure you want to go that route? We talked about how that could come back to bite you."

"I know but—just between you and me—I don't think I'll be around much longer. When I go, Emily will only have her grandparents to take care of her. I know they'll do their best, and Emily loves them, but she needs someone younger in her life. My parents don't have the energy it takes to raise a child. Does that make sense?"

Francis pondered that. "Yes, that makes sense. Did the doctor tell you something that has brought on this negativity?"

"Not in so many words, but I know what I'm feeling. I don't think the test results are going to be in my favour. I would feel better knowing Emily had her birth mom." Gloria covered her mouth and coughed again.

"Gloria, surely you know that could raise a lot of issues. What if her birth mom doesn't want her? That would be devastating for Emily."

"That's why I don't want Emily to know about it. I want to find her and talk with her. If she doesn't want Emily, then I'll have to think of something else. I just keep thinking of what the social worker told us at the time of adoption. She said the only request from the birth mother was that Emily be placed in a Christian home."

"So you think the birth mother is a Christian?"

"If she wasn't a Christian herself, I think she must have had a strong Christian influence in her life. It's been eight years. Her circumstances may have changed to where she wants her little girl back."

"And if she doesn't?" Francis asked. "She might be married now with a family, and she may never have told them about this

221

baby. Contacting her at this time in her life might have devastating effects for her."

"That could be, but I need to know." Francis had never known Gloria to be so adamant.

"Alright. Alright." Francis threw up her hands in mock defeat. "I'll help as much as I can. Where do we start?"

"I thought I'd set up an appointment to see the social worker who worked the case. Will you come with me? I don't want to go alone." Gloria turned her head and coughed. "I want you to be a part of this so if I don't live long enough to find her, you can continue the search."

Francis gasped. "What are you talking about?" Her panicked voice was too loud. She cleared her throat and lowered her voice. "Why are you talking like that? What did the doctor really say to you?"

Gloria leaned forward in her chair. Her voice was urgent. "I do not want Emily to know. Do you understand? I do not want Emily to know—but just between you and me—I know I'm dying."

"Gloria, did the doctor tell you that?" Francis softened her voice, her face a mask of concern. *How did this conversation go from tests to dying? What did I miss?*

Gloria leaned back in her chair and sighed. "You know doctors. They don't tell you anything. All he says is, 'I want you to go to the hospital tomorrow morning to run some tests.'" Her voice took on a professional tone as she mimicked the doctor's words. Then she changed back to her normal voice. "Francis, I just know. I have a feeling deep within my soul that I'm not long for this world. With the exception of leaving Emily, I'm at peace with dying. If only I could get her back with her birth mother," Gloria finished wistfully.

Francis pondered the situation Gloria and Emily found themselves in. There was no doubt Gloria had put a lot of thought into this. Francis knew she would go ahead with her plans with, or without, Francis. She could at least act as the mediator if they did find the birth mother.

Francis leaned over and took Gloria's hand. "I hope you're wrong and that you will be cured of cancer. In the meantime, I will help you try to find Emily's birth mother. Just remember that she may not be a suitable mother for Emily. I don't want you and Emily to get hurt in the process."

"What can I say? I have a feeling about this."

Francis leaned back on the sofa with a sigh. "Gloria, you are a dear soul. I will help wherever I can. Emily is special to me. I just want you to be sure you are doing the right thing."

"Thank you. I'm sure." Gloria's eyes looked tired, but Francis saw a spark of hope in them as her lips curved into a smile. "As soon as I get back from the hospital I'm making an appointment to see the social worker."

Tears threatened Mary's eyes as she watched John slowly step out of his car and close the door. He was but a fraction of the man he had been when she last saw him. *That whole ordeal in Mexico has done a good number on him,* she told herself as she watched him walk towards her with a pronounced limp. So much had happened since she had last seen him. *Thank you, Lord, for bringing him back!* As she went to meet him, trepidation overshadowed the joy in her heart. The hour of reckoning had come. She must tell him. *Lord, Thy will be done.*

John held out his arms, and Mary walked into them. Their emotional embrace spoke of years of heartache and loneliness. Years of waiting for this moment.

"I've missed you so much." John's voice was husky as he rested his cheek on top of her head.

"I missed you, too," Mary mumbled against his chest. She leaned her head back so she could look up into his face. The tenderness she saw in his eyes took her breath away. For a moment she considered not telling her secret. Maybe he didn't need to know. Mentally she gave herself a shake. That wouldn't be fair to him. She stepped out of his arms and took his hand.

"It's so good to see you." Clasping John's hand, Mary led him to the lawn swing behind the house. She sat down and patted the seat beside her. He carefully lowered himself onto the swing. "I was afraid I had lost you forever."

"You can't get rid of me that easily," John said. The twinkle in his eyes lightened the moment.

Mary laughed lightly. "Well, I'm glad you're back. I've been so worried about you—along with everyone else in this community."

"Yeah. That entire episode wasn't exactly what I had in mind when I went to Mexico. God's plans aren't always our plans, but he was with me through it all."

Mary nodded as she sought the right words. The time had come to be truthful about her past, but first there was one thing she needed to know.

"Before you left we agreed to write to each other," Mary said hesitantly, allowing her gaze to fall on the colourful fall leaves of distant trees. "I wrote to you, but I didn't get a response. Didn't you get my letter?" She missed the brief look of pain that crossed his face.

"Yes, I got your letter. I was very busy and didn't get around to writing back." He looked down at the small hand lying in his. He rubbed his thumb over the soft skin.

"I thought maybe you had found a girl in Mexico who stole your heart," she said.

"Never!" John exclaimed, astonished she would think that. "That never crossed my mind. I soon realized I had no idea what a teenage shelter for street kids does. I was honestly very busy." *That's honestly not the entire truth either,* his conscience reminded him.

Mary nodded, accepting his explanation. "Tell me about your ordeal," she said, relaxing a little. "It was terrible to know you were kidnapped. I imagined all sorts of things. Now I want to know what really happened."

John sighed as his thoughts went back to that drive through the mountains. Slowly he recounted how they were kidnapped, the long trek through the jungle, the guards, the hut, and finally their rescue. Mary sat quietly picturing each event in her mind.

"Cornelio thinks there was an informant in that group of guards because we ran into a full military check stop before we got to the first town."

"Do you remember when you were rescued?"

"Not really. I had a high fever, which—combined with the days of little food—had left me very weak. I was floating in a sea of fogginess."

"We had prayer meetings for you," Mary said.

"I am sure all those prayers are why I'm still here," John said. "I was in pretty rough shape. I can't remember all of it. I was already quite sick when we were rescued. I was in a coma for days afterward."

"Do the doctors think you'll make a full recovery?"

"If I rest enough and take care of myself, they are optimistic. The physio should help my walking."

"Then you'll have to take very good care of yourself. I don't need another big scare like that."

John chuckled. "Just seeing you makes me feel a lot better."

Mary felt the heat rise in her neck and a warm glow fill her heart. *Lord, please don't let me ruin that with what I have to tell him.*

"Mama gave me the letter you sent with her. Cornelio brought me the letter you mailed after I was captured. I loved what you said." He pulled out two folded pieces of paper from his shirt pocket. "I've kept the letters close to my heart."

Mary squirmed in her seat. She focused her sight on the distant trees. She couldn't look him in the eyes and tell him what she had to say. "I've told you before that there's much you don't know about me. I have not been honest with you, and that's not fair to you." She pulled her hand from John's grasp and clasped them tightly in her lap. "When you were kidnapped, I realized again how fragile life is. I was afraid I had waited too long to tell you the truth. So I wrote a letter telling you part of it—that I do love you—but there's more that I need to tell you."

"Mary," John said, "you don't need to tell me anything else. Those words—I love you—are all I need to hear." He put his hands on either side of her face and searched her eyes. "I love you. Nothing you tell me will change that."

She lost herself in John's tender eyes for a moment. "I have to tell you. It might change everything." John dropped his hands from her face and took both her hands in his. She took a deep breath before she continued.

"After David was killed I totally lost my way. There were times when I felt so angry inside I could hardly breathe. Other times I was so sad I couldn't stop crying. My friends tried hard to understand, but I pushed them away. In my sorrow, I didn't want to be close to anybody—yet I needed people to love me. I know that sounds mixed up, but that's how I felt. I rebelled against my parents. I was angry with God."

She inhaled deeply before going on. "One Sunday afternoon, when a bunch of us were at the river, Annie reached out to me. I started spending time with her and her friends. I went to parties with them. I started drinking and doing stuff I had never even thought of doing before." She let her mind go back in time to those dreadful days. John rubbed the back of her hand.

"It doesn't matter," he said softly. "You don't need to tell me anything."

"I have to tell you," she said, her breath ragged. *Lord, give me strength.* She took a deep breath and continued. "One evening, there was a guy at the party whom I'd never seen before. He was from the city. Everybody thought he was so cool—guys and girls alike. When he singled me out, I was the envy of all the girls there. He worked in the oilfields, so he wasn't always there, but when he was, we spent time together. I didn't realize he would use me. I didn't even know what that meant." She paused, not daring to look up. This was so hard. It could change their future.

"When I found out I was going to have a baby, he arranged for me to have an abortion. He put me on a bus headed for Edmonton, then walked out of my life. I haven't seen or heard from him since, nor did I want to. I felt so alone and desperate. By the grace of God, Francis was at that bus station and she took me in. She gave me an alternative to abortion. I babysat for her until I had the baby," Mary's voice broke as she wiped a tear from her eye. She took a deep breath, willing herself to continue. "I gave her up for adoption. I didn't know it would be so hard. I didn't want anyone to know the horrible thing I had done, and I thought if I gave my baby away, I could come back home and no one would ever know. I was wrong. I hadn't taken into account how I would feel. I sank into deep depression and the afternoon you found me, I had actually decided to end my life."

Mary heard John's sharp intake of breath.

"But you didn't," he whispered. His stomach dropped to his feet. *What if I hadn't stumbled upon her that day?*

"No." This time she dared to look into his face. "You saved my life."

His eyes were full of emotion as he squeezed her hands. "Thank you, Jesus." He breathed softly.

There was more he needed to know. Mary continued. "I had planned on going back home after the baby was born, but I couldn't. I hadn't taken into account that I wouldn't be able to leave her behind. The only connection I had with her was that maybe we were still in the same city." She wiped at the lone tear trickling down her cheek. "Then you came along and told me Papa was sick. I was so afraid he would die. That God would take him away to punish me for my sin. I couldn't believe it when Mama welcomed me back with open arms. No questions asked." Mary's voice cracked. She struggled to keep her emotions under control. "Francis encouraged me to accept Jesus as my Saviour, but I was sure my sin was too great. Finally one night, it all became clear to me. I knelt by my bed and accepted Jesus into my life."

"Praise the Lord!" John whispered. Mary looked up at him and was surprised to see tears in his eyes. It gave her the courage to go on.

"The Lord gave me the strength to come back home, but I vowed that no one would ever know about my baby. Mama and Papa know but—until now—they were the only ones." Mary swallowed hard. Her heart thumped wildly in her chest as she gathered all her courage together and looked into John's eyes.

GRACE TO FORGIVE

This was the hardest thing she had ever done. "I have loved you ever since I was a young girl. I have sinned so badly and treated you so horribly. Can you forgive me?"

To her surprise, John folded his arms around her and crushed her against his chest. She could feel his heart racing beneath her cheek. "Oh, Mary, how long I've waited to hear you say those words!"

Mary rested her head on John's shoulder as he spoke. "I'm sorry you went through so much. I should have been a better friend to you. All I could think of was getting away from here and all the reminders of David. Not that I wanted to forget him, but I felt I was suffocating. I do forgive you. You were hurting, you were young, and I had no claim on you. When you needed a friend, I wasn't there for you."

Mary lifted her head and looked into John's eyes. "How can you say that? Yes I needed a friend, but I turned away from my friends. I wouldn't let them help me." John's eyes were dark with emotion as their gaze held.

"I have things to confess as well," he said. "I have known about your daughter since before I went to Mexico."

Mary gasped. "How can that be? I didn't tell anyone!"

"You forget that Patrick is my friend."

Colour crept up into Mary's face as she remembered the connection. "He told you?"

"Let me explain." John kept his arm around Mary's shoulder as he spoke. "When Patrick picked me up at the bus station, we noticed a couple of no-good men talking to a young girl. Patrick went over to check it out—it's what he does a lot of these days. Turns out she was a runaway. He convinced the girl to go back home, and we waited with her until her father picked her up. On our way to his house, he told me about a girl he and Francis had rescued at the bus station years ago." Mary gasped as realization struck her between the eyes.

John squeezed her hand reassuringly. "He said that incident made him aware of the danger runaway teenagers place themselves into. Thus began his desire to help troubled kids get the help they need."

"How did you make the connection?" Mary asked.

"He mentioned that the girl was pregnant. He said that she ended up babysitting for Francis. Later that evening, Janelle mentioned the girl's name was Mary. That's when I made the connection. I asked Patrick if any other girl had babysat for Francis. He didn't think so. My flight left for Mexico the following day, but Patrick assured me he would talk to Francis. A few weeks later, I got a letter from him confirming my fears."

"That's why you didn't write back." Mary was mortified.

"*Your sin will find you out.*" The verse raced through her mind. Her heart pounded, and she struggled to breathe.

John rubbed her upper arms. "Mary, it's okay. I love you." She searched his eyes. They met hers without hesitation. Her heart rate slowed down until she was able to breathe easier.

"How can you?" Her voice squeaked.

"Please hear me out," John said. "I admit I was devastated. I was angry with you and with God. My faith was shaken. I didn't know what to think or what to do. Cornelio sensed I was struggling. That's why he asked me to go with him on a little trip he had to make into the mountains. That was when we were kidnapped. My thigh got slashed as we trekked through the jungle to the hut they locked us up in. During the days we were there, I confessed my concerns to Cornelio. He encouraged me to see things for what they were from your point of view. I got sicker with each day, and by the time we were rescued, I was in and out of consciousness. During the first days in the hospital

I was unconscious—fighting for my life." John paused, searching Mary's face.

"This might be hard for you to hear." He tightened his arm around Mary's shoulders. "While I was in a coma, I had a vision, or a dream, or an out-of-body experience. I don't know what it was exactly—but it was very real to me. I was walking in a beautiful garden. It was amazing with flowers of every colour and a beautiful river with the clearest water I've ever seen. When I saw David sitting on a park bench, I ran towards him and we embraced." Mary shivered—goose bumps appeared on her arms—her eyes grew teary. John kept rubbing her arm, his voice low as he continued. "David told me you needed me. I explained to him that you had a daughter. He said, 'She's a beautiful little girl who loves Jesus with all her heart.'"

Mary burst into tears, as she dropped her head into her hands. Her shoulders shook as a dam broke loose within her soul and released a bottled-up river of tears. John held her in his arms, gently massaging her back, until her tears slowed down. She sat up and wiped her face with her sleeve. Her voice choked as she whispered, "Oh John, do you think that's true? Do you think that my baby girl loves Jesus? I requested that she be placed in a Christian home."

"Like I said, I don't know if it was a dream, a vision, or an out-of-body experience. I'm just telling you what I experienced. If you asked for her to be placed into a Christian home, then it's quite likely that your daughter knows Jesus." John drew a deep breath before continuing. This part was going to be hard.

"I'm ashamed to say that I struggled to forgive you. It didn't come easy to me. I had all kinds of excuses that Cornelio chipped away at while we were held captive. Then David told me I had to forgive as Christ had forgiven me. He told me Jesus would give me the grace to forgive if I asked him. He said, 'Freely you have received, freely give.' When David started walking away, I begged him to take me with him, but he said it wasn't my time. He walked away from me down a path towards an arch filled with glorious light, while I felt myself being drawn back to my body. That's when I regained consciousness."

Mary was weeping softly as John held her close against his chest. He laid his head on her soft hair as he continued. "Ever since then, I couldn't wait to see you again. I needed to tell you how much I love you and forgive you. I realized that I was as much at fault as you because I wasn't there for you when you needed me. Can you forgive me for that?"

Mary turned her tear-stained face to look up at him. "Of course I forgive you. I love you so much." John looked deeply into her eyes.

"Thank you, Jesus," he whispered, as his lips claimed hers.

Anna looked up from the photo album that she and Jacob were looking at when Mary and John entered the room. Anna's gaze didn't miss the fact that they were holding hands or the happiness written on their faces. Her heart sang as a smile lit up her face.

"*Goonowent*, John," Jacob said haltingly, his face breaking into a smile as he patted the seat beside him. Anna was proud of how well he managed those few words. John shook hands with both of them before taking a seat on the other side of Jacob, pulling Mary down beside him.

"How are you doing, John?" Anna asked, closing the photo album and laying it on the coffee table.

"I'm doing well. My leg is still healing, but I'm getting stronger every day. I'm supposed to go to Edmonton next week for a check-up and more physiotherapy."

"I'm so glad to hear that," Anna said. The fact that John kept his fingers wrapped around Mary's hand didn't escape her. "Thank the Lord you pulled through. You gave us quite a scare, you know."

"It was quite the ordeal. I didn't know how sick I was until I came out of my coma," John said. He looked at Mary and then back at her parents. "It was only after I awoke that I realized how close to dying I had been."

He looked from Jacob to Anna Hildebrandt, gauging what to tell them and which parts to leave out. By now it sounded like a well-rehearsed story because he had to retell it so often. He never wanted to forget what had happened to him and how God had helped him, but not everyone needed to know all the details.

Mr. and Mrs. Hildebrandt are like my second parents. I'm sure they prayed for me as if I was their son. He decided they should know all of it. So he started with his work at the shelter. John did his best to bring his experiences to life for them.

"Tell them about seeing David," Mary urged when he told of his illness but omitted that part.

Anna gasped and Jacob's eyes grew wide. "What happened?" Anna asked, her voice just above a whisper. She covered Jacob's hand with her own.

John told them about the experience he had while in a coma. He told them of the gardens and seeing David. Anna quietly dabbed at a tear that snuck out of the corner of her eye as John told them, "He was so happy. He knew how much you missed him and what is going on in your lives. When he turned to leave, I felt myself being drawn back into my body. That's when I came out of the coma."

The room was quiet when John finished speaking. They were all caught up in their own thoughts and emotions.

Jacob cleared his throat. *"Dankschoen."*

Anna wiped her eyes and gently blew her nose into a tissue. "Yes, thank you for sharing. I feel like David is right here with us." Mary squeezed John's hand.

"I cannot describe the peace I felt. I have often felt at peace, but this was peace that truly passes all understanding. It was incredible," John said softly, still awed by the experience. "If that is what we have to look forward to, then we should never be sad when one of God's children passes into eternity."

Jacob nodded. "True." He pointed to himself.

Anna studied her husband closely. "Did you experience something similar after your stroke?"

Jacob nodded. He smiled, his eyes shining. *"Fraed."* He pointed at his chest again.

"Yes, peace," Anna repeated, laying her hand on his arm. "Oh, Jacob, you could never express that to us because you didn't have the words!"

The conversation turned to John's health and what he planned to do while he was recovering.

"Mary, will you help me make a snack?" Anna asked, getting up from the couch. "We'll have some coffee."

After the women left the room, John picked up the photo album lying on the coffee table. "Were you looking at pictures?" he asked. Jacob smiled and nodded.

John opened the albums one after the other, flipping through the pages while carrying on a mostly one-sided conversation with Jacob. His breath caught in his throat when he saw it. He brought the photo album closer to his face and studied the picture. He remembered when he'd seen the picture before. He'd been home for Christmas and had dropped by for a visit. They had been looking at photo albums that evening when this picture had caught his attention. He'd never seen Mary with short hair before. It made her look quite different. He remembered the story they had told that Mary had cut her own hair.

The face looking up at him from the picture was a good replica of a face he had seen a few days ago. Another little girl with the same shade of brown hair—only it was long and hanging down her back. The eyes smiling back at him from the picture were Mary's light brown eyes, not David's hazel ones that had looked at him from that other face. The dimple in the cheek had been David's as well.

"Coffee's ready," Anna said, coming into the living room.

John looked up at Mary's mama. "Would you mind if I took this picture with me?" he asked, pointing to the picture of Mary and David. "I would like to show it to a friend."

"Go right ahead," Anna said with a laugh. "I'm sure there are nicer pictures in that album that you could take."

John chuckled. "I'm kind of partial to this one." He removed the picture and put it in his shirt pocket. Then he got up, tucked Jacob's arm under his, and helped him to the kitchen table.

CHAPTER 18

Mike took Francis and the children shopping at the mall that weekend. The kids' wardrobes could use additional items, and with winter just around the corner, they would need new winter gear. None of the clothes they wore last winter fit.

"It's high time I pull my weight around here and start paying for my children's clothes," he had told Francis the night before. She had to admit that he could have done more over the years, but all the same, it felt like she was losing a little more control each time they were together. "Dad, can I get a new pair of hockey skates, too?" Brad asked as they entered the mall. "Mine are hand-me-downs from one of Mom's friends, and they don't fit very well."

"Well, I don't know a lot about hockey skates, but we can certainly check it out." Mike smiled at his son as they strolled through the mall.

"Cool!" Brad looked like he had scored on a clear-cut breakaway.

Is Mike trying to win me over or is he trying to win the children over? He comes into our lives after all these years and is able and willing to give the kids things they've always wanted, but that I could never afford to give them, Francis thought to herself.

"Brad, you can put skates on your Christmas wish list," Francis said, trying to keep the resentment she was feeling out of her voice. She was used to counting every penny. Going to the mall and buying expensive hockey skates on a whim was not something they normally did. "Those skates aren't perfect, but the way you're playing, I don't think they're that bad."

"But Mom, if you think I'm a pretty good player now, wait till you see me in new skates," Brad said.

Mike laughed. "I'm holding you to that. If you get new skates, you'll have to prove that they make a big difference." He cast a glance towards Francis. "Your mom has a good point though. Maybe it would be a better idea to put it on your Christmas list."

"Awe, Mom." Brad looked at her pleadingly.

"Don't put me in the middle of this," Francis said. Holding up both hands she looked at Mike. She hoped he'd get the message. She was bringing the children up to value a dollar, not to spend it on a whim. "I know you would love new skates. It's up to your dad if he wants to get them for you." She turned her eyes on Brad to drive home a point. "But I don't want you to think that your dad will get you anything and everything you want—when you want it—because that's not how life works."

"Your mother's right, Brad," Mike said, nodding his head to Francis. He got her message. "Today we'll see if we can find you some skates. But from now on 'wants' will have to go on a Christmas wish list."

Chantel was thrilled with the new jeans and denim jacket she got along with a ski-jacket, which was the latest fashion. When they finished shopping for clothes, they headed to the sports store to look for skates. After an hour of trying on skates and looking at all sorts of other sports equipment Brad would like—but knew enough not to ask for—they finally left the store with skates in hand.

By mid-afternoon, they stopped at the food court and purchased sticky cinnamon buns and drinks.

"Oh look," Chantel said, pointing to the centre of the food court where a magician was setting up to do tricks. "Can we go watch him?"

"You and Brad can go watch him while your mother and I finish our coffee," Mike said. "We'll watch from here." Francis let her eyes follow the children as they walked the short distance.

"This has been a really fun day for me," Mike said, watching Francis over the top of his paper coffee cup. "I'm so glad that Brad and Chantel have accepted me into their lives so readily."

Francis sighed. She lifted her coffee cup to her lips and took a drink. The ever-present question was on her mind: *Can I trust him?*

"You're right about the children not getting everything they want," Mike continued when Francis remained silent. "I'm glad you pointed that out because after all the lost time, I want to give them the world. You have done an excellent job in raising them, and there's no way that I want to interfere with that. I just want to make life easier for all of you. I should have been there for you, and I wasn't. I want to make it up to you. All of you."

Francis lifted her eyes to search his handsome face. Those baby blues still made butterflies appear in her midsection. He wasn't the young man she had fallen in love with—he was more mature, more confident, at peace with himself. Could she love him again?

"Part of me believes you. Another part of me doesn't know what to believe," she said. He could see the struggle in her eyes.

"As long as I can keep seeing you and the kids," Mike said. "That's all I ask. The rest is up to you and God."

She nodded. There were many hurdles still to cross.

Francis stopped at the supermarket for groceries on her way home from her secretarial job in the elementary school Chantel attended. She hated grocery shopping—especially after work. It was just one more thing on her long to-do list. She needed to get supper going. Brad had a hockey game tonight so that meant they had to eat supper early. He couldn't eat too close to the game, as it would make him sluggish. She stuffed the groceries into the back of her car and headed home. She'd have to put supper on, go get Chantel from piano, eat, and take Brad to the arena. He had to be there early for warm-ups and whatever the team did to prepare for the game. She edged the car into traffic and nearly ran into a pedestrian who stepped onto the street. Her first reaction was to honk the horn, but then she noticed that it was a crosswalk and the orange light was flashing.

"Slow down," she muttered to herself. "You don't need to get yourself into an accident." As soon as the pedestrian stepped onto the sidewalk on the other side of the street, she hit the gas.

Francis parked the car and unloaded groceries, lugging them up the flight of stairs to her apartment. She had just finished unloading the car when Mike drove up.

I don't have time for Mike now, Francis muttered to herself, her mind racing through her busy schedule. She watched him unfold his lanky body from the Mustang. He stooped back into the car and came out with a large pizza box.

"Supper." He held the box for her to see. "I thought you probably wouldn't have time to make supper since Brad has a game tonight."

Francis' shoulders sagged in relief. "I've done it lots of times," she told him. Mike covered the distance between them in a few steps.

"I know. I don't want you to have to anymore." His voice was low and husky. He smelled of soap. She felt a whisper in her heart. *Is it possible?*

"I was off work early so I figured—why not have a pizza night?" His voice was matter-of-fact as he walked past her and proceeded up the flight of stairs to her apartment.

The phone was ringing as Francis pushed the door in with her foot, her arms laden with groceries. She quickly set them on the counter and picked up the receiver.

"Hello."

"Hello." Gloria sounded like she'd been crying.

"Gloria? What's wrong?" Francis' heart started beating faster as she remembered Gloria's appointment at the hospital that day.

"I'm in the hospital." *Oh no!* Francis' mind scrambled to process the information. She grabbed the back of the chair. Gloria was supposed to go to the hospital for tests this morning.

"I was admitted. Can you come see me? I need to talk to you." She spoke with urgency and sounded stuffed up.

Francis' brain went off into a dozen different directions. "Where's Emily?" She knew she was stalling, but she needed to think.

"She's at my parents'."

Of course. I knew that.

"What is it?" Mike mouthed.

"Gloria, can you hold on a minute?" Gloria agreed and Francis covered the receiver with her hand. Turning to Mike, she quickly explained the situation.

"You go to the hospital. I'll take care of the kids," Mike said after just a few words from Francis.

"Are you sure? Brad has a game tonight and Chantel needs to be picked up from piano." Francis' brain reeled. *Can I trust Mike with the kids? Will he get Brad to practice on time?*

241

"I can do it," Mike insisted. "Francis—give me some credit—I am their father." Francis heard a trace of frustration in his voice. She gave one quick nod in Mike's direction and removed her hand from the receiver.

"I'll be right there. What room are you in?" Gloria told her the room number, and they hung up.

"You can pick Chantel up from piano," Francis said, glancing at the clock, "in ten minutes. Brad has to be at the arena by 6:15. I'll try to be there by the time his game starts at seven." She started putting the milk into the refrigerator. She needed to put the perishables away first.

"I'm on my way to pick up Chantel right now." He turned toward the door, thought better of it, and turned back to Francis. He took a few steps towards her and wrapped his arms around her in a hug. "Don't worry. I'll take good care of the kids. You stay with your friend as long as she needs you." Francis leaned her head momentarily on his chest. It felt so good to have someone be there for her.

Brad burst through the door and stopped short. A smile slowly spread across his face. Francis stepped back as Mike's arms fell to his side.

"It's not…" Francis said, but then changed her mind. Mumbling something to Brad about his dad explaining to him, she grabbed her purse and keys and headed to the door.

Minutes later, Francis pulled her car into a parking stall at the hospital. She grabbed her purse and keys, locked the door, and hurried into the tall, red brick building. She took the elevator up to the third floor and walked down the hall, reading room numbers. Gloria's door was open and Francis walked in.

"Hi Gloria. What happened?" Francis asked, giving Gloria a hug.

"Hi Francis. I'm glad you came so quickly." Gloria's eyes were red and swollen, and her pale face was blotchy from crying. "Remember I told you I had a feeling I was dying?" Gloria swabbed at her eyes with the balled-up tissue in her hand. "I thought I had prepared myself, but it sounds so final when the doctor says it."

The world stopped turning. *Dying? Gloria?*

"No!" Francis hugged her friend as their tears flowed freely. When they finally let go of each other, the world had started turning again, only now it was spinning out of control.

"The doctor says the cancer has metastasized, meaning it has spread to my lungs." Gloria laid her head back on her pillow and coughed. "They can't do anything for me now."

Emily is eight. How long till she loses her mother? Francis tried hard to wrap her head around the prognosis.

"The doctor couldn't say for certain how long I have—apparently each person is different—but I have a couple of months at the most." It was as if Gloria had read her mind.

Francis slumped back in her chair. "Have you told your parents?"

"Yes, they were here this afternoon."

"Does Emily know?"

"Not yet." At the mention of Emily, Gloria's tears overflowed, trickling down her cheek and onto her pillow. She swiped at them with the balled-up tissue in her hand. Francis set the box of tissues closer so Gloria could reach them. Grabbing a couple, she handed them to Gloria.

"How can I tell her?" Gloria turned to look at Francis. Urgency was written in her eyes. "We must find her birth mother."

Francis sighed and wiped the back of her hand over her eyes. "Right. You were going to make an appointment with the social worker."

"Yeah, that won't work," Gloria said. "I called the adoption department, and the lady that did our adoption doesn't work there anymore. I asked to speak to another social worker, but when I told her what I wanted, she wouldn't even give me an appointment. She told me in no uncertain terms that they could not give me any information." Gloria closed her eyes and coughed. The tears had dried up. She looked tiny in the hospital bed, with her bald head fading into the white bed sheets. She pierced Francis with her eyes. "We have to think of something."

A voice over the loudspeaker announced that visiting hours were over.

"Don't worry," Francis said, patting Gloria's hand. "We will pray that God will show us the way." Gloria nodded and together they prayed. Then Francis bid Gloria goodnight, promising to come see her the following day.

Francis was deep in thought as she drove to the arena to catch the end of Brad's game. *How will Emily respond? Poor girl; first her dad and now her mom. God, why does one little girl have to go through so much?* Her thoughts and prayers were all jumbled together as she manoeuvred her car through the traffic. *How does one go about finding a birth mother?*

Mike waved at her when Francis entered the arena. She picked her way through the crowd to sit with him and Chantel. Her eyes quickly scanned the ice and found the object of her search backing up in his zone with the opposing winger bearing down on him. Staying between the winger and the goal, he forced the winger towards the boards and stripped him of the puck.

"Way to go, Brad!" Mike yelled. As Brad skated off the ice on a line change, Francis saw the big smile on her son's face as he looked up towards them. *He loves having his dad in his life.*

Mommy, when will Daddy come home? In her mind, she heard Brad's frequently asked question after Mike had disappeared from their lives. It had broken her heart. *Will Mike break our hearts again?*

As if reading her thoughts, Mike covered her hand with his. When Francis looked up, he mouthed, "Trust me." For a moment she lost herself in the tender look in his eyes.

"Yay!" Chantel cheered, jumping up and down, and the moment was lost. They had both missed the goal.

They all went to A&W for burgers and root beer after the game to celebrate the win. Francis' growling stomach reminded her that she had missed supper. They waited in line to place their order and receive their food before finding a table.

It's kind of sad they don't have car hops anymore, Francis thought to herself. She didn't enjoy waiting in line to place an order and then standing around waiting to get the food. Chantel picked a table in the corner next to the window.

"How did you end up playing defense?" Mike asked Brad after they started eating.

"I'm bigger than some of the guys, and I'm pretty good at skating backwards, so the coach thought I'd be good at it." Brad took a big bite out of his burger.

"Is that where you want to be or is that just where your coach put you? Defensemen don't score many goals." Mike studied Brad over his burger.

"Naw, I like defense," Brad said. "I'm not the fastest skater, and I don't have the best shot, but I can take a player out pretty good."

"Yeah, you are good at it. I was just wondering if it was your choice," Mike said.

"He wanted to be a goalie, but Mom couldn't afford the equipment," Chantel piped up, sipping her root beer.

"Is that so?" Mike asked. Francis noticed his discomfort with Chantel's statement. "Would you like to be a goalie?"

245

"Naw." Brad shrugged his shoulders, popped the last fry into his mouth, and crumpled the paper into a ball. "I like defense. I've never played goalie, so I wouldn't be good at it."

After eating half of her burger, Francis pushed it aside. *How can I sit here and eat burgers while Gloria's dying? What will become of Emily? How does one find a birth mother?* Her stomach felt queasy as the long tentacles of anxiety tightened her insides. She looked up and caught Mike's eyes resting on her.

"Time to go guys," Mike said as he stood and picked up the trays. "School tomorrow."

After the kids were in bed that evening, Francis fixed them each a cup of coffee. She sat on the couch beside Mike and told him about Gloria's diagnosis and her determination to find Emily's birth mother.

Francis had a hard time sleeping that night. By morning she looked forward to going to work. Maybe the routine of a school day would clear her mind. One of the benefits of working at the elementary school in their neighbourhood was that she could take the kids with her. Brad had graduated to the high school across the street, but Chantel still attended the school where Francis worked.

How does one go about locating a birth mother? The question haunted Francis as the day dragged on. She had promised Gloria she would stop in at the hospital after school, so they could come up with a plan. Her fingers hit the wrong key. *Rats! Another mistake. Concentrate on your job, girl,* she told herself as she turned the knob on her typewriter and reached for the whiteout. She needed to get this report done. It had taken her too long already. She turned the knob in the opposite direction and returned to the correct place on the page, her fingers once again clicking away at the keys. The bell rang just as she released the page in her typewriter and yanked it out. Done. She put the cover over her typewriter and cleaned up her desk as teachers started wandering into the office, chattering about assignments and report cards.

"Mom, I'm starving," Chantel said, coming into the office.

"Me too," Emily said, tagging along close behind Chantel. Francis had offered to help take care of Emily while Gloria was in the hospital.

"Then let's get out of here." Francis picked up her keys and purse and put her arm around Emily's shoulders as she headed to the door. Brad joined them as they entered the boot room, and the four of them left the school.

"When are we going to see Mommy?" Emily asked when they got to Francis' apartment. Francis stuck her head in the refrigerator, getting out snacks and setting them on the counter, her heart aching for the girl. *Poor Emily.* Today Gloria was going to tell her daughter. It was bound to be a difficult night.

"As soon as you finish your snack," Francis said. "Right after we drop Brad off at the arena and Chantel at her piano lessons."

"Dad's picking us up, right?" Brad asked. He gulped down the last of his food and took a long swig of water.

"Yes, your dad will pick up both of you and take you out for supper." Mike had offered since Emily would need Francis after she was told the truth.

Lord, give Gloria the strength and courage to tell Emily. Please hold Emily in your arms and comfort her. This will be devastating for her. Francis had a hard time holding back her tears—knowing what lay ahead. It would be a long night.

At the hospital, Francis took Emily's hand as they walked down the long corridor. The little girl looked so innocent with her long brown hair swaying from side to side as she walked. Her warm hazel eyes took in everything. *Lord, Emily's world is about to turn upside down. Please hold her tight,* Francis prayed silently as they walked past the nursing station and turned into room 307.

"Hi sunshine," Gloria said as they entered the room. The big smile on her face was an attempt to hide the traces of tears on her face, and the dark circles under her sunken eyes. She was wearing her wig, which suited her well. "Come join me up here." Gloria patted the edge of her bed, and Emily climbed up and gave her a hug. "How was school?" Gloria asked, running her hands tenderly through Emily's soft hair.

Francis stayed back—taking in the poignant scene. Her heart broke with each word, each look, each caress that passed between mother and daughter. *Lord, you don't make mistakes, but I have a hard time believing that right now.*

"When are you coming home, Mommy?" Emily asked the fatal question. "Are you going to feel better soon?"

"Well honey…" Gloria said, her eyes dry and filled with love—willing Emily to understand.

Lord help Emily now, Francis prayed.

Gloria continued to stroke Emily's hair and her voice overflowed with love. "Honey, I am going to be better soon but not in the way you think."

Emily's forehead scrunched up. "What do you mean?"

"Emily, honey, you know I love you lots and lots, right?" Emily nodded, her eyes searching Gloria's face.

"I love you lots and lots too, Mommy."

Gloria pulled Emily into a hug as she fought for control. Cradling her daughter in her arms she continued. "You also know that Jesus loves you even more, right?" Emily's little head bobbed up and down. "You know that whatever happens,

Jesus will always take care of you, right?" Emily's nod came a little slower this time, and there were traces of fear in her eyes. "Emily, honey, never forget that. Whatever happens, Jesus will take care of you. Your grandma and grandpa will take care of you. Francis and Chantel will take care of you, too."

"What about you, Mommy?" Emily's voice was little more than a whisper. "Won't you take care of me?"

Gloria swallowed past the lump lodged in her throat. "Honey, Jesus wants me to go see him and Daddy in heaven."

Emily's eyes grew wide as they filled with big tears. "No." Her hair swished from side to side as she shook her head. "No."

Gloria crushed the little girl to her chest. "You'll be alright, honey, I promise." The little girl shook as sobs racked her tiny body. Gloria held her daughter tight as their tears mingled in a steady, heartbreaking flow. Tears streaming down her own face, Francis bent over the bed and encircled both of them with her arms. *Lord, I don't understand. How can this be your will?*

When the tears finally subsided, Francis pressed fresh tissues into Gloria's hand. Gloria gently wiped Emily's face, smiling through her tears. "Remember the verse we memorized when Jesus took Daddy to heaven?"

Emily nodded, looked up at Gloria, and together they repeated Philippians 4:13. "I can do all things through Christ which strengtheneth me."

"But I don't want you to leave me," Emily said, fresh tears threatening.

"I know, honey," Gloria said. She took Emily's hand and placed it over her heart. "I will always and forever live right here in your heart."

"But who will love me like you do?"

"Emily, sweetheart, do you remember I told you that when you were born you had a different mommy?"

Emily nodded.

"Gloria..." Francis interrupted. *What is she doing? This isn't the time to tell Emily!*

Gloria held up her hand towards Francis, stopping her from saying more. Her eyes held a mixture of peace and sorrow. She turned back to Emily.

"Do you remember I told you that your other mommy was too young to take care of you? That's why she gave you to Daddy and me so we could love you and take care of you."

Slowly Emily's little face bobbed up and down.

"Your first mommy is older now. I think Jesus wants her to take care of you. I'm sure she loves you very much and has missed you."

"Where is she?"

"I don't know yet, but Francis and I are going to find her. Until we find her, Francis and Grandma and Grandpa will take care of you. They all love you very much."

"But I want you to take care of me." The tears started again, and Gloria gathered Emily in her arms. "I know, Emily. I love you very much. Always remember that."

Francis took an emotionally exhausted Emily home that night. She promised her she could go back to the hospital every day to see her mommy. She curled up in bed beside the little girl and rubbed her back until she slept.

CHAPTER 19

John studied the picture in his hands as he lay sprawled across his bed. David's eyes. Mary's face. Complete with the same colour hair and bangs. *Is my imagination running away with me? Since I know Mary has a daughter somewhere will I always look at every little girl and wonder if she's Mary's daughter?*

Ever since he met Emily at Patrick's house that night, he couldn't get over the resemblance to Mary's face—but with David's eyes. Especially this picture where Mary's hair was cut short. He remembered the day he had seen the picture for the first time. He hadn't recognized Mary because she always wore her hair long and never wore bangs. Only after recognizing David in the picture had he figured out that the girl was Mary.

"Mama wasn't very happy with me," Mary had told him that Christmas Eve at her house. "I cut my hair, so Mama had to cut it really short because I had done such a bad job. I was probably six years old."

John had been back home from Bible College for the Christmas break. Mary had still been too young for him to ask out, so he'd paid a visit to her family. They had been looking through photo albums and reminiscing. It had been the year after David's accident, and they were still trying to find their way back to a new normal. John traced his finger over Mary's face in the picture. The following summer she had given birth to her daughter.

She must have been pregnant that Christmas! The thought made his stomach churn. *I can't imagine what Mary must be feeling every single day, yearning for her little girl.* He sat up in bed and placed the picture between the pages of his Bible. Then he placed the Bible in his suitcase—on top of his clothes—and zipped it shut. His mind conjured up Emily's image. *Lord, help me find Mary's daughter. It seems strange that Emily bears such a strong resemblance to Mary and David. Keep me open-minded about this, Lord. Don't let my imagination get away with me like this just because she's around the same age Mary's little girl would be.*

The whole episode with Emily had put a thought in his mind. *Maybe God is directing me to find Mary's daughter. Maybe that's why I had that reaction to Emily.* He strongly believed that everything happened for a reason.

John left his bedroom and went into the kitchen. Picking up the receiver from the wall phone, he dialled Mary's work number.

"J&H Accounting. Helen speaking."

"Hi Helen, this is John Hepner. May I speak with Mary, please?"

"Yes, of course. Would you hold, please?"

John waited a minute. It felt good that he was at liberty to pick up the phone and talk to Mary.

"Hi John." Mary's voice came across the line.

"Hi Mary, sorry for calling you at work. I had an idea that I want to tell you about." John sounded excited. "Can I call on you tonight?"

"Yeah, sure," Mary said, straightening her hair as she talked. "What did you have in mind?"

"I thought we could take the quad to the cabin." His leg still wasn't strong enough to walk that far.

"I would love that," Mary said happily. "I was hoping I'd see you before you leave."

"I wouldn't leave without saying goodbye." John chuckled.

"See you later, then." John returned the receiver to its cradle.

Later that evening, Mary grabbed her sweater on her way out the door as John's car pulled up. She had already brought the quad to the house so John wouldn't have to walk too far. The short ride to the cabin was exhilarating. The wind was sharp on her face and blew her hair into John's face behind her.

"Should I build a fire?" John asked when they entered the cabin.

"That's a good idea." Mary agreed. Evenings had a definite chill to them already.

"I should put a better heater in here." John chuckled as he laid the kindling in the ancient air-tight heater. "This old thing is out-dated."

"But it's always been here," Mary pointed out nostalgically. "It's part of what makes this place special."

"I could replace it with one of those new-fangled wood heaters with a glass door. Then we could sit and watch the fire."

"Oh yes, that would be nice," Mary agreed. "I guess we won't always be able to keep this little cabin exactly the same. Time goes on and updates need to happen."

John caught the wistfulness in her tone. He stood up and brushed a strand of hair from her face. "We'll always have the memories," he said.

"Yes, no one can take those away," Mary agreed, looking around the familiar cabin. The old paper posters sporting fast cars were curling around the edges. "So many memories."

John took her hand and led her to sit on the edge of David's bed—the bottom bunk.

"Mary," John said, weaving his fingers through hers and praying for the right words. "Ever since the other evening when you told me how hard it was to give your daughter up for adoption, I've been wondering—how do you feel about your little girl now?"

Tears leapt into Mary's eyes as she lifted them to meet John's. "How can I describe the heartache I live with every day? How can I describe the ache in my empty arms? The dreams that keep me awake at night? How every time I see a little girl I try to visualize what my little daughter looks like." Tears trickled unheeded down her cheeks. "She was eight years old in July. Eight years!" John's strong arms encircled her shoulders and drew her close.

"That's what I thought you would say," John said softly, stroking her hair. He couldn't imagine how difficult those eight years had been for her. "I've been wondering if there's any way we could get her back. Do you know who handled the adoption? Could they help us?"

Mary shook her head as she wiped her sleeve across her wet face. "I can't start looking for her until she's eighteen."

"What about the hospital? Maybe they would tell us something."

Mary studied John's face. Her heart warmed at the compassion she saw in his eyes. "Do you think there might be a way to find her?" Her voice was barely a whisper.

"Don't get your hopes up, but it can't hurt to try," John said, running his hand through his dark curls. "Since I'm going to be in the city for a while I might as well ask some questions—do some detective work. See where it goes."

"Mrs. Webber, I'm very sorry for your predicament, but the adoption records are sealed," the middle-aged social worker said from across the brown office desk.

"I understand that, Mrs. Kane," Francis said, trying to control her frustration. "But in this case, the adoptive father died a couple of years ago and the adoptive mother is dying of cancer. Is there any way that we could get word to the birth mother?"

"We cannot release any information until the child turns eighteen. Then we can release non-identifying information as long as the birth parents have not put a veto on the file."

"What does that mean?"

"If the birth parents don't want the child to find them, they can place a veto on the child's file. In that case, we wouldn't release any information to the child." Mrs. Kane stood up from her chair.

"If you can't release information, can you at least contact the birth mother?" Francis asked. "I'm not saying you should mention the child. Just feel her out—she might want the child back."

"We never contact the birth parents. Like I said, the adoption documents are sealed. It would take a court order to open them." Mrs. Kane walked around her desk. "I'm sorry I can't help you, Mrs. Webber. Please call us when the child's mother passes on." The social worker made it obvious that the meeting was over, but Francis remained seated. She wasn't going to be brushed off that easily.

"Why does Social Services want to know when the mother passes on?"

"If no suitable arrangements have been made for the child, then she will become a ward of the province," Mrs. Kane said matter-of-factly as she opened the door. "I'm afraid I have another appointment. Good-day, Mrs. Webber."

Francis stood up and walked to the door. She stopped in front of Mrs. Kane and pierced her with her eyes.

"That," Francis practically hissed the words, "will not happen." She turned and left the office.

How dare she threaten to make Emily a ward of the province! Francis fumed to herself as she walked through the glass doors and across the parking lot. *That lady has no compassion for children. Ward of the province, indeed! Not Emily!* Her hand shook as she unlocked her car door and then fitted the key in the ignition.

She was still fuming as she pulled the car into her apartment parking stall and ran up the single flight of stairs. She let herself in, allowing the door to slam shut behind her, and then flung herself face-down on the couch. Only then did she allow her frustration and fear to be released in a torrent of tears.

"Lord, where do I go from here? I won't allow Emily to become a ward of the province! Show me what to do, please," Francis begged and pleaded until she was totally spent.

"Be still, and know that I am God."

"What's that supposed to mean? I know you are God. I don't doubt that, but right now I have a situation that I need help with." Francis vented her frustrations to God.

"Lean not onto your own understanding."

"Okay, Lord, but you need to show me what to do."

Francis got up from the couch. She needed to get supper started. Emily was staying with her grandparents for the night, and since she didn't have good news for Gloria, Francis decided to take the evening off to be with her family. Mike was going to pick up Brad and Chantel, and then they were all having supper together. Tonight she would tell Mike her decision.

"What's going on with you and John?" Lena asked, pouring two cups of tea.

"What do you mean?" Mary's eyes twinkled in feigned bewilderment. She had decided to pay Lena a visit since it had been too long since the two of them had been able to have a good chat. Since John had gone to Edmonton, visiting her friends would make the time go by quicker.

Lena laughed. She set one of the cups on the table in front of Mary before sitting down across the table from her. "I've heard rumours that John's car has been seen at your house on occasion."

"Oh really?" Mary chuckled. She took a sip of tea. "You know how people like to gossip." She drew her eyebrows together in mock contempt as she looked over her teacup at Lena. Then she laughed.

Lena had always been her best friend. It was time to let her in on this part of her life. "The evening of your wedding, John told me he loved me." She paused. She'd never told Lena about her daughter. How could she tell her about John without telling her about the baby?

"I knew it! I knew it!" Lena exclaimed, jumping out of her chair as fast as her burgeoning belly would allow, throwing her arms around Mary. "Why didn't you tell me?"

"Because I told him I only wanted us to be friends."

"You what? Why would you do that?" Lena asked in astonishment. "You've loved that guy since sixth grade!"

257

Mary sighed. Could their friendship survive the truth? She set her cup down and shrugged her shoulders. "When John was kidnapped, I realized that I needed to be honest with him. I wrote to him, telling him I loved him, but there were things I needed to tell him that I couldn't do on paper." Mary took a sip of her tea. "When he came back, we talked—I'll tell you about it later—the bottom line is he still loves me."

"I don't understand." Lena looked confused as she sat down, gently rubbing her protruding belly.

Mary felt the familiar pain flash through her chest as she thought back to when her belly protruded like that. She leaned her elbows on the table, bringing her closer to her friend. "Lena, you've always been my best friend."

"Just like you've always been mine." Lena smiled, relaxing.

"I don't know how to tell you this. Something happened to me a long time ago that you don't know about." Mary paused, her heart pounding. *I don't want to lose her friendship, Lord,* she prayed silently.

"*Confess your faults one to another.*"

"What do you mean?" Lena asked, her forehead furrowed.

Mary took a deep breath. "It goes back to when David died."

Lena's face softened visibly. She remembered well. It had been a trying time.

"I felt so lost." Mary's voice was soft. "I was mad at the guy that caused the accident, the world, God—everything. I was so angry."

Lena reached for Mary's hand. "I know. That was a horrible time for you. For all of us who knew David."

"Everywhere I looked I was reminded of David, how life had been, and how much I had lost when he was killed. I had so many emotions warring within me—the grief and anger were unbearable. Being with my friends reminded me of the fun times we had that were no longer possible. He was missing from every activity. I pushed you and all my friends out of my life."

This was not going to be easy. "I took up with Annie, Tina, and their friends. They didn't remind me of David because I had never been friends with them before. The things they did and places they went were so different from anything I had ever done, it was easier not to think about him constantly."

"Yes, I remember," Lena said, nodding her head slightly. She had been at her wits' end trying to remain a true friend to Mary. Then she smiled, her eyes twinkling again. "But you figured it out and came back."

Mary smiled wistfully. If only she could turn back the clock, she would handle the whole situation differently. "The first time I went to a party someone handed me a beer. I didn't like the taste, but it made me feel different inside. I could loosen up and have fun. It gave me some relief from the constant agony of living life without my brother." She paused, searching Lena's face. *Is our friendship strong enough to survive the truth?* She lifted the teacup to her lips and took a sip.

"The truth shall make you free." The voice encouraged her.

Mary took a deep breath. "Remember I went away?"

Tears sparkled in Lena's eyes. "How could I ever forget? I was heartbroken. I prayed for you every day."

Mary studied Lena's hand that covered hers on the table between them. She couldn't look her friend in the eyes. This was hard. *Lord, help me.* "At one of those parties I met a boy from the city. He was fun and good looking. I felt lucky when he singled me out. Looking back I realize he probably saw me for who I was—a sheltered and naïve girl. One evening, I got really drunk. I can't remember everything that happened. I found out later," she kept her eyes on their hands, "I was pregnant."

Lena gasped. She must have heard wrong. It couldn't be. "Pregnant?" she choked out.

Mary nodded as she looked up, her eyes imploring her friend to understand. "That's when I went away. I had a baby girl. She was adopted."

Lena's jaw dropped. She was stunned. Speechless. Pregnant? Adopted? She couldn't breathe. She got up from her chair and stumbled to the bathroom. She felt sick to her stomach. Splashing cold water on her face she lifted her eyes to the mirror and saw Mary standing in the doorway behind her.

"Are you okay?" Mary's voice was filled with concern. "I'm sorry. I shouldn't have told you."

Lena pulled a towel off the rack and wiped her face. "I can't believe it." She turned around to face Mary. "That was years ago. You never said anything."

"I couldn't." Mary turned around and went back to the kitchen. She should leave now. Lena would want her to leave. She had to get her purse.

"That's why you told John you didn't love him—just so you wouldn't have to tell him?" Lena asked, following her into the kitchen. Sitting down, she waved at the chair Mary had vacated. "Sit down."

"I thought I could keep him as a friend as long as he didn't know. If he knew my past, I would lose him completely. That's why I didn't tell you either." Mary sat down. She lifted pleading eyes to Lena's face. "I'm so very sorry. Please forgive me?"

Lena blinked. "Forgive you? For what?"

"For living a lie. For not telling you all those years ago. For shutting you out of my life. For getting into trouble. For not being the person you thought I was." Tears spilled over her cheeks. Mary took a deep breath.

Lena's face was wet as she came around the table and put her arms around Mary. "Of course, I forgive you!" Her body heaved in a single sob as she clung to Mary. Her heart was breaking for her friend—for the pain she'd had no idea Mary was living with.

Mary spent the evening telling Lena all the things she hadn't dared talk of before. Lena was compassionate and remorseful that Mary had not felt secure enough in their relationship to talk about the subject that lay heaviest on her heart—the baby girl she hadn't seen for eight long years.

"Okay guys, bedtime," Francis said as she slid her chair back from the table where they had spent the evening playing games.

"Awe, Mom," Chantel said, in her whiny I-don't-want-to-go-to-bed voice.

"Don't 'awe mom' me," Francis said, cutting her short. "School tomorrow."

"I still have some math homework," Brad said, pushing back his chair.

"Now you tell me! Then you better get at it. I want you in bed in half an hour." Francis turned to Chantel, who hadn't moved yet.

"Chantel, I'm giving you ten minutes to get to bed," Francis said in her no-nonsense voice.

Chantel scraped her chair back and stood up, dragging her feet as she slowly headed to the bathroom.

"Every night's the same," Francis told Mike after both children had gone to their rooms. She laughed as she added, "They're getting comfortable having you around so they're starting to show their true colours."

Mike chuckled. "I like how that sounds."

Francis opened the door to the refrigerator to hide the colour creeping up into her cheeks.

"You want a pop?"

"Sure. I'll have a Pepsi if you have it."

Francis grabbed two Pepsis, handing one to Mike as she walked past him, and sat down on the couch in the living room. She put her feet up on the ottoman and popped the can open. Mike sat down beside her. Francis took a sip and set the can on the table beside her. She turned to face Mike.

"I'm ready," she said, looking up into his clear blue eyes.

"Ready for what?" Mike's look was guarded.

"I'm ready for you to move in with us."

Mike threw back his head and laughed. Francis felt the colour rise in her cheeks again. Isn't that what he wanted? Had he changed his mind? She was mortified. Mike saw her confusion and stopped laughing.

"That's it?" he asked. "I'm ready? No mushy 'I love you'? Just 'I'm ready'?" He chuckled again, but this time she saw the teasing in his eyes.

"I thought that's what you wanted to hear!" Francis retorted. "You told me the ball was in my court and to let you know whenever I was ready—and now you want mushy stuff too! You should have told me." She crossed her arms in indignation.

Mike's smile faded. His eyes were serious as he took her hands in his. He rubbed his hand over her bare ring finger.

"Do you still have your engagement ring?"

"Yes." Francis felt a lump growing in her throat.

"Would you please get it?"

Francis went into her bedroom, opened her jewellery case, and retrieved the engagement ring she had placed there years ago. A solitary diamond. Memories flooded over her as she stood there looking at the ring. Mike had surprised her with this ring on the evening of her graduation from high school. They had been so in love. They got married that same summer, and Brad was born the next spring. She could never have imagined the heartbreak that was in store for them. After Mike walked out on her and the children, she had placed her rings in this jewellery box. She didn't have the heart to pawn them, even though she could have used the money. It was a reminder of the young, carefree love she once knew.

She closed the box and rejoined Mike, holding out her hand so he could see the ring in her palm. He reached out and took it from her, pulling her down beside him at the same time. He rolled the ring over in his hands, studying it. When he looked up, his eyes shone with love.

"Francis, I don't deserve you. I messed up badly, and I will always regret that. You don't know how much it means to me that you are giving me a second chance." His voice cracked, and he took a moment before continuing. "I promise you with my whole being that I will cherish you to the end of my life. I will be a good husband to you and a good father to our children. Because one thing I know now— more than ever before—that you are the only woman that can make me happy. I love you, Francis Webber. I love you so much it hurts."

"I love you too, Mike," Francis whispered. As she spoke she felt the last piece of wall around her heart crumble. She opened her heart, revealing the love that had lain dormant for so long. She blinked back the tears that sprang to her eyes.

Mike rolled the ring over in the palm of his hand. "This is the ring that I gave you when I fell in love with you. It's a symbol of the love we had, and for that reason, I want you to wear it." He picked up a small box from the coffee table and removed a ring. Francis gasped when she saw it. It was a solitaire diamond but the band—it was more like two bands with a space between them. Mike worked the original ring into the space, clasping the two rings together as one, with the two diamonds nestled against each other. "This second ring signifies the love we have now. Encompassing our first love but making it so much better." He looked deep into her eyes. "Francis Webber, I love you. Will you be my wife again?"

"Yes, I will." Francis couldn't hold her tears back as Mike slipped the ring on her finger. "I love you, Mike."

Time stood still as Mike took her in his arms. The years peeled away as Francis melted into her husband. She was home again where she belonged. This is what God wanted for them. They had lost their way for a season, but God in his infinite wisdom had brought them back together. Only this time, they were both God's children. A three-fold cord is not easily broken.

Mike held Francis at arms-length. The love she saw in the eyes that searched hers took her breath away.

"I want to do this right, Francis. We've been apart so long, and with the kids and all, it might be a little awkward if I just move in with you."

"I've thought of that," Francis said. "What do you have in mind?"

"I asked you to be my wife, but we're already married, so I thought we could renew our vows. Have a mini-wedding including the kids."

"That's sounds adorable." Francis' eyes lit up. "What a great idea! I forgot what a romantic you are."

Mike chuckled. "I have one stipulation—let's not wait too long."

CHAPTER 20

It seemed to Francis that every time she saw her, Gloria's cancer-ravaged body looked tinier between the stark white sheets of the hospital bed. Without her gorgeous black curls, her eyes looked big and sunk into their sockets. Emily ran to her mother, crawling up onto the bed to give her a hug. Francis swallowed to release the lump in her throat as she approached Gloria's bed.

"Hi Gloria." Francis gave Gloria a hug, pulled a chair close to the bed, and sat down. "How's it going?"

"Hi." Gloria shrugged, fingering the edge of the thin blanket that covered her frail body. "About the same." She lifted her hand, stroking her fingers across Emily's cheek. "How was school, honey?"

"It was okay." Emily smiled at her mother. "I work hard to make the time go by fast so I can come see you."

"Oh honey." Gloria pulled Emily close, fighting to control her emotions. "I miss you, too." Over Emily's head, Gloria raised questioning eyes to Francis. Francis sighed as she gave her head a slight shake. She hadn't been able to get any information on Emily's birth mother.

Every afternoon, Francis brought Emily to see Gloria. Sometimes Emily would come home with her and spend the night or her grandpa would pick her up to spend the night with them. Her heart ached for her friends. *What will happen to Emily when Gloria passes?*

"Is that an engagement ring on your finger?" Gloria asked, excitement in her voice. "I haven't seen you wear it before."

"Mike asked me to be his wife." Francis beamed as she held up her ring finger for Gloria's inspection.

"That's wonderful!" Gloria exclaimed, reaching for Francis' hand to better inspect the ring. "I didn't know you guys were divorced."

"We're not," Francis said quickly. "We decided that since we've been separated for so many years, it would be proper for us to renew our vows before we start living together."

"I'm very happy for you." Gloria's voice was wistful.

"Chantel said she's going to be the maid of honour!" Emily told her mom excitedly. "She's very excited to have her daddy live with them. She never had a daddy before." She paused. The happiness in her eyes overshadowed the sadness as she looked at her mother. "I'm glad she's going to have a daddy."

"That is exciting." Gloria tightened her arm around the little girl. "It's very good of you to be happy for Chantel." Gloria put her finger under Emily's chin, turning her face up to meet her eyes. "I promise you that you'll have a happy life, too. I know right now is a sad time for us, but God has a plan for you—a plan to give you a good future. Sometimes we need to go through hard times so we can appreciate the good times more."

"You mean like Chantel will appreciate having a daddy more because she didn't have one all her life?" Emily's eyes were serious, displaying wisdom beyond her years. Francis' eyes filled with tears at the tender moment between mother and daughter.

"Yes, that's what I mean," Gloria said, her voice filled with compassion. "Jesus will take good care of you because he loves you."

"Why doesn't he heal you then? That would make me the happiest. Why do you have to go be with daddy now?" Big tears threatened to spill onto Emily's cheeks. Glory wiped at them with her hand. "I've been praying for you to get better."

"Oh honey, Jesus doesn't always answer our prayers the way we want him too. Sometimes he has even better things in store for us, but he does always answer our prayers. That's why I know he'll look out for you. He has even better things for you in the future."

Francis silently left the room—giving mother and daughter some time alone—her heart heavy for the two of them. She entered a small waiting area down the hallway and sank into a chair. *Jesus, how is it possible for Emily to have a better future than she has with Gloria? They love each other so much. Why is this happening?*

"All things work together for good..."

Her thoughts went back to the struggles she'd had in the years after Mike left. She'd had to work hard to raise her children, often doing without just so they could eat. Eventually she had been able to create a decent life for them. Now that Mike was back—a better man than before—her joy had been restored and multiplied.

Oh Lord, please don't make Emily go through years of hard times, she prayed. She couldn't pray, 'Thy will be done.' What if his will was for that very thing?

"Trust me."

I do want to trust you, Lord. Please help my unbelief! She knew Jesus would take care of Emily, but how? *I want to know how, Lord.* How often had she cried out in prayer during the years Mike had been gone from her life? God had answered, but it took a long time. She didn't want that for little Emily.

When Francis returned to Gloria's room, they were both asleep. Gloria was holding her daughter's little body tightly curled into her side. Dried tear stains were evident on both faces; they were emotionally exhausted. Francis quietly left the room.

John was frustrated as he entered the hospital cafeteria. He bought a coffee and a sandwich before looking for a table. Somewhere quiet.

"Hi John." He hadn't noticed Francis until she called out to him as he passed her table.

"Hi Francis." He set down his tray to shake hands with her. "Is anyone joining you?"

"No. Sit down." Francis motioned to the seat opposite her. "How are you doing?"

John took a seat and pulled his food tray closer. "I saw the doctor today, and he's happy with my progress, so that's a good thing."

"Do I detect a 'but'?" Francis asked, leaning forward and crossing her arms on the table.

John laughed, took a sip of coffee, and shrugged. "I guess I was hoping the recovery would be faster."

"You were a very sick man," Francis pointed out as John took a bite of his sandwich.

"You're right," John said, eyeing Francis over his sandwich. "Why is it that it's never enough? People prayed for me to pull through and I did. Now I want more. I want my complete health back. No lingering effects."

Francis sighed. "Isn't that a fact—we always want more."

"So what brings you here?" John asked.

"My friend is dying of cancer. I come to see her daily."

"I'm sorry." John was empathetic. "I know what losing a friend is like."

"Her husband died a couple of years ago, and they have a little daughter." Francis' voice caught in her throat.

"That's rough. An only child?"

"Yes. They adopted her." Francis twirled the remaining coffee around in the paper cup. "She has it in her head to find the birth mother before she passes on."

"Really?" John looked sceptical. "Isn't that a huge risk?"

"That's what I tell her." Francis sighed. Setting her cup down, she lifted her eyes to meet John's. "She's adamant."

"Has she had any success?"

"No. Social Services say the adoption file is sealed and can only be opened when the child turns eighteen years of age, provided a veto hasn't been placed on the file."

"What about the hospital? Do they have any information?"

Francis shook her head. "I've hit solid brick walls in every direction."

"That's not very encouraging." John finished the last bite of his sandwich and crumbled the plastic wrap into a ball. "I told Mary I'd try to find information about her little daughter while I'm in the city, but it sounds like it won't be easy."

"How is Mary?" Francis asked, her eyes lighting up. "I haven't thought about her in a while."

"She's doing well." John smiled, his eyes taking on a softer light. "My ordeal in Mexico changed her mind about letting me in on her little secret; freeing us up to pursue a relationship."

Francis' face lit up. "Good for you! She's a good person." She glanced at her watch. "I should see if Gloria and her daughter are awake yet. They had both fallen asleep, so I thought I'd take some time to get a coffee. Do you want to come up and meet them?"

"If you think they wouldn't mind," John said as they both got to their feet, dropping their garbage into the big brown garbage receptacle on their way out.

"They'll love it," Francis said with confidence, slowing her step to match John's limp.

They took the elevator to the third floor, walked passed the nurses' station, and into Gloria's room. There on the hospital bed, beside a wisp of a woman lying beneath the sheets, was the little girl who haunted John's dreams.

Francis was busy making arrangements for their upcoming mini-wedding to renew their vows. When they had gotten married, they had exchanged vows before a justice of the peace with only a few friends in attendance. Now, they would renew their vows in church, in front of family and friends, with Pastor Bob officiating. Their church family would be called on to hold them accountable in their renewed marriage.

After work, Francis did some shopping for the wedding before picking Brad up from hockey practice and Chantel from piano lessons.

"Chantel, help me carry this stuff in," Francis said, getting out of the car. Brad got his hockey bag from the trunk as Francis and Chantel loaded up with shopping bags.

The phone was ringing as they pushed through the front door. Brad dropped his hockey bag and grabbed the receiver off the wall phone. Francis and Chantel deposited their bags in the living room to be unpacked later.

"Mom, it's for you," Brad said, holding the receiver towards his mom.

Francis took the receiver. Holding her hand over the mouthpiece, she told Brad, "Put your hockey bag away. Chantel, please put the water on to boil." She removed her hand from the mouthpiece. "Hello."

"Hi Francis." Patrick's voice came over the wire. "John is dying to talk to you, but he can't navigate stairs real well. Would you mind coming over after supper?"

Francis bit her lip as she looked at the clock. "Mike is coming for supper. I promised Gloria I'd stop in at the hospital this evening. Would after visiting hours work?"

"Yes, that works for us," Patrick said.

"Okay. I'll stop in on my way home from the hospital." They hung up, and Francis got busy making spaghetti and meat sauce.

Francis was tired and dejected as she pulled away from the hospital and turned her car towards Patrick and Janelle's townhouse. She would have liked to go straight home and spend some time with Mike and the kids. She was glad that Emily was spending the night with her grandparents. It gave her a break from dealing with the little girl's emotions. Gloria was deteriorating but still refused to give up hope that they would find Emily's birth mother. Francis had mixed emotions about that and questioned the wisdom of their pursuit. It probably didn't matter since they weren't getting anywhere. She suspected it might be good for Gloria to have a goal to work towards. It kept her mind occupied by something other than the fact she wouldn't be around to see Emily grow up.

Traffic was light at this late hour, so it didn't take long before she pulled up at her friend's house. She locked her car and walked up the grey-pebbled sidewalk to the front door.

"Hi. Come on in." Patrick greeted her with a welcoming smile, opening the door wide.

271

"Hi," Francis said. She followed him into the living room where Janelle and John were sitting on black leather couches.

"I'm so glad you could make it." John motioned for her to join him on the couch as Patrick took a seat beside his wife.

"How are Gloria and Emily doing?" John asked as Francis settled herself on the couch.

Francis sighed. "I can't see Gloria holding on much longer. Emily is obviously going through a hard time. Having laid her dad to rest a few years ago, she realizes the finality of death."

"I can't imagine what she's going through," John said. "Losing a parent must be a lot harder than losing a friend, but to lose both within a few years—it's unthinkable." John paused as he handed Francis the picture of Mary and David. "Does this girl look familiar to you?"

Francis studied the picture. John reminded himself to breathe as his heart thumped in his chest. Francis lifted confused eyes to meet John's. "Who is this?"

"Does she look familiar?" John asked again, avoiding her question.

"Yes, she does," Francis said, her consternation obvious in the way her eyebrows furrowed as she looked back at the picture. "Where did you get this photo? The girl almost looks like Emily but not quite. The boy's eyes look like Emily's but his face doesn't. This is obviously an older photo so it can't be Emily." Francis' heart was starting to beat erratically.

John knew he had to proceed carefully. He shouldn't jump to conclusions. He needed more concrete evidence. A smile played around the corners of his mouth. "Francis, when is Emily's birthday?"

Francis stared at John. What was he getting at? "July eighth. She celebrated her birthday shortly after they moved here last summer. I remember it was July eighth."

"Do you know where she was born?"

"Yes. Gloria told me she was born in the University of Alberta hospital." Francis' hands were shaking. "John, what are you saying?" Her voice was barely above a whisper.

"Francis," John said, "the girl in the picture is Mary. The boy is her brother David."

A tear trickled down Francis' face as her mind grappled with what John was saying. "Mary's baby girl was born July eighth, eight years ago, at the U of A." She looked up at John, a slow smile dawning on her face. "I remember because I drove her there myself. Did we just find Emily's mother?"

"It seems almost too coincidental to be anything else." John's eyes clouded with frustration. "I don't see how we can be sure without the adoption files being opened."

Francis shook her head. "No chance of that happening."

Patrick cleared his throat. "They could do a DNA test."

"I would hate to get Mary's hopes up only to have them crushed if the test turns out negative," John said.

They agreed to keep their hypothetical findings to themselves until they could figure out how to go about making sure they were on the right path.

The following day, Gloria was moved to the palliative care unit. Francis' heart was heavy as she took the elevator up to Gloria's floor. Emily held tightly onto her hand.

Gloria's eyes were closed when they entered the room. Francis caught Emily's eye and put her finger on her lips. Emily nodded. They would let her mommy sleep.

Francis let her eyes roam around the room. It was larger than the other room she'd had. A picture of Gloria, Richard, and Emily smiled back at them from Gloria's nightstand.

"No hug?" Gloria asked, turning her head toward them. Emily scampered onto the bed and hugged her mother before settling into the bed next to her.

Francis stooped over for a hug. Gloria's skin felt clammy.

"How are you doing?" Francis asked.

Gloria smiled ruefully. "As good as can be expected." She looked around the room. "How do you like my new digs?"

"I like it, Mommy," Emily said, pulling her knees up. "It looks cheery. It looks more like it's your bedroom."

"That's true," Francis said. The tan walls and pastel curtains were a welcome reprieve from the stark white walls in the regular room. Family pictures lined the windowsill—pictures of happier times. The green vinyl chairs—although not spectacular—were more comfortable than the previous stacking chairs.

"Mom decorated the room." Gloria waved her hand to encompass the pictures. "Those chairs open up as beds."

"Does that mean I can spend the night with you?" Emily asked, turning her head so she could look at Gloria's face. Gloria stroked her daughter's cheek.

"Would you like to?"

"Yes." Emily didn't hesitate. "I miss you so much when you're not at home."

"I miss you too, honey." Gloria turned her eyes to Francis. "Maybe we can figure something out for the weekend. We'll have to ask the nurses." She looked at her daughter and pretended to put a stern look on her face. "But you definitely cannot stay here on a school night."

"Oh goody! It would be fun to have a sleepover," Emily said with more excitement than she had shown in a while.

"Time for your meds." An elderly nurse rolled a blood pressure machine into the room. "How's my newest patient tonight?" She was all smiles as she worked with the blood pressure machine, wrapping the cuff around Gloria's thin arm. "This gorgeous young lady must be your daughter." She winked at Emily. "I see you're getting your cuddles in."

"Yes, this is my Emily," Gloria said, smiling at her daughter.

"Pleased to meet you, Emily. I'm Linda."

"Hi Linda. Can I stay here for the night?" Emily asked, wasting no time. "Mommy said I had to ask you." Emily looked up at the nurse with hopeful eyes.

"Well, honey, I don't know. We don't usually have children spend the night," the nurse said matter-of-factly as she continued her routine check. She had read the patient's chart. A widow with an only child. Her heart went out to the little girl. "I won't make any promises, but I'll see if I can pull some strings."

Linda adjusted the bed and tidied the sink in the corner. She pulled down the blinds part way, and then picked up a picture of Richard, Gloria, and Emily.

"Is this your family?" she asked. Although Gloria's hair had started growing back, it was nothing like the luscious black curls that had fallen out from the treatments. The young woman in the picture didn't look anything like the woman lying in the bed.

"Yes," Emily answered. Scrambling off the bed she padded over to Linda and pointed to each person in the picture. "That's my daddy. He already went to live with Jesus. That's my mommy and that's me. I was just little," she chuckled, as if she was so much bigger now. "My mommy and daddy adopted me when I was a baby. I was born right here in this hospital," Emily told Linda proudly.

"Did they?" Linda glanced over at Gloria, who was watching the exchange. "I used to work in the nursery."

"In this hospital?" Gloria asked, her interest piqued.

"Yes. I've worked here my entire career. I met and married a local man when I attended university, so this is where I stayed."

Emily had lost interest in the conversation and was digging around in her book bag.

When Linda left the room, Francis followed her.

CHAPTER 21

"A hospital?" Mary asked, raising her eyebrows in confusion as John turned into the U of A hospital parking lot. John had called her a few days ago and told her it was urgent that she come to Edmonton. He couldn't tell her why on the phone, but he had assured her it was a good thing. She had asked for some time off from her job, packed her bags, and driven all day. *Just to have John take me to a hospital?*

Pulling into a parking stall, John parked the car before turning to face Mary. "Bear with me, Mary. Trust me." He smiled into her eyes and saw her relax.

"I trust you," she said, meeting his eyes. "I don't know what you're up to, but I trust you."

"Good," John said, getting out of the car. He caught her hand as they walked across the parking lot and into the hospital. *Lord, guide the way,* he prayed silently as they walked down the hall.

Mary hesitated as they entered Gloria's hospital room. She didn't recognize the frail woman lying on the bed and hooked up to oxygen with an IV needle in her arm.

Then her eyes fell on the little girl who was looking up to her from a green vinyl chair in the corner. Long, brown hair framed her angelic face, but it was the eyes that attracted her: David's eyes. Mary walked across the room as if a magnetic field pulled her. She knelt beside the little girl, so they were at face level.

"You are beautiful, sweetheart," she said softly, around the lump in her throat. "What's your name?"

"Emily." Emily studied Mary's face.

"What a pretty name," Mary said. She reached out her hand to touch Emily's hair.

"Are you my other mommy?" Emily asked. "Mommy said Jesus told her my other mommy would come."

Mary's eyes glistened with tears as she met John's tender gaze. He nodded, too choked up to speak. She turned back to the little girl who she hadn't seen for over eight years—who had always haunted her dreams—who she had prayed for and loved.

"Yes, I am." Happy tears tumbled over her cheeks as she smiled at Emily. "Your mommy was right. Jesus brought me here. May I hug you?"

Emily climbed off the chair and stepped into Mary's arms. "Thank you, Jesus," Mary whispered as she held Emily tight, her heart exploding in her chest. "I love you, Emily. I have always loved you."

The years of waiting and praying for the chance to hold her baby one more time were worth every minute. Not wanting to overwhelm her, Mary drew back and feasted her eyes on her beautiful little girl.

"Emily." Mary let the name roll over her tongue. "That's a beautiful name. What a lovely young lady you are," Mary told her, fondling her hair, "just like I always imagined."

"Mommy tried to find you," Emily said, her eyes moving beyond Mary to the woman on the bed. Mary turned around to see tears streaming down the face of the woman lying there. Slowly getting to her feet, she walked over to the bed and took the woman's outstretched hand.

"Thank you for coming," Gloria said, not even trying to wipe her tears away. "Jesus told me you would come."

"I don't understand," Mary said, looking from Gloria to John. Then she noticed Francis standing on the other side of the bed. "Francis?"

Francis smiled through her tears as she came around the bed. She hugged Mary tightly before stepping back to the foot of the bed.

"Gloria was determined to find Emily's birth mother," Francis explained. "We tried every angle we could think of, but we couldn't get any information. Then John showed me a picture of you and your brother. I was astonished by the similarities. Emily's birthdate was the same as your baby's, but still we needed to be sure."

She looked from Mary to Gloria. "When Gloria was moved to this ward, her nurse mentioned she'd worked on every floor of this hospital." Her gaze landed on Emily, who was listening closely, her little hand engulfed in Mary's hand. John had his arm around Mary's waist. "When the nurse left the room I followed her. I questioned her, and she told me that the year Emily was born there were three newborn adoptions out of this hospital. The others were born in January and October." Francis smiled at Gloria. "She remembered giving the baby to the birth mother right after the birth, which was not normal procedure for adoptions. She also remembered Richard and Gloria picking the baby up."

"Emily, sweetheart, come sit with me," Gloria said to the daughter she'd been blessed with a few days after her birth. Mary lifted Emily onto the bed.

Mary looked up to see Francis and John quietly leaving the room. She took a step toward them, but Gloria gestured for her to stay, and then she turned to Emily. "Emily, sweetheart, I love you—you know that, right?" Her voice was as tender a voice as Mary had ever heard.

Emily's head bobbed up and down. "I love you too, Mommy."

"I know you do." Gloria smiled through the tears shining in her eyes. "I will always love you." She glanced at Mary then back at Emily. "Always remember that Jesus loves you very much too. Things might not always go the way we want them to, but Jesus will always work things out." Gloria wiped at the single tear that rolled down Emily's cheek. "Jesus is calling me to go live with him and Daddy, but he didn't want you to be alone. That's why he wanted me to find your other mommy because he knew that she loves you very much as well."

"But I want you to stay with me." Emily's tears flowed in earnest as Gloria pulled her down to her chest—stroking her hair as the floodgates opened and soaked the sheets around her.

Mary's own tears flowed unheeded as she watched her newly found daughter's heart break. She put one arm around Emily and her other hand on Gloria's shoulder as she prayed: "Jesus, we don't understand why things happen the way they do. Your ways, Lord, are different from our ways, but you say in the Bible that all things work out for good for those who love the Lord, and Jesus, we love you. We come to you with deep joy and with deep sorrow. Show us the way, Lord. Touch Gloria's body with your healing hand. Touch sweet Emily's heart with your love. Surround us with your comfort and fill our hearts with your peace. We pray that your will be done. In Jesus' name, we pray. Amen."

Emily stretched her legs out alongside Gloria's, and Mary silently stole out of the room. She found a small waiting room down the hall, and there she prayed. When she finally finished talking to God, she went back to the room and found Gloria and Emily asleep—exhausted from the emotional trauma. She took the elevator down to the cafeteria, where she knew she'd find John and Francis.

Gloria's funeral was beautiful. The church was decked out with flowers and photos of Gloria's life. As she studied one picture after another, Mary thanked God for the happy childhood these people had given Emily. God had been merciful, allowing both mothers to spend Gloria's last days together with Emily—creating a bond between the three of them. Mary and Emily had spent the last few nights with Gloria, sleeping on the chairs that doubled as beds. It had been a time of reflection and planning—of letting go and of binding together. They had talked and prayed.

At the end, Gloria had taken Emily's hand and placed it into Mary's hand—praying over them as she gave Emily back to the mother who had borne her. They had agreed that Emily would call Mary 'Mama' since Gloria was her mommy, and Mary would never take Gloria's special place in Emily's heart. She would create her own place. Mary blinked back the tears as she felt a small hand tugging at her arm.

"Mama, Grandma said to get you," Emily said, looking up at Mary.

Mary was amazed at how well Emily was coping with all the emotion and upheaval in her life. Gloria had done a fantastic job in raising her little girl. Mary wasn't sure she could have done better.

Mary allowed her daughter to lead her to where Gloria's parents and the rest of the funeral procession were waiting to enter the church sanctuary. Mary and John held Emily's hands as she walked between them, following Gloria's parents to the front pews. The fact they had invited Mary and John to sit with the family showed the same grace that had been evident in Gloria. Mary could see evidence of that grace instilled in Emily. It was a grace that was borne in love. Love for their fellow man by the grace of God.

EPILOGUE

Mary swallowed the lump in her throat as she watched Emily. In her flowing pink dress and with a sparkling tiara on her head, she spread rose petals as she walked down the aisle to the front of the church.

Her dear little Emily. The light of her life. Everyone who got to know her, fell in love with her. Emily loved the freedom of living on a farm. Every day was an adventure for her.

The music changed, and Pastor Penner asked the congregation to rise. Mary smiled up into Benny's kind eyes—for once they held no mischief—as together they stepped into the aisle. Her papa's face beamed at her from his wheelchair while her mama stood beside him, wiping a tear from her eye. *Mama cried on the phone when I called to tell her I found my daughter. She's loving every minute she gets to spend with Emily. The little girl has Papa and Benny wrapped around her little finger.*

Standing beside Pastor Penner at the front of the sanctuary was John; tall and handsome, with a sparkle in his eye and a grin lighting his face. Beside him stood his best friends and groomsmen, Henry and Patrick. Her bridesmaids, Lena and Annie, smiled back at her from their positions on the stage. Emily stood beside them, her face glowing.

For a moment, Mary let her eyes scan the congregation. There were Francis and Mike—they had renewed their vows a few months ago—with Brad and Chantel. She saw Isaac, Annie's husband, with their three little children. He was slowly finding his way to the Lord. There were Gloria's parents. They had made the trip to see their granddaughter on this special day. Mary was thankful for their love and support. The pews were filled with a sea of faces, extended family and friends, who had accepted Emily wholeheartedly.

Joy radiated from Mary's face as she fixed her eyes on John. Every step took her closer to him and the future that awaited them. A forever future. Her heart was overwhelmed with love as her prayer of thanksgiving lifted high above the rafters.

Lord, thank you for John, for Emily, and for all these people. Thank you for granting them the grace to forgive me and accept me and Emily into their lives.

ACKNOWLEDGEMENTS

First and foremost, I want to thank the Lord Jesus Christ for his finished work on the cross: that "whosoever shall call upon the name of the Lord shall be saved." (Romans 10:9) What a promise!

A big thank you to my husband, who loves me even when I mess up; to my children, who are my inspiration; and to my grandchildren, who make me feel young. I love you all. May the Lord bless you!

I thank my parents, who have both passed on to their heavenly home, for teaching me about Jesus and for instilling in me a love for writing. I look forward to seeing you again.

Thank you to everyone who reads this book. Without you, there would be no point in writing. I pray that you are encouraged.

A big thank you goes out to each FriesenPress staff member who diligently guided me through the publishing process.